The Devil of Dunakin Castle
Highland Isles Series

The Devil of Dunakin Castle

Highland Isles Series

HEATHER McCOLLUM

This book is a work of fiction. Names, characters, places, and incidents are the product of the author's imagination or are used fictitiously. Any resemblance to actual events, locales, or persons, living or dead, is coincidental.

Copyright © 2017 by Heather McCollum. All rights reserved, including the right to reproduce, distribute, or transmit in any form or by any means. For information regarding subsidiary rights, please contact the Publisher.

Entangled Publishing, LLC
2614 South Timberline Road
Suite 109
Fort Collins, CO 80525
Visit our website at www.entangledpublishing.com.

Scandalous is an imprint of Entangled Publishing, LLC.

Edited by Alethea Spiridon
Cover design by Erin Dameron-Hill
Cover art from DepositPhotos and Period Images

Manufactured in the United States of America

First Edition November 2017

This book is dedicated to all the women who feel like they are secondary characters in the novel of life. Grace Ellington was a secondary character, yet see what she has become! Behind our masks of self-doubt, we are all heroines.

Chapter One

Aros on the Isle of Mull, Scotland
Winter 1523

"*Magairlean*," Grace Ellington swore as she clung to the thick log, suspended over the half-frozen river.

"Ye know I speak Gaelic, lass," Thomas Maclean called from the bank. The elderly blacksmith, whom she'd helped heal when she'd first come to the Isle of Mull, had volunteered to take her hunting for winter holly.

"I don't rightly care if you hear me cursing," she said, her teeth and eyes clenched.

"The good God understands Gaelic, too," Thomas said. "In fact, I like to think it is his native tongue."

At the moment, she worried more about falling into the freezing river that ran past Aros Castle than falling into the devil's burning hole. *Bloody hell.* She never would have gone with Thomas if she'd known the greenery, with its bright red berries, was on the other side of the river. Terrified of water since her brother had held her under as a child, Grace made it a point to stay away from rivers and streams, especially in midwinter, when cold water could also bring on illness.

"Come now, ye caught yourself on the log," Thomas said, his voice coaxing. "Now crawl backward to me."

"Have you ever crawled on a log wearing a kirtle, petticoats, and cloak?" Grace swallowed hard as the edges of her skirts caught in the flow of water under her, bits of ice rushing by, catching and tugging on the wool.

"Can't say I have," the elderly Highlander said. He huffed. "I'll come get ye."

"No," Grace called, determination and disgust over her paralyzing fear shuddering through her. "I will make it."

"That's a lass," Thomas called.

Grace raised up, the bones of her kneecaps wobbling on the thick creases of her kirtle. Her fingernails dug into the log, and she moved one knee backward. Then the other. One inch at a time. *Dear God. Dear God. Dear God.*

Crack. Upstream, ice broke free, caught in the current. Grace watched in horror as a large chunk rushed toward her. Panic gripped her with ferocity, and she grabbed tighter, trying to lie flat, but she wavered. She gasped one last time before—

Splash! Cold raked across Grace's skin as the deep water embraced her. A need to survive overrode the panic, and she threw her arms out, clawing at the icy water. Wet wool dragged her with the current as she tried to dig the heels of her boots into the rocks on the bottom. Gurgling water and bubbles filled her ears, and she broke the surface, gasping for air.

"I've got ye," Thomas said, his hand encircling her flailing wrist. Up to his waist in the river, he dragged her to shore.

Grace's heart pounded so hard she couldn't fully catch her breath. Freezing, she crawled under her sopping gown up the bank. *Mo chreach.* Fear had beaten her again. Self-loathing made tears press in her eyes, and she blinked to clear the ache.

She'd cry later, when she was alone with her humiliation.

"Let's get ye home, lass. Ye'll freeze to the ground if we stay out here."

Grace let the man pull her up. Numbly, she accepted the wool blanket he'd brought to catch the holly twigs they never reached. Thomas walked her back to her little cottage on the edge of Aros Village. A far cry from the estate Grace had inherited down in York, England as the daughter of the Earl of Somerset, she still loved her cozy cottage with its thatched roof and wooden walls.

"Get dry and warm," Thomas said.

She managed to glare despite her chattering teeth. "I'm the healer, Thomas. I know that."

He grinned. "Aye, ye do." He shook his head. "Ye need a husband to take care of ye, lass. And there's plenty around wanting to. Say aye to one of them."

"Not you, too."

He shrugged. "Gavin Maclean is an upright, strong lad who'd be happy to watch out for your every step."

"I don't need someone watching out for my every step."

He raised one eyebrow, his gaze dipping to her soaked clothes. "Aye, lass, ye do."

She huffed loudly. Very unladylike, but she wasn't in England anymore, being groomed and corrected by her mother. She was in the wilds of Scotland where she could huff, curse, and stack her hands on her hips. She frowned. "Thank you, Thomas."

He grinned, showing several holes where teeth used to sit. "Now get ye warm."

Grace pushed inside her cottage, the warmth of the little home surrounding her immediately. She leaned back against the door and let her shoulders curve forward.

"Grace?"

She shot upward, her heart jumping back toward panic.

But it was her half sister, Ava, who pushed her pregnant bulk out of the bed. Waddling into the living area, Ava stopped. "What happened?"

"What does it look like happened?" Grace asked and let the wool blanket drop from her shoulders as she went to the hearth to stir the coals and add more peat.

"You fell in the river?" Ava asked, a shocked grin on her beautiful face. "And I wasn't anywhere near you." She walked over and helped Grace out of her dripping cloak and untied the knots of her bodice.

"I panicked again," Grace said, a sinking feeling in her middle. "It makes me lose my balance and turns me to stone." She scrunched her face. "Oh Ava. I hate it, my cowardice." Ava hugged her as best her large stomach would allow. Grace pushed back. "I'll get you wet."

"I don't care."

Grace sniffed softly. "If you get ill, Tor will throw me back in the river."

Ava laughed. "I'm healthy as a two-ton horse." She patted her stomach, which was much too large to be one baby at only six months along.

Grace changed behind her privacy screen, throwing her warm day gown on over a fresh smock. "Thank the Lord Tor's mother is such a talented healer."

"Cullen wants Rose here when it's her time to birth their first baby in another month or so. They arrived this morning."

"Is that why you're hiding in my cottage?" Grace asked, coming out to sit at the table near the hearth.

Ava sighed, lowering into the seat across from her. "Yes. It's a bit noisy, and I gave Rose our bedchamber to nap in while her chamber is dusted."

Grace sighed as she fingered through her damp hair. Ava reached across for her other hand, squeezing it. "What's wrong?"

Grace shook her head. "Everyone is having babies. You, Rose, even Mairi now up on Barra Island. People are falling in love, marrying and starting families, moving on, and I'm just…falling in the river."

"You could marry Gavin," Ava said, catching her gaze. "He's handsome and sweet and wants only to take care of you."

A mutinous frown curved Grace's lips. "I don't want to be taken care of like some broodmare who's always getting into trouble and swooning. I'm tired of being afraid." Grace's gaze beseeched Ava. "I want to be courageous like you."

"You are. I wish you could see it."

"But I'm frightened all the time, it seems," Grace whispered. Especially where water was concerned.

"Courage is action in the face of fear," Ava whispered back as if she shared a secret. "I'm frightened a lot, too." She rested her hand on her large belly. "Like whether I can handle birthing all this baby. You can be afraid as much as you want," she said. "We just need to work on helping you move forward."

Grace met her sister's kind gaze. "I want an adventure. I want to feel the passion that you have with Tor, and that will never be with Gavin. I think I must leave Aros."

Ava's face tightened. "Somerset? Back to England?" Grace shook her head, and Ava rolled her eyes. "Thank God. I'd never see you again."

"I need to go somewhere on my own without Gavin or any of the other would-be suitors following me around, asking to help me or carry me." She waved her hands around. "Or pull me out of the river or cut my meat so I won't choke."

Ava covered her mouth with her hand, but couldn't stop the chuckle. "Really, Grace. No one cuts your meat."

Grace straightened in her chair, an idea surfacing in her mind. "Has Tor decided who will go to Barra to help Mairi deliver her baby?"

"No. Tor won't let his mother go with my stomach so large. And I can't, obviously. It's some months before Mairi is due, but she's worried about the weather keeping us away."

"I will go," Grace said, her stomach squeezing with excitement. "I've helped you with several births now. I can help Mairi, and get away from Aros for a while. Maybe long enough for Gavin to find another helpless wee lass to marry." She stood from the table.

"Grace, you don't—"

"Yes, I do." She opened her eyes wide and nodded. "I really do."

...

"A short ride to Kilchoan now," Thomas said as he and Grace rode away from the ferry that had brought them from Mull. He coughed into his fist and cleared his throat. "Escorts from Barra Isle will meet ye to take ye to Mairi." He coughed again.

"I don't like the sound of that," Grace said, searching his face from her seat. His eyes looked a bit shiny, like sickness was setting in.

"I'm too old and ornery to be ill." He led them down the road that was covered with several inches of snow.

"Thank you for escorting me, Thomas," Grace said, patting her mare's neck. "Gavin wouldn't stop asking to take me until you stepped forward."

Snow began to fall as they trotted past a small church on the outskirts. They slowed, pulling the horses to walk alongside each another. Grace watched the swirling flakes.

"Thomas?" she said, her voice muffled in her scarf.

"Aye?"

"How do warriors stay so brave?"

He chuckled and cleared his throat. "From wee lads,

we are taught to be prepared for harm, how to fend it off, outsmart it."

"Can you teach me to be prepared?" She looked up, and flakes caught on her eyelashes. "To start, how do you stay warm in all this snow?"

"That depends. If ye're caught in a storm without shelter, ye make shelter. Ye put pine boughs under ye and a blanket, if ye have it, on top, or more boughs. 'Tis better to find a cave to hide in out of the wind. Ye can start a fire with flint, a bit of wool, and dry twigs."

Grace carried a leather satchel on her back with basic provisions, including flint, just in case. "Ye can cut the boughs or kindling with a dagger. Ye do have one?" he asked.

"Yes," Grace said, patting her leg where a short, black handled, *sgian dubh* was strapped. "Gavin was teaching me to throw it."

Thomas nodded. "A lass should be able to defend herself." He pointed up ahead and shivered in his cloak. "There now, we've made it to Kilchoan port."

Grace stared through a curtain of snow toward a small village on the ocean, the MacInnes Castle sitting beyond it. Mairi, Tor's sister, had one time lived there, married to the elderly MacInnes chief and harassed by his horrible son, Normond MacInnes. But the elder chief had died, and Mairi now lived on Barra Island with her true love, her husband, Alec MacNeil.

Thomas coughed into his woolen glove; the sound seemed raspier than when they'd left the day before. She could pick out a wheezing sound in his inhale. Or was that the wind? "We should get you inside," she called to him above a gust. "This is turning into a blizzard."

The tavern had one open room above, and Grace worked quickly to secure it for Thomas. He felt hot to the touch, and his eyes looked damp, sure signs of a growing fever. "Is there an apothecary close?" she asked the friendly maid who'd showed them upstairs.

"Aye, on the far side of town. But milady, ye can hardly see out there in this storm. 'Tis right wicked."

Grace's lips tightened with determination. "I need some licorice root for my escort's cough."

"I'll take some honey up to him and brewed feverfew," she said. "And watch him while ye are gone."

"Thank you." Grace wrapped up once more in the cumbersome layers and pushed out into the blowing snow. Wind blew the flakes sideways, creating drifts half a foot high between the thatched buildings. Grace threaded her way between two cottages and trudged uphill along the line of trees, which helped buffer her. Her boots sunk until the accumulation came up to her calves, freezing the hem of her skirts. Thinking of poor Thomas, she trudged on.

A root caught Grace's toe, and she gasped as she fell forward onto her knees. Scrambling in her heavy skirts and wraps, she turned several times before standing. She parted the scarf to see better, but there wasn't anything to see. The snow was thick, and the wind was so fierce that all she saw was white, a grayish white that warned of sundown.

"Ballocks," she shouted, the curse caught with her wet breath in the scarf. Fear reared up inside her, and she cursed more, throwing the words out at the storm. It was better to be angry than afraid. Grace grabbed hold of a thin tree and walked around it, looking out at the swirl of white.

It truly was a blizzard. And she was lost.

Chapter Two

Keir Mackinnon, brother to the chief of the powerful Mackinnon clan of the Isle of Skye, sat atop his black charger, looking toward where the small village of Kilchoan should be. But instead he saw snow, mounds of it, gale winds full of it, undulating white and gray. It covered his fur wraps and melted on his face.

"It shrieks like a bloody banshee," his best friend and cousin, Brodie Mackinnon, yelled across to him.

Ignoring what he could not change, Keir pointed forward. "Rab said the healer should be either at Kilchoan or on the Isle of Mull at Aros," Keir said. "We will wait out the storm at Kilchoan."

Brodie leaned toward him so he'd be more likely to hear. "Or we could return to that snug hunting cabin back a way."

"If we find the healer in Kilchoan, we can return to Skye with her tomorrow."

"Not in this damn snow," Brodie said. "Your grandmother and Dara are taking care of little Lachlan. He may be well when we return."

"Unlikely," Keir said. Keir's nephew, Lachlan, had been ill for two weeks, his seven-year-old body growing weaker by the day as he vomited his meals. So his father, Rab, had sent Keir off the Isle of Skye to find and return with the renowned Maclean healer to help his only son grow strong again.

Inhaling, Keir caught the tang of woodsmoke. Aye, the village was close. He pointed between the trees. "There. I saw a steeple."

With the slightest of pressure, his horse, Cogadh, moved forward with Brodie on his left. Only a foot away, the snow obscured him. Aye, this was a blizzard, one of the worst he'd seen.

A sound in the wind made Keir turn in the saddle to look back the way they'd come through the woods. A scream? Or was it the shrieking wind? Again it came, a thin, high-pitched scream. "I hear something," Keir said.

"What?" Brodie called.

Keir cupped his hands around his mouth and yelled. "Go on. I'll find ye in the village." The reins gripped in his gloved hand, he turned Cogadh around. His war horse was used to discomfort, as was Keir, but he was glad he'd put the wool drape on Cogadh under his saddle. He guided them blindly through the white in the direction he'd heard the cry. His ears trained on the woods.

A shriek sliced through the wail of the wind, ahead to the right. "*Siuthad!*" he yelled, making Cogadh jump forward as Keir leaned low over the horse's neck. His loyal beast churned the snow under his hooves, trusting Keir to guide him between the trees that appeared out of the white at the last second. They moved together, man and war horse, a single creature of power and perseverance.

Keir pulled back as they neared a stony cliff face. He and Brodie had ridden around it to avoid the caves cut underneath where animals likely slumbered. There, backed against a thick tree, was a cloaked woman. The cliff blocked some of the wind, and Keir could pick out three gray shapes in the snow, advancing toward her. Wolves. Hungry, no doubt.

He leaped down and drew his sword. The woman's face jerked toward him, and she screamed again. "Shite," she yelled through the scarf, covering her mouth.

Keir could see only wide, lash-framed eyes staring at him, full of panic. "Stay back!" he yelled and stepped between her and the wolves. He swung his blade through the frost-filled air, and it sang with the wind.

"Don't kill them," the woman called from behind. "They have a cave on the backside of this rock, with babies in it. Cubs, pups, whatever they're called."

Bloody hell. The woman had walked into a den of wolves protecting their pups. He sheathed his sword and threw his arms out wide. He frightened grown warriors; perhaps he could frighten hungry wolves. He growled, showed his teeth and stomped forward. One of the wolves immediately withdrew, dodging to disappear around the corner, but the other two snapped back, apparently not impressed. While one growled at him, the other began to circle behind him, realizing that the woman was the weakest and easily culled.

Cogadh snorted and reared up on his hind legs, helping with intimidation. The wolves didn't seem to care, but the woman screamed again. She grabbed onto Keir's back, pressing against him, and a weaker man would have ended up face down in the snow. Backing slowly, Keir kept the advancing beasts before him. "Ye're going in the tree," he said over the wind.

"What?" the woman asked, but there wasn't time to explain. With a swift glance over his shoulder, he turned and lifted the woman onto a branch above his head. Snow tumbled off the branch, momentarily blinding him as she scrambled. Her boots kicked, and fighting the slippery branches, she stood to balance on the thick extension.

A growl broke through the shrill of the tempest, and fire bit into Keir's thigh. "*Mo chreach*!" He swung his fist backward, making contact with the wolf's snout. It released his leg, shaking its massive head. It hunched down to spring at him. "Don't make me kill ye," he said low and slipped his sword free. The familiar feel of it, heavy in his hand, overrode the deep ache from the bite.

Cogadh, the smell of blood familiar to him, shrieked into the wind as he charged forward, his forelegs stomping down in force. The second wolf turned in time to gnash his teeth against the horse's leg. Cogadh, a born warrior, raised his front legs, bringing them down on the wolf's back end.

With a yelp, the animal rolled and sprung up, limping as he trotted in retreat around the corner of the cliff. Keir yelled and sliced the air with his sword before the remaining wolf's face.

"Watch out," the woman called and—

Crack! Something hit the back of Keir's head. "Sard!" he cursed and looked down to see a dagger in the snow, a throbbing in his head now joining with the throbbing in his thigh. Luckily, the wolf was losing its courage as Keir's horse continued to stamp and paw the ground next to him. With one last glance, the beast dodged out into the continuing blizzard, hopefully to burrow back into its cozy den.

Keir turned to the tree. The branch creaked overhead with the woman balanced on it, clinging to the trunk. "I'm sorry. I meant to hit the wolf." Wind gusted against them, blowing the woman's skirts about her legs as the branch swayed, creaking. "You were bit," she yelled down. "I'm a healer."

A healer? Was she from Kilchoan or Aros? He wouldn't have left her stranded in a tree regardless, but if she could be of help to his nephew, he wasn't going anywhere without her. Keir stood below. Perhaps good fortune had called him to her.

"Sit on the branch and lower down." The woman continued to cling to the tree. "Let go," he said.

"I will. I am," she said. "I'm just...I hate this. Cold, wolves, being up in a tree."

"Sit, woman," he said.

With painstakingly slow movements, she bent down, still gripping the thick trunk, until she sat on the limb. "I'm... I think I'll fall," she said as the limb shook and cracked in the wind.

He moved under her. "I'll catch ye."

A gust blew up over the rock wall, slicing down to hit the tree as the woman slid out farther away from the trunk, preparing to drop down. "Good Lord," she yelled as the branch let out a snap and crack, breaking. Pain shattered the white scene before Keir as the heavy limb slammed the side of his head. His last thought of the woman with large, blue eyes was that good fortune had absolutely nothing to do with her. Then all went black.

...

Snow shot up Grace's skirts, wetting her wool stockings, as she landed in a heap under the tree. Gasping, she pushed up off the man who'd come to her rescue. "Good God," she yelled as she saw the blood trickling from his scalp. Yanking off her gloves, her freezing fingers dug against his collar to find the pulse in his neck. She dropped her head in relief at the heavy thudding she felt below his skin. Still alive.

Wind gusted against her, throwing her hair out like thin whips to sting her eyes, eyes that swam with tears. Pushing off his chest, her gaze swiveled around. Horse with blood dripping down a leg. A stranger unconscious and bleeding beneath her. Blizzard blowing like white death. Wolves not too far away. Good God, what was she going to do? "Shite, shite, shite," she cursed as tears caught in her scarf, turning to salty ice against her skin. She pulled it from her mouth and chin to suck in gulps of cold air. Small pinpricks of light flashed in her periphery, and heavy sobs broke from her with the rushing of her shallow breaths flooding her ears. She blinked. *Oh God. We will all die.*

The horse neighed and walked over, holding its one leg up. His large body hovered close, over them as if shielding them from the frantic wind. Grace lifted her hand to touch its warm side. She'd always loved animals and had been a wonderful horsewoman in England. She glanced toward the direction the wolf had skulked off. It would smell the blood.

She had to do something, and passing out to die numbly was not an option. Grace shoved her glove back on. She inhaled, counting to four and exhaled counting out. The *sgian dubh*. Where was it? Grace churned through the feathery snow under the tree until she found her dagger. Running back to the man and horse, she used the knife to cut the bottom of her linen smock under her skirt, ripping it until a long strip came off. She dropped back next to the man's leg. The wolf had bitten his thigh, so she jerked up his kilt, exposing his powerful legs and—

"Oh, good Lord," she said, feeling her cheeks warm even though they were frozen. No time for polite sensibilities with him turning the snow red under his leg. She plucked the plaid from the puncture wounds that swelled with blood. She pressed clean snow on it until it turned into a macabre version of the snow cream dessert her mother used to make when she and Ava were children.

"Bloody hell, oh God." She continued to curse in whispers, occasionally passing the sign of the cross before her when unholy words about God's ballocks issued forth in her near panic. Wiping the snow off the Highlander's muscular thigh, she wrapped his leg tightly and tied it off. Moving up to his head, she ran her fingers through his thick hair and felt the stickiness of blood where the limb had hit him. Scalp wounds always bled profusely. She cleaned it with the heaping snow and cut off more of her smock to bind it.

Rising and whirling around, she saw the poor horse standing with bowed head. "Your turn," she said. Wipe, wash, cut smock, and bind. She ran her hands along the noble creature to his head. With a flick of the billets on each side of the saddle, she loosened the girth and guided the saddle off the horse's back, dropping it into the snow. There was a blanket under the saddle, which she pulled forward to cover more of the horse's head.

Breathing heavily, Grace focused on each task at hand while the white swirled around them. Lost, alone, and injured, if she allowed herself to think further than the circle of need around the three of them, she'd lose her mind to hysterics. Warriors were trained to prepare for disaster, not gentle ladies from English drawing rooms. Although, how could anyone prepare for this day? If she wasn't certain they were all going to die out in this freezing Hell, she'd have laughed. She'd wanted adventure, and by God she'd found one. And damnation, it was going to kill her.

Grabbing another blanket tied to the saddle, she lowered it over the man. Recalling the advice Thomas had given her, she trudged to an evergreen, its limbs heavy with snow. Using her *sgian dubh*, she sawed at several bushy evergreen boughs. Panting, her arms shaking with the effort, she dragged them back and jumped away as the horse lowered to the ground next to him.

"Oh, no, no," she said, leaping up to fix the blanket back over the animal. Stepping back around, she squatted at the man's side and pushed against him, trying to roll his heavy frame toward the horse. "I…have…to…get…these under you," she said, her teeth gritted as her heels dug in behind her.

"Sard it all!" she yelled, using the flame of anger to give her something besides fear to hold onto.

Grace shoved the pine boughs up against the man's side and laid two over the horse's back. She cut a few more, dragged them back, and laid them over the man, who was now completely covered with the blanket, snow, and evergreens. Yes! She'd done what Thomas had explained, well, most of it. And the horse would help keep the man warm. Hands on her hips, she turned in a tight circle and let her arms drop back down. Now what?

She had absolutely no idea which way to go. She'd wandered through the storm for nearly an hour before trying to duck into the cave where she'd come face-to-face with an immature wolf. Adorable in its youth, its parents were anything but. Now, as she struggled against the buffeting wind and snow that stung her eyes, she realized that her efforts for rescuing anyone were at an end. There was nothing else she could do. Gloved hands pressed to the side of her head, Grace looked down at the lumps of man and horse. At least she'd be warmer up against them, under the boughs and blanket and accumulating snow.

She looked out at the white where she could hardly see to the evergreen. There was no choice. Grace dropped to her knees, digging in the snow to find the edge of the wool blanket. Shaking flakes from her clothes, she lifted it and crawled underneath. The horse lay against one side of the stranger, a massive boulder of warm flesh. It was either lay half in the cold or on top of the man, so she wiggled her way across him, fixing the edge of the wool blanket to block the wind. Body heat filled the space, and the wool and boughs muted the bite of the gale. Grace worked the scarf away from her face for easier breathing, arching her back where she pressed over the massive body under her. In the dimness of the crude tent, she stared at the stranger, studying him for the first time.

Dark lashes lay against his skin that she guessed would be tanned from the sun. The shadow of a beard coated a strong, square jaw. His lips were the perfect shape, adding to the overall ruggedly handsome look. The strength and courage he'd shown in saving her, the compassion for not slaughtering the wolves and thus dooming the wolf pups, combined with his handsome face and thick, dark hair that fell in waves to his broad shoulders… "Good God," she whispered. "I'm in love with you already." She huffed at her ridiculous declaration. The cold was numbing her mind.

His chest filled with an inhale, lifting her under the shelter, and she braced her legs over his to stop from rolling off. Grace watched, unmoving, as the man's eyes blinked open.

"Oh," she whispered and inhaled past the fear tightening her throat. "Hello." He stared up at her, a crease forming between his brows.

"I am dead," he said. "Finally."

Finally? Did he wish to die?

His lips rubbed together, and she felt him shift, his gaze connected to hers. Before she could utter anything, his hand came up to cup her cheek. "And ye are my reward."

Chapter Three

Disoriented, Keir gave in to the desire that woke his aching body. He guided the angel before him, her wide eyes and smooth skin shadowed in the dimness. Her lips were cold but soft as he met them. He caught her gasp in his mouth but pressed on, lifting his other arm to hug her against his body. The pangs of pain shot through his thigh as she shifted against it, and the throbbing in his head made him pause. She'd slanted her mouth against his, returning his kiss, but when he stopped for the space of a heartbeat, she reared back.

Ice slammed against the side of his face. "*Mhac na galla*," he yelled and wiped the snow from his cheek. The angel had hit him.

"I know enough Gaelic to know what that means," she yelled back, rolling off his body, her leg hitting his thigh. He grunted, the pain clearing more of his mind.

"What the bloody hell is all this?" He turned his head from one side to the other, and his arms came up to throw off the heaviness overtop of the two of them.

"You're ruining our shelter," she said. "And there's a

bloody blizzard still going on."

The heavily clothed woman rose, throwing the blanket, snow, and what looked like branches down over his face. "There's a tree on me," he called up through the layers. He remembered the branch breaking, knocking him out, but this seemed to be a pine. Och. Beaten by a dead tree limb. If Brodie found out, Keir would never hear the end of it.

The woman cursed again, but the rest of her words were caught in the wind. Keir pushed up on his elbows and realized Cogadh was lying beside him. "Shite," he said and threw off the blanket and tree limbs. "Cogadh," he yelled, rising despite his leg.

"He's lame," she said. "I wrapped the wound on his right hock."

Keir rubbed a gloved hand along his horse's side under the wool blanket, feeling his friend's strong breaths.

"He's well enough for now," the woman yelled over the wind. "But we all need to find shelter."

Keir turned, sitting against Cogadh in the snow. The lass stood, white swirling around her, making her look like a small snow goddess come to earth. The lowering sun, blocked by the thick clouds, obscured her coloring, but her long hair whipped out from around her hood. The fur-lined cloak framed a heart-shaped face and large eyes. Brave and fierce, ignoring the gales shoving against her, molding her clothes to her body, she frowned. She wasn't afraid of him, didn't look like she was afraid of anything. Although, when he'd first found her screaming, she had been terrified.

"Either we cover back up and let your steed keep us alive with his body heat," she called, "or we find our way back to Kilchoan."

"Ye're from Kilchoan?" Pushing up, he stood closer to hear her words before the tempest snatched them away.

"From Aros on Mull. I am trying to find the apothecary

for a friend ill at Kilchoan, but I am lost."

Keir looked to the rock wall that he and Brodie had ridden around. Snow blew over the top, dropping into growing drifts. "There is a cabin close," he said, shaking the wool blanket free of snow and pine. He pushed the boughs off his horse and leaned down to peer into his face. "Up, friend."

Cogadh flicked his ears, snorting out warm steam into the frosty air. Using muscle and a rocking motion, he rose, his strong chest working to hold his weight. He lifted his back leg where the lass had tied a bandage. Keir rubbed the thick binding on his head. Where had she found wrappings?

"Come," he called as he led his steed by the bridle. He stepped around the snow-covered lump he assumed was the saddle. He'd return for it later.

A healer from Aros? Could she be the one he sought? Once Brodie tracked them down, they could return to Dunakin Castle when the storm ceased. Blast this snow. Foul weather and illness were the only enemies Keir couldn't slay.

"Do you know where you're going? How can you even see?" she asked. Her breath came in loud rasps through her scarf.

"I just traveled this way," he answered.

The pain in his leg ached, but he'd endured worse… however, never from an animal bite. Hopefully the lass had something for fever.

Heads bent into the wind, Keir looped his arm through the woman's to keep them together. Several times he helped her find her footing as they floundered up a hill, battered by the driving snow, which felt like ice daggers slicing his bare face. They rounded a dense strand of trees, and the rough sides of the small cabin came into view.

"Praise be," the woman called, relief so heavy it sounded like a sob.

He pushed open the door, sword out, but nothing stirred in the darkness. Abandoned and sturdy, a palace in this freezing world of ice.

The woman passed him, stepping barely inside the door, and Keir led Cogadh into the shelter.

"There are no stables?" she asked, unwinding the scarf from her face.

"He helped save your life, and he's injured."

"Of course. It's just…" She held out an arm to the small room. "I don't see any hay for the floor."

"He can shite without hay under him," Keir said, shutting the door firmly against the wind.

"That's what I'm afraid of," she mumbled and slapped the snow off her skirts.

Dropping his outer cloak on a wooden chair that looked barely able to withstand its weight, he went to the small hearth made of round stones. A searing pain mixed with the deep ache in his thigh. He grunted as he knelt.

"I'll do that," the woman said. "You need to lie down on that…moldy lump that's supposed to be a bed." She grabbed his arm, attempting to lift him. Startled by the contact, Keir let her lead him to the bed. When was the last time a woman had been concerned about his welfare, or had even touched him without clawing at him with desire? Ten years ago. The last time his mother had hugged him.

"I have flint in my satchel," she said, turning from him, her shoulders straight. He couldn't see much of her, but he was fairly certain there was a wee lass under all the layers. One with soft lips and the face of an angel. The memory of her pressed overtop of him made him wonder if the rest of her was fashioned more for sin than angelic endeavors.

"I will check your wound, sir, when I'm finished warming us." She dodged around Cogadh, reaching out to pat the horse's shoulder, ducking under his muzzle. She wasn't afraid of his gigantic war horse, either.

"I am not a sir," he said, his voice gruff from yelling in the storm.

"Give me a name to call you by then," she said, lowering onto her knees and striking against a small piece of flint to catch on a bit of wool. Luckily, there were dry twigs and peat already inside the small hearth.

"Keir. Keir Mackinnon of the Isle of Skye. From Dunakin Castle." He waited. Would she recognize his infamous name? It had been known to steal the breath from people.

She glanced over her shoulder and nodded to him. "I am Grace Ellington. Since we have both worked hard to save each other's lives this day, you may call me Grace."

"Ye are a *Sassenach*."

"Yes, I'm English, originally from York, but lately from Mull." The sparks caught on the wool and then the kindling, and she bent low to blow life into them.

"Aros? Ye are a healer there?"

She sat back on her heels and added some more dry grasses to feed the little flame. "Yes, and I'm on my way to Barra Isle to help a friend. But first, I must return to Kilchoan to help Thomas."

"Your husband?" The word tasted like bile on his tongue. If the fearless lass had a husband, she certainly wouldn't let him kiss her again. And he'd like to see if she tasted as sweet as he thought when he'd first awoken.

"No, he is a friend."

"A lover?"

Grace stood to look at him. It was dark with the fire beginning to grow behind her, but he was sure she glared. "A friend. An elderly friend who is married to a lovely, elderly woman back at Aros. He was escorting me to Kilchoan to sail to Barra when he was taken ill. I need to tend him before I continue my journey."

"Ye are going to Barra to heal someone?"

"To help with a birth."

He watched from his seat on the bed as she unwound the scarf and slid her wet cloak off her shoulders. Would she be a fragile waif, cold and easily crushed? He watched as she pulled off an overgown, leaving her in a kirtle and bodice that hugged her ample bosom. She turned, and her lush body silhouetted against the fire. Bloody hell, she was all womanly curves, sloping to a middle that was perfect for a man's hands. She raked fingers through her long hair before the heat of the fire, drying the length. Despite a body perfect for loving, she was more angel than devilish siren. An unwed virgin, perhaps, and someone who would want nothing to do with him.

The fire lit the small room, and she pulled the blanket from off Cogadh, snapping the melted snow from it and hanging it on a peg. "We should dry everything out." She dumped the contents of her leather bag on the crude table. "And dine on two oatcakes, dried venison, and a crushed tart." She looked up, meeting his eyes. "A feast."

"Your feast. Cogadh and I can do without." Deprivation was part of war, and they were both familiar with hunger pangs.

"Pish. Healing wounds need sustenance." She walked over to Cogadh and let him sniff her hand. Patiently waiting, she raised her palm, giving his horse ample time to examine her smell. Shifting slowly, his mighty warhorse leaned forward until his muzzle pressed into her palm. "There now," she said softly and stroked down his muzzle. She held up a bit of broken-off bannock for him to lap out of her hand. "You are a beauty, and I thank you."

Keir watched in amazement as she bent her forehead to touch his horse's. *Humph.* "I also saved your life," he said.

"Yes, you did," she said, still stroking his horse's face. She glanced his way. "Thank you." The fire glowed against her face, revealing the woman's creamy skin, perfect, straight nose, rosy, round cheeks, and large eyes. But it was the lovely bow of her full lips that caught his full attention. She smiled pleasantly without a hint of fear or lust. Slowly, one of her brows rose, and her smile flattened. "And I saved your life," she said, dragging out the last of the sentence in a blatant encouragement for him to thank her.

"I wouldn't have been bitten if I hadn't been saving ye."

A frown darkened her face. "The limb may still have dropped on you."

He shrugged. "I wouldn't have been near it or on the ground, but even so, I would simply have woken up and gone on my way."

"Arrogant," she mumbled and returned to stir up the fire. "You'd be a large, plaid-wrapped icicle, frozen until spring."

"Ye'll find Cogadh is as arrogant," he said as she fed his horse another bit of bannock. "He just doesn't talk."

"Maybe you should follow his example."

Keir snorted and felt his mouth curve into a grin. The lass was feisty, like his sister, Dara.

"What does his name mean?" she asked, taking an iron pot from the hearth.

"Cogadh means war in Gaelic."

"You named your horse 'war'?" She looked at him like he was insane. "When he was a sweet foal, toddling around the pen, nuzzling his mother to nurse, you named him 'war'?"

"My sister called him Little Laoch when he was a foal. It means Little Warrior."

Grace patted Cogadh on his hindquarters and shook her head. When she opened the door, the wind blew about the room, killing the warmth. She scooped up snow with the pot and slammed the door. "God's teeth, we aren't going anywhere tonight."

She sounded furious and forlorn at the same time. It was fortunate she could not read Keir's mind. Snug up in a dry, warm cottage with a lass as brave and beautiful as a goddess, Keir couldn't remember a more promising predicament.

Chapter Four

"You are hot," Grace said, her palm flat on Keir's forehead.

"'Tis better than dead cold," he said, eyes closed, but a grin transformed his serious face into something more playful.

She snorted and laid a damp piece of her torn smock on his forehead. "Too hot leads to dead cold." Grace had boiled the snow and washed his wolf bite, as well as the shallow wound on his horse's hock. She had some honey and several bulbs of garlic, so she mashed and mixed them together to make a poultice. "I need to pack your leg and wrap it."

With a flick of his hand, he yanked off the blanket that she'd been tucking and raised his kilt. Grace's cheeks flamed at the sight of his muscular thighs, the kilt barely hiding his manhood, which she remembered only too well. "Thank you," she said and patted his hand to get him to drop the plaid.

Reaching back, he cradled his head so that his elbows jutted outward, making his biceps strain against the linen of his shirt. Lowering her gaze to his wound, she dabbed globs of the honey-garlic mixture onto each of the puncture holes and gashes from the wolf's teeth. "'Tis a good thing for you that I don't believe in men turning into werewolves. Else you'd need to worry about me planting my dagger in your heart when you fall asleep."

"And ruin all your hard work at keeping me alive?" he asked.

Lifting her kirtle, she used the dagger to start the tear of another round of somewhat clean linen fabric. The warrior shifted and cracked his eyes open at the ripping sound. "Ye'll have little left of your smock by the time we are healed," he said, his low voice strumming a warm path through Grace. It was an intimate voice, as if they were lovers, and he was imagining her out of her smock.

"Be happy I have it, and wasn't instead running about the forest naked," she murmured, bending closer to work the cloth under his thigh, which seemed as thick with muscle as a tree trunk. "Else you could have bled to death."

"Ye would be an angelic, ice-blue, naked icicle," he said.

She turned her head to look up at him from her bent position and paused, caught by his stare. The fire crackled in the hearth, while the blizzard whipped around the eves. Nothing else stirred. Even his horse had closed his eyes, dozing while standing near the door. "You called me an angel when you woke." She should look away, finish the wrapping, but she wondered what thoughts might twist inside him. His dark eyes were mesmerizing.

He shrugged. "I thought I was dead," he said. "And ye have the look of one."

She straightened up. "You thought you were dead, and you kissed me? Sinfully kissed me."

"Aye." He lowered his arms.

She raised an eyebrow. "So, that is what you plan to do when you reach the gates of Heaven? Kiss an angel and hope God doesn't throw you down to Hell?"

A lazy smile curved his mouth. "If a kiss from an angel

tastes as good as ye, I'd gladly risk damnation."

She exhaled a laugh in a huff and shook her head to look back at his swollen leg. "You are definitely feverish, Keir Mackinnon."

"I wasn't when I kissed ye," he said, his eyes closing.

Tying the ends of the poultice, she stood. "I will say a prayer for your sinful soul."

"Good," he murmured. "For God doesn't listen to my prayers."

She frowned. "God listens to all prayers." Taking the dry leaves of feverfew, Grace added them to some melted snow in a small crock and set it on the smoldering coals. She needed to get it into Keir before his fever grew out of control. Once the storm blew out, she must try to hike back to Kilchoan to find help and see to Thomas. Hopefully, the maid was tending him.

Grace took the shovel for the ashes to the door. A horse in the house, good God. Forcing her overused muscles into more action, she scraped the refuse, shoving the mess out the front door before struggling against the wind to shut it again, lowering the bar. She turned to lean against the door, breathing heavily as her eyes went back to the bed. Gone?

"Keir?" she called and stopped when she heard the obvious sound of him urinating in the privy pot set in the back corner. "Oh," she whispered and turned to face the door. What had she gotten herself into? A blizzard, wolves, a heated kiss from a stranger, and now mucking out a house occupied by a horse named War and a man who had no modesty. She'd asked for an adventure, and God, or Satan, had provided.

"Ye can turn back around now, lass," he called, and she heard the creak of the bed.

Grace retrieved the crock from the coals with her gloves. "I have some brewed feverfew for you to drink," she said and stopped, her eyes taking in the sight before her.

Keir sat up in the bed, the blanket over only his feet. He'd taken off his linen shirt and leaned against the wall at his back. Broad shoulders, thickly muscled arms, and his entire toned chest lay bare, down past his navel where the low edge of his kilt wrapped his narrow waist. Dark swaths of pigment painted his one arm from shoulder to elbow in pointed curves around his biceps like intricate blades. Grace swallowed and walked closer, noticing the scars lining his physique.

In the dim light, she hoped he couldn't see the blush that rushed up her neck and into her face. She was a healer, after all, and shouldn't be affected by the sight of a man's naked body. "'Tis hot," she said, but he took the crock, holding it around the rim.

Grace watched as he lifted it to his beautiful lips and sipped. "You should drink it all to help bring down your fever." Her gaze fell on his chest and shoulder where more dark marks lined up in rows that ran down his right side. She blinked, leaning in. "Are those…crosses?"

He swallowed. "Aye."

She bent to look closer at the small, simple marks of gray and black. "You have been…branded?" With crosses, hundreds of them, in lines running down the side of his torso and across his hip to sweep along his back where she couldn't see. She noticed other designs on his chest, too, under the light sprinkling of hair, over his heart.

"Not with fire, but with ink," he said. "They represent those I've killed in battle." He drank the rest of the feverfew.

"So many?"

All teasing from earlier had vanished, leaving a hard, hollow look to his glassy eyes. "Five hundred eighty-seven."

Grace's entire body tensed as they stared at each other in the shadows. She was face-to-face with the most lethal person she'd ever known. Only the memory of him throwing down his sword to save the wolf pups, by not killing their parents, allowed her to inhale. "Five hundred eighty-seven men?"

"One woman," he said, sliding a finger down his side to a white cross on his hip bone. "She was a warrior from the Isle of Lewis. Fierce." He said the word with respect.

"Oh," Grace whispered. "You…have been a warrior for a long time." Five hundred eighty-seven people. The little crosses printed permanently on his smooth, tan skin took on the solemnness of a battle memorial. Bloody hell, that's exactly what it was.

"Aonghus Mackinnon took me into battle starting when I was sixteen." His finger slid up to his shoulder, resting on a cross at the top. "My first kill was an Irishman warring with the Macleods for money, a mercenary."

"You remember him?" she asked softly.

His eyes were dark in the shadows. "I remember them all."

She let her gaze slide down the line of crosses. Finger extended, she touched one with the tip. "This one then?"

He looked down. "That row, and half the next, was a battle at Kyle of Lochalsh, inland from Skye, about seven years ago. A raid to repay a raid on Skye." He turned to lean his head back on the wall and closed his eyes. "That particular warrior was old, no teeth, but still very brutal. He died well."

"And the marks running down your arm?" she asked, peering at the dark, smooth marks curving along the muscles of his shoulder and mountainous biceps.

"To remind people who I am."

"Who are you?" she whispered.

His eyes opened to meet her stare. "The Devil of Dunakin Castle."

"Oh." Grace's mind churned through images she'd seen of devils. She felt his forehead, sliding her hand up to touch the spot where the scalp wound had scabbed over. "No horns? Maybe a forked tail painted down the back of a leg?"

The hard lines of Keir's mouth relaxed, followed by the

quake of a chuckle in his chest. "Nay, not yet, but I could talk to Brodie to see if he could do it."

"I think it will be hard enough to get into Heaven with five hundred eighty-seven crosses on your body. Horns and a forked tail might doom you beyond redemption," she said.

A grin spread across his lips. "Especially when I'm kissing an angel first thing."

"Exactly." She pulled the blanket up higher over his kilt and stomach. "When you first woke up out there in the snow, before you lost your mind and kissed a strange woman—"

"Who was lying on top of me."

She ignored his comment. "You said…'I am dead. Finally.'" She paused, watching his face. Firelight and shadows played along his sloped nose and darkly chiseled features. "What did you mean by 'finally'?"

His grin faded. "When a tree falls on a man, it can make him think and say odd things, lass." She met his stare, waiting, but he closed his eyes and worked his way back down the bed to lie flat.

She stood up. "Tomorrow you will need to teach me how to set a trap."

"Aye, milady," he answered, his voice thick with the beginnings of sleep as he turned toward the back of the room.

Grace traced, with her gaze, the rows of crosses that extended around his side onto his back. He'd memorized the lives he'd taken, using his own skin to mark their passing. A chill spider-walked along Grace's spine, and she wrapped her arms around herself as she went to tend the fire. The Devil of Dunakin, a warrior who remembered those fallen. Powerful and obviously fierce, but with a heart of compassion for a family of wolves out to kill him. A man willing to help a woman stranded in a blizzard.

She looked to his horse, War, who blinked at her with large, dark brown eyes. "You deserve a rest," she whispered to the animal, her gaze shifting to the man in the bed. "You and your warrior."

• • •

Keir ached. He knew this ache, the pain of resolving infection and the stiffness from lying in bed. It ran through his body, weakening him, and he hated it. Weakness was not allowed. Only strength honored his clan. He'd rather die than be weak. However, he'd been in this position often as he healed from battle wounds, and knew that the fastest way to regain strength was to let the healing take place. But it made him sour.

He opened his eyes to a gray dawn light filling an empty cabin, and the snowstorm came back to him. Keir pushed up onto one elbow and exhaled in frustration at the ache running down his back muscles and the throbbing pain in his thigh. Where was Cogadh and the woman, Grace?

Keir wiped his brow and looked at his hand. Wet. His stomach growled, and a wave of thirst made him rub a hand over his dry lips. All good signs that his fever was ended.

A sound outside the unbarred door caught his attention, and the door opened. "Bloody, blasted snow," Grace murmured as she pushed into the cabin, striding directly to the fire to drop her load. Stretching her back, she turned toward him, her breasts jutting outward with her arch, and gasped. "You're awake." Throwing off her gloves, she rushed over, hair standing on end from dragging her scarf away.

Her golden-brown hair flew about as if lightning lit her from within. He raised his palm to feel the brush of the ends. "Your hair, lass, seems to be alive."

"What? Oh," she said and almost hit him as she ran her free hand over her head. "'Tis from the scarf."

He sat against the wall at his back, the ache in his thigh reminding him why he had slumbered instead of completing his mission. "The blizzard blew out," he said. "As did my fever."

Grace studied him. Even with her hair sticking out at odd angles, her high cheeks, flushed pink from the cold, and her brilliant blue eyes made her the bonniest lass he'd ever seen. "Yes, the blizzard stopped trying to topple this cottage. But your fever…" She touched his head and then his chest. He looked down at her small hand, flattened over the tattoos emblazoned across his heart. So soft. Most women were afraid to touch his markings.

A smile bloomed across her mouth, making her lips look incredibly inviting. "But your fever took three days to break."

Keir's brows lowered. "I've been asleep for three days?"

"Going on your fourth, really. I've nearly lost track of time trying to force liquid into you and keeping us warm."

"Where is Cogadh?"

"Little Warrior is doing better than you. He's snug and comfortable in a little barn out back. He has a blanket and fresh water and hay to munch. Unlike us." She gestured toward some sticks and rope near the hearth. "I tried to rig some traps, but I have no idea what I'm doing. Anytime I tried to get you to help me, you'd mumble names." She crossed her arms over her ample chest. "I assume of people those crosses represent, because you also would say how they died. Spear to heart. Slashed throat and so on. I stopped asking you about the traps."

Grace turned and shucked her fur-lined cape. "You mentioned two women," she said. "Margaret and Bradana."

He didn't say anything, and she turned to look at him. "Is one your wife?"

"Nay," he answered. "Margaret was my mother, and Bradana was my brother's wife."

"Was?"

"They are both dead," he said, his voice going flat.

"I…I am sorry, Keir. Are they marked on your skin, too?"

"Aye, the crosses over my heart."

Her gaze moved to his bare chest, but Keir grabbed his shirt that lay folded to one side and threw it on. "Did ye put the table and chairs out with Cogadh?" he asked, changing the subject.

She glanced around the bare room. "I had to break apart the furniture to feed the fire."

"Quite resourceful and clever. Ye've done a valiant job at keeping us alive."

Her features lightened, and she smiled, as if his praise was as valuable as firewood and food. "One twitch of you growing fur and fangs, and I'd have been forced to kill you, though. I'd have had to put one of those little crosses somewhere on me." She placed another slat of wood on the fire.

"Ye've done well to heal me, but I thought the healer of Aros was Mairi Maclean," he said, watching her closely.

She brushed her hands and shrugged, standing. "There are several healers at Aros, myself included. Mairi's mother is much more talented at working cures than she." She looked at him, her lovely face bright. "And Mairi's not at Aros anymore. I am actually on my way to help her birth her first child on the Isle of Barra."

"Barra?" he asked, his brows lowering. "Where Kisimul Castle sits in the bay?"

"Yes. She's married to the chief of the MacNeils, the Wolf of Barra." She laughed quietly. "Down in England titles like Earl, Duke and Baron are given to people. Up here, titles like Wolf and Beast and"— she indicated him—"Devil are much more common."

"The Scots are fiercer," he murmured, his mind chewing on this new information. Was Grace misleading him about Mairi? Why would she? She had no reason to guess his urgent mission or the lengths to which he would go to complete it.

He'd been tasked to find the talented healer, Mairi Maclean, but she was about ready to have a bairn, and she was wed to the chief of Kisimul, a castle that had never been breached. To retrieve the woman, he'd have to sail all the way to Barra, find a way into the castle, and take her without harming the bairn. And if she wasn't a talented healer, the risk and time required warranted a change in strategy.

"How is Cogadh?" he asked as he considered the timing.

"Little Warrior is nearly healed, and he's too sweet to be called War in any language." She brought over a hot cup of brewed feverfew and half a tart she'd saved, which he took greedily. The bitter taste of the hot drink was familiar, bringing back snatches of warped memory. Grace wiping his chest with a rag. Grace forcing him to drink the brew. Grace praying over him.

Praying? Not even the priest on Skye prayed for Keir. He swallowed the last drop, his mind latching onto a new mission, and handed the cup back. She smiled broadly without a hint of disgust or fear. The lass didn't know his past sins and wicked reputation. And she surely didn't know what he had planned for her, or she'd have left him to die, frozen to the ground.

Chapter Five

"There are more wolf tracks in the snow," Grace said, pushing into the cottage, her heart beating in her throat. "They've been around the cabin since the storm stopped." Which was why she had delayed attempting to find Kilchoan, for fear of getting lost again and eaten. She swallowed and looked to Keir, frowning. "Why are you standing?"

"I'm going to see my horse."

She'd managed to keep him in bed for another day, but he was obviously not accustomed to resting. "You shouldn't put pressure on your leg. I sewed in a few stitches to keep the puncture wounds closed. Strain could open them."

Grace watched Keir check his thick thigh, which did seem to be healing with her poultice. She'd been watching him for a week, mostly alone with her thoughts as she washed his chest, legs, amazing arms. There wasn't an inch of fat on his lean, muscled body. The marks, swirling up his arm, only accented the curves of his biceps.

"I must insist—" she started.

"It's healing well, thanks to ye." He grabbed the cloak

he'd worn when he'd rescued her, and brushed past her on the way to the door. "I will come back."

Grace's breath stuttered at his nearness and kind words. Her whole body thrummed with the possibility of… Of what? Asking him to kiss her again? Seducing him? She felt her cheeks warm and watched the man step out into the deep snow. Such things didn't happen to her. She was the woman who smiled politely while a handsome man asked the lady next to her to dance. She was the friend or sister or assistant to the woman people wanted to meet. But then again, she'd never been on an adventure by herself before.

Grace threw her cape back on and grabbed her scarf, following him out the door. "I will accompany you to make sure you don't fall," she called, running to catch up to him.

The snow lay in two-foot drifts, and they walked the path that she and Little Warrior had blazed the morning after the storm when she'd spotted the barn. Grace pointed to the tracks that circled both the cabin and the barn. "Those are wolf tracks, aren't they?"

"Aye," Keir said. He walked beside her without the aid of a crutch. His face was set in a hard line, but he didn't grimace. Despite his display, Grace knew he must be in pain. When they stopped at the barn door, she could see the line of sweat on his forehead, but he didn't hesitate and pushed inside.

His horse turned toward them, ears twitching. He snorted, bobbing his large head. Grace laughed lightly. "I think he's smiling."

Keir walked up and stroked Little Warrior's nose. Leaning in, he rested his forehead there. Grace stayed back, feeling a bit like she was interrupting a private reunion.

"He is well?" Keir asked, still pressed to Little Warrior's face, his fingers scratching around his ears.

"I've changed the bandage daily. His injuries were not too deep, and I cleaned them as soon as we arrived before any taint could set in. We will need to wait until he can accept your weight before we leave with your leg still healing."

"I can walk."

"No," she said, her chin and voice rising with determination. "You will ride or you will re-injure all the good I've done."

Keir moved to the horse's right hock wrapped with her smock. Grace came around to lift the leg so Keir didn't have to bend his knee. The obedient horse didn't move as she unwrapped the binding. "See, he's healing well. Another week and he'll be able to carry you."

"A week is too long," he said, frowning. "A day or two at most." He stroked the horse's side.

Grace propped her hands on her hips, something she'd never have done down in England as the Earl of Somerset's daughter. But now she was a wild Scotswoman, free and knowledgeable about healing. "*If* you are better."

She rewrapped the horse's leg. "I will leave you two to your visit," she said, cooling her voice to seem disinterested instead of being slightly jealous of a horse being stroked. "If you are strong enough, we can check on the snares when you return to the cottage."

He glanced her way from the pile of hay in the far corner of the small building. "I'm always strong enough."

Grace rolled her eyes. Men, warriors especially, were stubborn arses about their health and strength. "Yes, yes, you could lift mountains and wrestle lions with one leg cut clean off," she said with a flip of her hand.

...

Keir watched the barn door close and turned to Cogadh. "If she screams, I'll have to go." The wolves might return.

He sat on the edge of a built-in wooden seat that Grace hadn't yet splintered with an axe to burn. The woman had accomplished much for a gentle creature. Keir's sister would have killed and gutted a buck by now, but Grace… She was made of softer stuff. Aye, much softer, in all aspects. That golden-brown hair felt like silk when he'd risked a touch earlier. Her skin looked like pure cream, and he knew her lips were soft, although the memory was more like a half-forgotten dream after his fever.

If he wanted to kiss her again, he must before they left the cabin. He frowned, but the twisted feeling that came with fulfilling duty above all else was familiar to Keir. As the feared Devil of Dunakin, protecting the clan and serving out justice was his life. He needed to carry a healer back to Dunakin as fast as possible. Hopefully, his sister, Dara, and his wise grandmother were keeping his nephew, Lachlan, alive. If Keir's brother, Rabbie, lost his only surviving child, after his wife and daughter had died in childbirth last year, he would surely forfeit his mind. As it was, Rabbie seemed to balance on the edge of irate madness most of the time now. No, young Lachlan must live, and that required a talented healer.

In the silence of the barn, Keir's stomach growled in a low, twisting echo within his empty stomach. Cogadh snorted, his ears twitching. "Ballocks," Keir said, pushing up into a stiff stance, his thigh feeling bruised and tight. He narrowed his eyes at his faithful horse. "Ye have your food stacked up in here, while my stomach's been empty for nearly five days."

He checked Cogadh's water and headed out into the blinding white landscape. Squinting, Keir turned in the direction of a small creek where he'd told Grace to set the rock trap, to knock an unsuspecting animal into the water to drown, tied to the tethered buoy.

"Where are you going?" Grace asked from the doorstep of the cabin, apparently waiting for him. She strode through the snow.

"Checking the traps," he said as she reached him. "If ye

didn't set them perfectly right, they won't work." A hungry belly was worse than bruised feelings.

Stepping up to the creek, Keir noticed Grace remained behind several feet. He knelt by the edge where her earlier footprints marked the spot, but the rock wasn't there. It had already fallen into the water. "It's been triggered," he said. "Come see."

"I go near water only when absolutely necessary," she said. "Did I catch something?"

"Or ye didn't set it right." He grabbed the rope tied to the rock and pulled it up from the freezing current. "Well, bloody hell," he said.

"What?" Grace stood yards behind him.

He looked over his shoulder and opened his eyes wide with shock. "Ye actually trapped us a meal." He lifted the large rabbit from the stream. "Maybe ye are an angel if ye can work such miracles," he teased.

As he turned, a snowball flew straight into his face.

Chapter Six

Grace clamped a hand over her smile as Keir wiped his snow-covered cheek. "I didn't mean to hit your face," she said and squeaked as he rose. She grabbed up her skirts and leaped forward through the snow.

"Revenge is cold." His deep voice didn't sound amused. "Icy cold."

Was he running after her? "You'll pull your stitches," she yelled and gasped as a ball of snow hit her in the back. She bent down to make another ball and turned.

Keir stood in the snow-draped woods, looking like some Norse god from one of the ancient manuscripts she'd seen in her father's library as a child. Powerful and lethal, he was fodder for nightmares, except he held a snowball instead of a bloody axe. Ducking back down, she gathered another ball and volleyed it at him. But with the extended distance and lack of surprise, he easily dodged, hurling one back at her.

"No fair," she said laughing, brushing her cape, which was crusted now with a circular ice patch.

"More fair than hitting a man with no warning." He

stalked toward her, a snowball in hand.

"I meant to hit your shoulder," she said and dodged the icy ball by a mere inch. Turning, she ran, arms pumping. Surely she could move faster than a man with tooth marks boring into his thigh. Leaping to cut through the snow toward the cabin, Grace took three strides before Keir's arms stretched around her.

"Bloody hell," she yelled, laughing as his momentum felled them both, their bodies breaking through the crisp surface of an unblemished drift. He turned them so that they landed on his unhurt leg, plowing half of Grace's face into the snow.

She spit the ice from her mouth. "Horrible wretch," she said, attempting to roll away from him, but the height of the drift didn't allow her to gain distance. She flopped onto her back, where Keir's face loomed above her, framed by the blue, sun-filled sky.

His smile matched her own, making him all the more handsome. Longish hair hung about his ruggedly chiseled features, and his eyes sparked with unguarded merriment. "Never attack without a planned retreat."

"I had a plan." She laughed, her eyes wide.

"One that has half a chance to work."

She watched his lips move over white teeth. Her heart beat faster as she realized he pinned her to the ground. A giddy feeling thrummed through Grace. Was this what Ava felt every time Tor touched her?

Inhaling smoothly to cover her reaction, she poked his shoulder. "It had a good chance of working, since you are supposed to be injured, but I suppose I am such a skilled healer that you are able to run faster than I thought."

"And my aim is true," he replied, smiling down at her.

She rolled her eyes. "You've had much more training than me. It was hardly a contest."

"And yet ye started it." He shifted slightly so that both his arms framed her head, but he kept his body off to the side. "What in bloody hell were ye thinking, lass?"

She opened her eyes wide, imitating his look at the streamside. Pursing her lips, she imitated his Scot's accent. "Maybe ye are an angel if ye can work such miracles," she said.

His smile broadened. "Ye took that poorly."

Her face pinched into a frown, and she reached out to grab another gloveful of snow. He dodged to the side as she tried to smear it in his face, catching her wrists easily in his hands. She laughed at his grin, both of them breathing with their stomachs rising against each other. They were hidden down in the snow, the powerful sun slaking across them to warm Grace's cheeks. Grace grew silent as she stared into Keir's dark brown eyes. The world around them faded away.

Without a word, she slid one hand from his grasp to touch the side of his face. Even through her glove, she could feel the strength in his jaw as she stroked down his neck to his shoulder. He leaned closer, casting her face in shadow, and she closed her eyes. She knew his kiss was coming, but when his lips touched hers, her heart leaped high within her. She grasped his shoulders to draw him in, slanting her face to meet him fully.

Keir's fingers curled in the edge of the shawl covering her head, raking into her hair. His mouth moved over hers, meeting her, yet seeming to hold back, too. Did he think she was fragile, a coy virgin afraid to experience passion? She was a virgin, but passion was not something that frightened her. Quite the contrary, Grace yearned for it.

Yanking at her gloves, to toss away in the snow, Grace plunged her fingers through Keir's wavy hair, pulling his face closer until their kiss grew more urgent, more reckless. His free hand stroked down her neck and lower across her breasts. Even with the many layers separating her skin from his touch, his caress teased her senses, causing heat to ache down through her very center. Grace pushed upward against his hard body, instincts taking over her rational mind. She wanted more—more kissing, more touching, more of this large, powerful warrior pressing against her.

Keir leaned farther over her so he could hold her face in both of his hands. The hardness of his body thrilled Grace, and she molded herself upward against him, her knees parting at the feel of his erection. She was wanton, hot and achingly wanton. "Keir," she whispered against him, the chill tingling her kiss-dampened lips.

"Aye?" He left her mouth to kiss the side of her jaw, his fingers licking a path of fire along her neck.

She hadn't a clue what to say, and her rational, cautious self abandoned her completely. "More," she said, feeling drunk on the word.

He paused for the slightest of seconds, a low growl issuing from the back of his throat as he met her gaze before lowering to kiss and tease her neck with nibbles. Good Lord, she'd just thrown all constraint to the winter wind, with a man called a devil. What was she thinking? Things like this didn't happen to her. Her mother had warned her to refuse carnal desires. At the time, Grace had had no idea what those were, but now she felt them. They were desires so fierce that she was tempted to ruck up her skirts for a virtual stranger, in a snowdrift, no less.

Forcing her eyes open, Grace slapped her palm at one of Keir's large shoulders as she stared at his bent head where he kissed the hollow of her exposed throat. He lifted, shifting his weight, and gazed down into her face. She stared up at his deep brown eyes, filled with desire, and rubbed her kiss-moistened lips together.

"We…" She breathed hard, trying to let the coolness of the air beat back the heat raging within her body. "We…we left the hare back at the stream. Some other animal might be dining on the meal I caught for us."

He stared at her for a long moment, as if her words were nonsensical gibberish. "The rabbit by the stream. We should retrieve it," she repeated. Her breath came rapidly, and she watched as his face relaxed, the haze of passion cooling back to sense.

Pushing up, he gave her a wry smile. "Of course. We wouldn't want to lose your lucky catch." As he stood, Grace could tell he favored the injured leg, but he still reached down to help pull her from the snowdrift. He brushed down her back, even over her backside. "Ye're coated in snow."

Face heated, Grace stepped away from the outline their bodies had made in the drift. "I will melt," she said and chanced a look up at him despite her blush. "Shall I collect the hare?"

He studied her, curiosity in the narrowness of his eyes. Did he think her fickle? A frivolous girl who sought to push virile men to the edge of sanity and then joyfully refuse them? The flames in her cheeks flooded down her neck, and she opened her mouth to say something.

"Nay," he answered before she could come up with a defense or apology or whatever was suitable. "If ye prepare the fire inside the cabin, I'll skin and gut it. We'll have roast rabbit for supper." He turned to trudge back, following the path they'd blazed before.

• • •

Lasses were impossible to understand.

He worked his knife under the skin of the large hare, freeing it from the meat that would soon be spitted and roasting. His stomach growled even if his mind focused on the strange twist of events less than an hour ago. Grace had pulled him down to her, hadn't she? She'd shut her eyes, her lips parting in anticipation of his kiss. And she'd pressed against him, and blast it, she'd said "more." He cursed softly and slit the small animal to remove the entrails.

He exhaled long, watching his breath puff out in a quickly fading cloud. It was true that he'd never kissed a virgin before, and with her unguarded, innocent look, Keir was fairly certain Grace was a virgin. Inexperienced lasses stayed far away from him, their mothers collecting them like hens after chicks when a fox roams near. As if he'd eat them up and spit out their young bones. His only experience with females was confined to brazen, vastly experienced women who were drawn to his dangerous personage, his strength, and his reputation for loving a lass vigorously.

Working the thick iron spit through the rabbit, he thought back over the snow fight and subsequent kiss. She was innocent, but what he'd felt in her response was enticing beyond anything he'd ever known. He rubbed his chin where his beard was growing in during the journey.

"Bloody hell," he said low. She had no idea who he really was, no idea the jeopardy she was in, no idea what he planned to do with her. He should stay far away from Grace Ellington. Grabbing up the heavily weighted spit, he walked around the cabin, opening the door.

Grace pivoted toward him from near the hearth, her hand across her breast like he'd startled her.

"My apologies." He held up the rabbit. "Ready to roast."

"No," Grace said, her hands clasping together.

"No?" he asked. "'Tis better to cook it. Raw rabbit will likely give ye worms, lass."

Her face scrunched in beautiful confusion, and her eyes dipped to the spit in his hand. "Not the rabbit. I mean, no, you don't need to apologize. I'm the one who must apologize." She stepped back, motioning him to place the spit in the iron holders over the low fire that she'd banked.

"And what are ye apologizing for?"

She exhaled long, walking over to sit on the edge of the bed that she'd straightened. "I didn't mean to attack you out there." She waved an arm toward the wall.

Keir leaned back against the hearth and crossed his arms. He barely noticed the ache in his thigh, not with the most fascinating words coming out of the bonniest mouth he'd ever kissed. He'd never been apologized to before, either. "Attack me?"

"Yes. It was… I didn't mean to…" She was having a hard time speaking a full sentence. "I am not usually wanton, Keir, especially with someone I've helped heal. I don't usually make men kiss me."

He tipped his head to the side. "So ye made me kiss ye." He uncrossed his arms.

"Yes, and I apologize."

He took a step closer. To hell with his decision to stay away from her. "Ye did, lass."

"I know," she said, folding her slender fingers in her lap, fingers that he'd felt claw through his hair.

He shook his head, for she had no bloody idea what she was doing to him. "Your damnably soft lips and your smooth skin and silky hair. It was a trap, along with that sweet laughter of yours and cleverness. All of it in your arsenal of weapons to use against an innocent man."

She stared at him, eyes growing wide. Her lips parted. "I…I meant when I pulled you down to kiss me," she said.

If she was experienced, he'd swear her declaration was merely an act to entice him to ravish her. Because her wide-eyed innocence was shattering any remnants of resolve to stay away from her.

Keir rubbed the back of his neck and walked over to stand before her where she sat on the bed. "I accept your apology."

He gazed down at her, taking in the soft beauty. "And seeing that ye are an angel, without much experience dealing with devils, I want to let ye know…" He lowered his voice to an intimate level. "All ye need to do is say 'more' again, and I will love ye so fiercely that your angel wings will melt off like Icarus flying too close to the sun."

For the space of several heartbeats she stared, chin dropped open, as if she were frozen.

Keir inhaled fully and turned to walk toward the door. "I'll be back when I smell cooked rabbit." He stepped out of the cabin. *Damnation.* He'd need to take another snow bath to cool his blood. The woman didn't know her allure nor her jeopardy at being trapped with him. If she continued to stare at him with those wide blue eyes, devoid of fear, he'd kiss the very breath from her. And heaven help her if she uttered that one syllable: *more*.

Ignoring the ache in his leg, he threw off his clothes near the barn and washed with icy white until his body numbed enough for comfort. "Bloody hell. Icarus?" he murmured as he scrubbed the melting snow over his skin. If Brodie had heard his poetry he'd laugh for hours, or until Keir punched him in the mouth. Keir grunted and washed around the binding on his leg. He fingered the bit of lace attached to it. Once, the bandage had been Grace's smock, brushed her legs as she walked. What would those legs feel like, bare and wrapped around his arse?

Was he enough of a devil to find out?

Chapter Seven

Grace sat on the bed for long minutes, her palms flat against her cheeks. "More," she whispered. "Good God." The word had nearly rolled from her mouth. What would be happening right now if it had? The thought brought back the ache she'd felt while kissing Keir in the snow. But was she willing to give up her maidenhead to find out exactly how it felt to be loved by a man as powerful and passionate as Keir Mackinnon?

Some women were known to throw honor to the wind, but titled English ladies knew their innocence was highly prized and required to secure an advantageous marriage. Grace slid her hands off her cheeks to fist in her lap. *But I'm not in England anymore.* The thought coiled through her like the biblical serpent tempting Eve.

In fact, she didn't plan to ever return to York or Somerset Estate. It held too many terrible memories of her brother torturing her. With his death, she planned to sell it off to some Englishman. She didn't want an advantageous marriage, because it would mean leaving Scotland, a rugged land that she'd grown to love over the last year and a half. No, she would never leave. Living a pampered life on a grand estate was not something she'd ever truly desired, which was why she'd been eager to leave Somerset with Ava to escape her brother. No, she'd much rather live an adventure, and this was definitely an adventure.

Grace realized she'd walked to the hearth and bent to turn the roasting rabbit. *God's teeth!* It was damn hot in the cottage. Or was that the effects of thinking about the brawny warrior who'd just given her the power to choose what would occupy their time tonight?

Taking off her outer kirtle, Grace went to the door to let in a little fresh air. She pulled it open and froze. Standing beside the barn was Keir, completely naked. His perfect buttocks curved tightly from his narrow waist. His legs were thick and long, and his back muscles flexed as he grabbed more snow, scrubbing it over his skin. He raised his arms over his head to smash snow into his hair and over his face. When he began to turn, Grace pivoted and slammed the door.

"*Mo chreach,*" she cursed in Gaelic. He'd have to be deaf not to hear the bang. Would he think she'd been spying on him? She hurried back to the hearth to turn the rabbit. "Trapped," she whispered. This whole reaction, the heat and heart thumping, the clenching in her loins, the pearling of her nipples, and the kiss she'd initiated. It was all from being trapped with the handsome, virile man for five days.

The sun lowered outside, casting the room in shadow as she turned the spit and considered her options. One, she could do nothing and avoid Keir. Although that would be difficult in the small space. Maybe if she asked, he'd sleep in the barn. Or two, she could call him in, look him straight in the face and say "more." Was she brave enough? She snorted. Doubtful.

The Devil of Dunakin? Yes, Keir Mackinnon could definitely turn her toward sin. She looked around her. Caught together in this small cottage, they could fornicate in the most inventive, pleasure-eliciting ways all night and day without anyone knowing. It would be an adventure that could live in her fondest memories for the rest of her non-adventurous life.

Grace looked to the pot of melted snow she kept heated over the back of the hearth. If Keir had washed the week's grime away, she would do the same. Just in case. The thought made another surge of passion tighten through her body. She used the extra energy to lift the pot, carrying it behind the blanket she'd hung in the dark corner. There was nothing she could do about her poor smock, ripped around and around up her legs, so she abandoned it altogether. She used a rag from it and a small bit of floral-smelling soap from her satchel and washed as best she could. Her hair would have to wait, but at least her skin was rosy, clean, and freshly scented.

The door opened. "Do I smell rabbit?" Keir asked, making Grace's fingers fly to tie on her long sleeves.

"Turn the spit, please," she called. "I'll be right out." Without the smock, the dress rubbed against her naked body. Her legs and womanly *V* felt exposed, adding to the indecent thoughts that kept sliding into her mind. She brushed a comb through her long waves, letting them fall naturally down to her hips. She pinched her cheeks and smoothed a finger over her lips. It was the best she could do without provisions.

Grace stepped out from behind the screen and walked toward Keir. Since she'd burned all the furniture except the bed, he was slicing the rabbit meat on the flat stone built into the hearth. "It seems cooked through," he said. He skewered a chunk of moist cooked meat onto his dagger and turned, holding it out to Grace. His gaze met her face but slid along her hair and frame. He tipped his head to her. "Ye look fresh. Here, first bite."

"Thank you," she murmured, feeling her heart hammer. He thought she looked fresh. From any dandy Englishman the term would have seemed a slander, but from the rugged warrior, it felt like he'd called her exquisite. "I suppose we will have to eat picnic style, since I burned the table."

He sat, his long legs stretched out and crossed at the ankles. "Some of my best meals have been eaten on the ground."

Grace lowered, tucking her skirt under her to protect her naked backside from the cold floor. "Mmmm," she murmured, chewing the roasted rabbit. "The best I've ever tasted."

He leaned forward. "Hunger makes the meal sweeter." He held a piece to her lips, his direct gaze making it plain that he could be talking about something much more carnal than eating food. Or was it all in her wanton mind?

She hesitated for a moment before opening her mouth to close her lips around the piece of meat. His gaze drifted to her mouth and back up to her eyes. The intensity tightened her stomach, and she blinked, sitting back. "Hunger can make a person desperate, which can lead to foolish actions." She looked off to the side and flipped her hand. "Like a person stealing bread right before a magistrate."

Keir chewed and swallowed. "One could argue that giving in to a hunger should be done in private so worries about judgments couldn't sour the feast."

He wasn't speaking about sharing the rabbit but slaking a different kind of hunger, wasn't he? "Like…we are doing," she said, her voice low. "Alone in the dark woods, in this snug little cabin." Her breathing was shallow, as if she held part of her breath, anticipation heating her blood as she waited to see what he'd say or do next.

"Aye," he said without looking away. "I could…taste this rabbit in many different ways." His voice was gruff, like a rough caress, his rolling Scots accent a temptation in itself.

"Different ways?" she asked, trying to smile, but the excitement thrumming through her made it falter.

"Certainly," he said, his eyes becoming more playful,

giving Grace a bit of space in which to breathe fully. "I can inhale its tantalizing aroma, breathing in its delicious essence. I can nibble along it, tasting it slowly, squeezing every drop of enjoyment from its juicy flesh."

Grace's mouth went dry, as if all her moisture had traveled to her core, adding to the ache between her legs. She shifted. "Nibbling," she repeated.

"Aye." He pulled off one of the cooked legs, the tender, moist meat peeling away from the rest of the roast. He bit into the meat, his teeth showing as he broke off a piece.

Grace's body sat at full alert, her eyes wide as he chewed, their gazes tethered together. She raised a hand to her lips, unable to hold in the tension any longer. "God's ballocks," she said, her mouth turning up as she laughed loudly, leaning back on her hands to stare at the dark ceiling.

"I didn't know *Sassenach* lasses cursed with such foulness," Keir said, and Grace brought her gaze back down from the rafters.

She quickly passed the sign of the cross before her. "I never cursed before I came to Scotland." Breathing deeply, she leaned forward to peel more of the rabbit from the spit. She pointed the piece of meat to Keir. "And you, sir, are sinful."

His gaze was merry, making him ravishingly handsome. "What else would ye expect from a devil?"

She laughed softly, the two of them eating and licking their fingers. When they'd picked all the meat from the bones, Grace stood, throwing them out the door into the snow. While Keir added some bundles of hay he'd twisted to the small fire and some slats from the barn, Grace retrieved her bathing bucket to empty and fill with clean snow.

She worked in silence, but the warmth of their exchange remained within her. The man could certainly taste, nibble, and devour her. He literally waited for her to say the word.

They sat before the fire, and Keir cleared his throat, his arms crossed over his chest as he leaned against the edge of the stone encircling it. "So ye say that Mairi Maclean is wed to the MacNeil and is expecting a bairn?"

"Yes. I am headed there to help with the birth." Grace tucked her skirt and crossed her legs under her.

"Ye must be a talented healer." He patted his leg. "Ye helped me and Cogadh. Is Mairi expecting a dangerous birth?"

"No, but she'd like someone she knows to help." Grace watched Keir, his playfulness faded. "You were traveling here to find her. Was it to help someone at your home?"

Keir nodded, his gaze searching. "Aye, my nephew. He's only seven summers old."

"What ails him?"

Keir shrugged. "No one knows for certain, but he won't rise from his bed. Even my *seanmhair* isn't sure what plagues him. My brother worries he will die. He has no other children."

Silence draped heavily around them. "Will you brand yourself with another cross over your heart if he dies?"

"Aye, but I will do everything I can not to let him die. In small Lachlan lies the future of our clan. My sister wishes to be a warrior, rather than a mother, and my brother has not remarried."

"And you?"

"A warrior makes a poor mate. I have no children."

Grace watched him. "Lachlan is very important to all of you," she said low, the muscles across her shoulders tightening. "And to make such a long journey only to find that the healer you'd sought is unavailable to ask for help…"

Worry prickled up Grace's spine, adding knots to her shoulders. "I'm sure you can find someone else at Kilchoan. There are numerous healers about," Grace said. "More talented than Mairi or I."

He nodded, and some of her worry faded at his easy response. He leaned back on bent wrists behind him, and the linen stretched across his chest, reminding Grace of the ridges of muscles that sat beneath it. His biceps were large where they flexed in his shirt down from his broad shoulders. Keir's hair was longer, reaching nearly to those shoulders. After his snow bath it had dried in waves of brown, giving him a free, tousled look, like a wild adventure within reach.

Grace shook her head. "You are completely comfortable being who you are, aren't you? Such confidence must be freeing, knowing you could survive in any situation." She shrugged, trying to keep envy out of her tone. "Against a wolf pack, or falling in a cold stream, or getting waylaid by a blizzard. You're strong and know how to trap and skin animals to eat. Nothing frightens you, does it?" She matched his relaxed posture and studied him closely. "I can't even imagine the freedom that comes with courage. I possess very little."

A shadow tightened his face. "None of us are truly free, Grace Ellington. We all have our demons. Even though death doesn't concern me much, doesn't mean that I don't fear. Even the mightiest warrior knows pain and avoids it, not only physical pain." He rubbed his leg absently.

"I suppose," Grace said, watching the muscles flex in his exposed leg. "But a helpless woman has much more to fear than a warrior. We are easily captured, where mighty warriors are never trapped at all." She watched him to see if his posture changed, warning her that he might be more enemy than savior.

His gaze met hers directly. "A warrior is trapped by his duty, his honor to uphold the dictates of his chief, the judgment of his people. It can consume a man's life," he said, his voice dropping lower, yet he didn't look away.

All worry about his intentions faded at the hint of vulnerability Grace caught in Keir's fierce image. "A woman, too, can be trapped by all those things," she said. "It is a human affliction, I fear." She leaned slightly closer. "Right now, though, there is no one to judge either of us," she said. "I'm currently not plagued by fear, and you don't have to do anything for your clan tonight. In a way, trapped here together…" She swallowed and inhaled. "We are free, holed up in this little house, surrounded by darkness and snow, with no one nearby expecting us to be a lady or a warrior." Her voice crept softer with each word. "Just a woman and a man. No one to hear…if one of us was to say…" Grace shrugged one of her shoulders. "More."

He stared at her for a long moment, until Grace began to wonder if she'd actually spoken out loud or had only thought the powerful word. His gaze searched her face. "Ye are not afraid of me?"

She gave small shakes of her head. Could he see a hint of unease in her, like a familiar wound she wanted desperately to ignore? "No fear. No duty. Just the two of us." Desire and thudding eagerness prickled up her skin. She could feel it under the fabric of her sleeves, making her hands tingle and her body come alive. It was like fire curling out from her middle to heat her, awakening places within her that Keir had only started to unearth when she'd kissed him earlier in the snow.

Keir's intense gaze shifted over her as he pressed forward. "And ye know what happens between a man and a woman? When they are alone?" he asked.

"Yes," she said. "Not personally…but I've watched two people…tupping."

His brows rose slightly, as did her blush. "Ye spy on people tupping?"

She opened her mouth and closed it with a little huff. "My sister—"

"Ye've watched your sister tupping?"

"No!" She huffed. "She and I were going to the barn on Somerset Estate, and we came across a maid and a groom together…alone." She moved her hand instead of adding more.

"And ye stayed to watch."

"No, well…yes. They were enraptured of each other." She shook her head. "Their pleasure was so fierce it seemed almost painful." She swallowed. "Perhaps the same way Icarus felt in the heat of the sun."

He brushed her cheek with his thumb. The simple touch shot tingles down through Grace. "Icarus felt hot and melting," he said.

"Oh…" Grace curled her fingers into the blanket under her. "The maid and groom were quite flushed." She wet her lips, looking away for a moment to give her rational mind a chance to decide if she was actually going to give in to the adventure her body was craving. Would regret haunt her if she surrendered her body to this powerful, kind man? Rather, if she walked away without tasting the pleasure he offered, she'd wonder about it her entire life. Looking back, she met his stare. "I think 'more' encompasses all of that," she whispered, mesmerized by the desire in his gaze.

She gave a small nod and wet her lips, watching his gaze dip to them and return to her eyes. "Yes, Keir. I am asking for more."

As if a wild stallion had been allowed out of his gate, Keir pulled her in to him, his mouth melting over hers. Her heart leaped inside, her toes curling to prop her up, meeting him there on bent knees. She threaded fingers into his soft hair, raking his head and slanting against his mouth. Wild. Passionate. Free. Grace lost herself quickly, releasing her confined heat into the kiss. Pressing against him, she wrapped her arms around his shoulders, clinging to him while they kissed. Her nails raked down Keir's back, feeling his shoulder blades move under the fabric of his shirt. She wanted the shirt gone, wanted his skin on her skin.

With a small growl in the back of her throat, Grace yanked on the edge of his shirt, freeing it from the waist of his kilt. Keir's large hands clasped her head as he tasted her. When she slid her hands underneath his shirt, along the hot skin of his chest, he groaned, rubbing his hands down her to squeeze her backside.

Ravenous. Grace hungered for the sensations whipping around inside her, pooling to ache down in her pelvis. She kissed him, working his shirt higher until he finished the task by shucking it, throwing it off toward the door. She inhaled, her eyes fastened on his glorious bare chest. She grasped his shoulders, sliding her palms down along his skin and moving muscles. "Good Lord, you are beautiful," she said, making him pull her against all that hot skin to kiss her, his hands sliding along her neck to her scalp.

Kneeling, Grace held herself level with his face. Keir's hands rucked up the back of her skirt, baring her legs, caressing the skin, teasing it and rubbing. Without a smock to work around, he had immediate access to all her naked flesh. His hands found and cupped her rounded backside.

"Touch me," she said against his lips and inched her legs apart. He answered her with a growl that filled her with fluttery anticipation. "Touch my heat," she said. The words that filled her head instantly came out on her tongue. Honest words of passion and want. Whispered things she'd fantasized about all afternoon and while she'd bathed. "I want you, Keir Mackinnon. I want you to feel how wet I am, how hot I am inside." Did people talk while fornicating? It didn't matter one way or another. No one was present to hear, and every word she said seemed to drive Keir more and more frantic. Speaking them aloud licked passion up through Grace.

Working down under her hips, Keir's fingers slid along

her intimately, and Grace leaned into him. "Oh God, yes," she breathed, arching her back and opening to him. Strong, gentle fingers filled her, pressing and stroking. Grace kissed him, opening her mouth as much as she opened her body to him. Running her hands down his chest, she reached under his kilt to capture the heaviness she'd felt pressing against her stomach.

Large, hot, and heavy, he filled her hands. Velvet soft over the hardest of steel, she stroked up and down to the rhythm he'd begun. He groaned in her mouth, and they slanted against each other, wild with unleashed passion. Keir left her lips to trail kisses along her neck and over to her ear as he stroked her backside, cupping and stroking below. "Ye smell like flowers and hot, wet woman," he said, his voice a whispered rasp.

"That's because I am a hot, wet woman," she said back.

He breathed against her. "Aye, ye certainly are, and I like hearing about it."

She looked into his face and saw only sincere appreciation and passion. She grinned. "Good, because I seem to really like telling you about it."

His fingers worked to loosen her bodice until it gaped away from her breasts. With a small shrug, Grace slid off each sleeve, baring her arms, and pulled the bodice away to fall on the floor. Her breasts fell heavily before her, nipples hard and completely open to his view. Part of her couldn't believe she was baring herself to a man she'd met only a week ago, but a much louder part of her mind couldn't believe she'd waited so long to discover what it felt like to be with a man. And not any man, but a chiseled, brawny, fiercely passionate man like Keir Mackinnon.

He whispered something in Gaelic, something that sounded reverent. Grace lifted her breasts with her hands, pinching her nipples like she did when she fantasized alone in her bed. Watching him view her made it even more erotic, and she reached down to ruck up her skirts in front.

"Och, lass," he said. "Ye are exquisite." He reached forward to cup her one breast while pulling her back in for another heart-pounding kiss. Lost in the feel of her nipples brushing against the light hair sprinkling his chest, Grace felt clenching below. Keir followed her own fingers, finding her sweet spot without her even having to tell him about it.

Grace breathed hard on a moan as he rubbed, feeling herself grow hotter by the heartbeat. "More, Keir. I want more."

"Bloody beautiful," he rasped. "Ye are soaked, lass. I want to taste ye."

She kissed him boldly. "You are," she said against his lips.

He smiled wickedly against her mouth. "I want to taste more of ye."

"You may feast on any part of me," she whispered.

Keir pulled back, and she watched the firelight carve across the planes of his face. "Every word ye say amazes me," he said.

She rubbed her breasts against his chest. "Every touch you give amazes me." Her lips curled up as she narrowed her eyes in a seductively teasing glare. "Touch me until I burn like the sun."

"Aye," he said, wrapping her in his warm arms, kissing her senseless. When he broke away she nearly cried out, but the promise in his eyes thrilled her anew. Palming and teasing her breasts, he lowered his mouth to one peak, and Grace gasped at the hot, wet tug that seemed to stretch down through her body. "More," she said out loud, but he continued his slow tease. Each kiss, each tug and lick coiled tighter inside her middle, until she bent her knees, exposing herself. Reaching down his hot skin, she rubbed against his huge length, stroking until he groaned.

"Keir, watch me," she whispered at his ear. She felt his shoulders contract, and he sat back.

One hand on her own breast, one hand down below, her fingers moving and diving, he gritted his teeth, his own fist riding up and down over his bared member. "Bloody hell, Grace," he said, joining her in working her tender flesh.

Grace gasped. "Oh bloody... Oh good God," Grace called out as she felt her insides grow with a tide of passion.

"Och, Grace. I want to taste ye."

"Yes," she nearly yelled, and he lowered his mouth.

Bam! Bam! Bam! Someone pounded on the outside door.

Grace gasped, a scream flying from her already open mouth.

Chapter Eight

Keir leaped off the bed, ignoring the cramping pain in his thigh and his aching yard. Grace rolled to the back, nearly falling off the bed as she scrambled to reach the cover of the blanket in the back corner. Where was his bloody sword?

"Keir Mackinnon," called the arsehole outside the cabin. "Are ye in there?"

"Bloody bastard," Keir said, his curse seething out from behind clenched teeth as the familiar voice registered in his mind. "Brodie," he yelled back.

"Aye, what's going on in there? I found your saddle near the boulders and then Cogadh in the barn, so I knew ye must be about."

Keir retrieved his sword by the door and lifted the bar. It swung inward with a gust. "What are ye doing here?" Keir asked in Gaelic.

Brodie's gaze scanned the interior of the cabin. "Looking for ye." He raised one eyebrow at the pile of lady's sleeves and bodice near the hearth. "Thought I heard something… interesting," he said and glanced down at Keir's tented kilt.

"And yet, ye knocked anyway," Keir said, his words low and lethal as he adjusted himself.

Brodie smiled broadly, unfazed by Keir's deadly stare, and walked farther into the room. "What a cozy cabin," he said in English. "It's the one we passed before the storm turned terrible. I could have sworn I heard a woman scream." He tramped to the hearth, tracking snow.

A movement behind the blanket screen pulled Brodie's gaze. "I saw a mouse," Grace called out. "I always scream when I see a mouse. Silly really, but I do."

Brodie looked at Keir's shirt on the floor, his brows raised nearly to his hairline. Keir shrugged, grabbing it up. "I threw my shirt at it." He tossed it on over his head.

"Who's the lady?" Brodie asked in Gaelic.

"An answer to Rabbie's prayers," Keir continued in their language.

Brodie pulled off his heavy wraps. "You found Mairi Maclean?" His eyes went wide. "And you tupped her. Rabbie's friend isn't going to be happy about that."

"What's being said?" Grace asked, her face peeking around the blanket. "Hello."

Brodie gave a little bow, his smile almost leering when he saw how beautiful Grace was. Called Keir's nicer twin, the good warrior to temper the brutal warrior, Brodie often loved the lasses who were too frightened by Keir. Brodie was as tall and broad as he, with pigmented crosses etched on his back, though only half the number as Keir.

"Hello, lass," he said.

"She isn't the one we sought," Keir said in Gaelic, hoping Grace didn't know more than curse words in their language. "But she's a talented healer and will do. The other is wed to the Wolf of Kisimul and about to birth her first bairn."

Brodie nodded. "Milady, I'm sure the mouse was more frightened of you." He laughed. "Usually, Keir is the scariest creature in a room. He eats mice for breakfast."

Keir shoved Brodie as he walked toward the blanket, but before he could reach it, Grace stepped out wearing what little was left of her smock. The linen hung right above her knees, exposing the long, shapely legs that should be locked around his hips at the moment. Sleeves torn away, a low neckline and short skirt made the ensemble arousing as hell.

"I was changing out here," Grace said, pointing to her skirt pooled by the bed. "While Keir waited like a gentleman behind the screen. I screamed when I saw the mouse, and he came out to rescue me." She smiled sweetly. "I am Grace Ellington, lately of Aros Castle on the Isle of Mull. My sister is the new Lady Maclean, and your friend rescued me from the storm at the expense of his leg." Grace took a full breath and continued while both men stood in silence. "I used my smock to bind his wound and the hock of his horse, leaving me with very little in which to sleep."

She stepped forward with a tilt of her lovely head. "And you are?"

Brodie stood as if stunned for a moment, his mouth open. Was he looking at Grace's naked arms and legs? Keir strode past Grace and yanked the blanket from the hooks in the walls. Walking up behind her, he wrapped her in it.

Brodie had closed his mouth and found his grin. "I am Brodie Mackinnon, second-in-command of the warriors at Dunakin Castle."

Grace pulled the blanket around her shoulders to grasp in front of her. She stared back at his friend as if she were a regal queen in her ermine-lined robes. "And you also know Mairi Maclean?" she asked. She glanced at Keir. "I heard him say her name, and you told him about Kisimul."

The lass was quick. She looked between them as if trying to decipher a riddle. Brodie glanced to Keir, obviously not sure how much he could reveal. "Aye," Keir said. "Brodie and

I were journeying down to Aros to ask her to return with us to cure my nephew, like I mentioned."

"Perhaps," Brodie said, glancing around as if for a chair. He ended up lowering to sit against the wall. "Ye could return with us to help poor Lachlan."

"I'm afraid I cannot," Grace said, her gaze moving to Keir. "I am expected on Barra Isle, and I left an ill man back in Kilchoan."

"At the inn?" Brodie asked.

"Yes. You were there?" she asked.

Brodie nodded. "The maid was taking soup and bread to him when I inquired about a room. Said she was taking care of him, and he was doing quite well."

Ballocks, Brodie. Don't push the explanation too far. But Keir couldn't say anything, and crossed his arms over his chest, his gaze on the angel standing in the center of the small room.

"Truthfully?"

Brodie smiled. "Aye."

Grace sighed, her shoulders lowering a bit. "That is fortunate. So, the roads are passable now?"

"Nay," Brodie said, crossing his big feet at the ankles as if he was settling in for the bloody night. "For horses, but not carriages."

"Did ye put your horse in the barn?" Keir asked.

"Aye. That's when I saw your charger looking quite cozy and well fed."

"'Tis a cozy place for ye to sleep, too," Keir said. "We can talk in the morning about…plans."

"Little Warrior is lame, and Keir can't walk far with his wolf bite still healing," Grace said, sitting on the edge of the bed. She scooped up her skirt and lay it across her lap.

"Little Warrior?" Brodie asked. "Wolf bite? Those can turn foul."

"Very," Grace said. "Luckily I had the makings for a

poultice that pulled out the taint and some feverfew to brew. Keir was unconscious for three days with fever."

"Ye seem hardy now," Brodie said. "Fully functional again." His dastardly grin told Keir that he meant tupping and not walking.

"Weakness still plagues him," she said.

"It does not," Keir replied immediately.

She ignored him. "He still can't walk long distances, hence the problem if Little Warrior is lame," Grace said.

"She calls Cogadh Little Warrior because he's too sweet to be called War," Keir said.

"Sweet? I've seen that horse kick a man's teeth out." Brodie stretched and rolled forward to stand. He picked his heavy cloak from over the iron poker and shrugged into it. "I will go bed down with the horses, and I'll let the two of ye get back to…hunting your mouse."

Grace's lovely lips opened in dismay. "Oh, Keir will join you soon. Once he was fully up and vigorous, I mean awake… he's stayed in the barn with his horse."

Bloody hell. He was being banished. Instead of a glorious night of heady passion with a deliciously vocal angel, he'd be tossing in the cold hay next to Brodie. If Brodie smiled at him, he'd end up with his teeth at his feet. Realizing his danger, Brodie nodded and slipped out the door without anything more than a neutral grin.

Keir lowered the bar across the door and turned to Grace. He shot his fingers through his hair to cup the back of his head. "I can stay."

"What will your friend think?" Grace whispered, clutching the blanket around her so that only her face stuck out.

"I don't give a damn what he thinks."

"I do." Embarrassment had changed her drastically from the sensual woman who'd told him to watch her pleasure herself.

Keir walked closer, and she turned big eyes up to him. He touched her cheek. "Bloody hell," he whispered. "Ye don't need to look scared. Brodie isn't going to say anything to anyone." He'd lived his whole life frightening people. The only lasses who dared his bed were experienced and uncaring as to what society thought of them. Grace was different. She was a virgin and a lady. The shame she felt from being caught with him was evident. What was he thinking? Tupping a beautiful, untried, gentle lass? She deserved a hero, not a devil.

His jaw tensed. With a small nod, he stepped back. "Ye sleep here. Bar the door, and don't let anyone in unless it's me. I'll bed down in the barn. Tomorrow we leave."

"Leave? I don't think—"

"Cogadh's wounds have healed, and my leg can withstand walking, if need be. It's time to go." Spending more time in the cabin would be torture if he couldn't finish what they'd begun. And Brodie's presence had ruined the possibility of getting closer to Grace. If they could leave, they must, to get her back to Rabbie's sick son.

With one last look at the angel, standing alone, questions in her gaze, he turned and walked out into the freezing night.

・・・

The rising sun was breaking through the forest, its rays sparkling on the snow as Grace braced herself for seeing Keir in the light of day after what they'd shared.

She yawned, blinking at the brightness, exhausted from tossing most of the night. Her body had ached for hours, and she'd nearly walked to the barn to invite him back into the cabin. After all, they would be parting today, and she hadn't finished her adventure. Perhaps she could send word to Barra, letting Mairi know she'd be there as soon as she helped Keir's nephew. But first she must check on Thomas.

Her boots broke through the thin crust of ice on top of the snow as she hiked to the barn, her breath puffing out in white clouds. At the door, she rapped and stepped inside.

The heat from the horses and the hay acting as insulation made the barn cozy. Little Warrior and another horse turned their heads her way, ears flicking. Pushing up through the bedding, like a corpse coming out of its grave, came Brodie, yellow spikes of hay sticking out from his hair. But what drew Grace's immediate attention was the half-clad familiar form of Keir turning toward her.

He stood naked from the waist up, the black markings on his arms swirling about his muscles as he hefted his sword. A slight sheen along his skin showed that he'd been working or practicing with his heavy claymore. Biceps curved with muscle as he lowered his sword and crossed his arms over his chest. His plaid kilt had been replaced with a black one, and he wore a black leather band around each upper arm. If she didn't know the man behind the warrior, fear would certainly cast her mute and frozen to the spot.

"What?" Brodie asked. "Good God, is the sun even up yet?"

Grace swallowed, blinking, but couldn't tear her gaze from Keir's display of fierce strength. She cleared her throat. "How are you feeling?" she asked. Maybe he'd be too sore to journey today.

In the hayloft, Brodie rolled around, trying to brush the straw from himself. Keir raised the edge of his kilt, exposing the inside of his thick thigh. A little higher and Grace would see the heavy member that she'd held and stroked. The memory of it alone caused heat to flood her cheeks. She stepped closer as he unwound the fabric to show the healing holes and scratches. "Does it ache?" she asked. "Your thigh," she added quickly.

"No more than normal for a healing wound," he answered,

and her heart dipped lower at the distance in his words. They were cold, as if he'd already said good-bye to her. "I am sound enough to ride, and your care has helped Cogadh's leg heal. He can carry me."

Disappointment hollowed her stomach. "Good," she said. "We can go, I suppose. I should check on Thomas. Perhaps we could discuss…your nephew's illness in Kilchoan."

Grace watched Brodie glance between her and Keir, as if waiting for something. He seemed surprised. The hairs on the back of her neck rose under her scarf. Something didn't feel right. Could she have misread Keir's integrity? Hadn't he nodded when she'd suggested he find someone else in Kilchoan to help his nephew?

Grace swallowed past the dryness in her throat, watching them carefully. Brodie asked something in Gaelic, but Keir cut him off with a raised hand. His steely gaze centered on Grace as if determining the extent of her understanding. And even though she didn't know the words, she very clearly understood.

Keir had no intention of taking her back to Kilchoan. Her tight stomach dropped through her to the packed ground. "Bloody hell," she said and pivoted toward the door, slamming through it out into the snow.

"Grace," Keir called, but she kept going, leaping through the frozen drifts into a run, although she had no idea how to get back to Kilchoan. "Grace, there are wolves out here." She heard his footfalls behind her growing closer, snow-muted thumps overriding the rush of blood in her ears. Anger and hurt twisted together, filling her with desperate strength.

"I'd rather brave the forest!" she yelled, yanking her skirts higher to run. But there was no escaping him in an all-out chase, so she stopped, spinning to confront him. Panting with her exertion, the fact that he didn't even look winded doubled her fury. "You weren't ever going to take me back to Kilchoan, were you?" she asked and lowered her voice, hissing through her clenched teeth. "Even last night, before Brodie showed up. As soon as your horse could hold us, you were taking me to Dunakin."

He stared in her face, his features a blank mask.

She tipped her gaze to the sky. "It was always your plan, wasn't it? Wasn't it?" she yelled and shook her head. "And I fell for…" She flapped her hands toward the cabin. "Everything."

She waited, but he didn't say a word, which was as terrible as if he'd nodded. She huffed out an angry, warlike sound and tried to kick him with her boot, but her skirts hindered her movements. *Bloody damn skirts!*

He sidestepped, pulling her in to him. "Come back to the barn. We are leaving." His voice was cold, heart-piercingly different from last night when he'd held her in the cabin.

She frowned deeply until her face hurt. "They are right," she seethed. "Everyone who calls you a devil."

"Aye," he said, easily accepting her condemnation.

She tried to turn back to the woods, but his fingers manacled around her wrist, reeling her in like an impotent fish. Hands dropping to her waist, he hoisted her up, throwing her over one of his massive shoulders. "Let me down." She pounded the muscles across his back and attempted to kick him. Bucking with an arch of her back, she screamed, "After all I did to save your life, you carry me like a sack of wheat."

He grabbed her flailing legs, pinning them down his front, and continued to stalk toward the barn. When they reached it, he set her inside the door. Her face flushed deeply from being upside down and from being carried like a caught goose in front of his staring friend. She glared at them both.

Brodie led the two saddled horses toward Grace. "Ye are safe with us, lass."

"Highly doubtful!"

Brodie grinned, though his eyes remained cold. "Nay.

Even when he looks like he wants to slice ye in two, Keir never kills lasses."

"Unless she raises a sword against him," Grace said, remembering the one white cross on his skin. "And at present, I just might do that."

Chapter Nine

Keir watched Grace's full mouth, the soft, pink lips that had opened to scream in passion the evening before, tighten with her fury. She hated him now. It was better this way. The Devil of Dunakin couldn't have attachments. Duty would always come first, and Grace was needed to help Lachlan live.

"Ye will ride before me on Cogadh," he said, stepping closer to lift her up.

"Perhaps she should ride with me," Brodie called. "I'm less likely to end up with a *sgian dubh* in my gut."

Keir hadn't taken away her weapon. He'd already stripped her of her pride and trust, and he wouldn't leave her feeling even more defenseless.

"I will take my chances," Keir said, reaching for her.

She slapped at his hands and turned toward the horse. "I can climb up on my own." Her words were colder than the blizzard winds that had drawn them together. He stood there watching as she stepped on a hay bale and pulled herself up the side of Cogadh, straddling him to stare forward.

"I've never seen a woman able to climb your warhorse,

Keir," Brodie said with his lighter tone, but nothing was melting the ice Grace had encased herself within.

"I've been riding since I could walk," Grace said. "There isn't a horse I can't befriend, mend, or climb upon." Her gaze dipped to Keir. "So beware. Little Warrior knows who saved him from lameness."

Keir had no doubt that his horse was faithful to him, but he nodded anyway and climbed up behind her. There was barely room for them both to sit in the saddle, and his thighs rested along the curve of her lovely round arse. But she held her back straight, leaning slightly forward so as not to touch him. It was going to be a long ride with a very bitter lass.

"How long will we journey?" she asked as they started out.

"It took us two days to ride down from Mallaig where there is a ferryman to take us across to Skye," Brodie said. "Though with the snow, and a lady riding along, it may take three days."

She snorted as if his comment was ludicrous.

"And Keir's horse should not overstress his leg," Brodie said.

"And where will we sleep?" Grace asked. She gazed at the cabin as they passed. Did she loathe the reminder of their intimacy?

"Brodie carries a tent folded on the back of his mount," Keir said. "It's not as sturdy as the cabin, but it will do."

"It kept us dry on the way down," Brodie said. "Until the blizzard hit with the fury of a banshee." Brodie smiled across at Grace, giving her a roguish grin. "We will keep ye warm, lass."

Grace said nothing, but when Brodie glanced his way, Keir made it obvious from the ice in his gaze that there would be no "we" when it came to warming Grace. Brodie's grin soured, and he looked forward.

They rode for most of the morning, Grace sitting straight for hours before she slumped slightly forward as if her back ached. He halted them near a stream to eat some bannocks and cured beef that Brodie had brought from Kilchoan. When Grace stepped around a series of boulders to relieve herself, Keir and Brodie led the horses to the stream to drink.

Without preamble, Keir advanced on Brodie, stopping right before him. "Ye will not warm or touch Grace," he said, his voice low, the threat evident. "I am responsible for her. Me, on my own. Is that clear?"

Brodie's ready smile flattened, and though he had to look up at Keir, he didn't back away. "Quite, though the reason behind it is not."

"I don't owe ye a reason. 'Tis none of your business," Keir said and turned toward the stream.

Brodie snorted. "Everything about the Devil of Dunakin is my business, Keir." He rubbed his horse's side, adjusting the saddle. "Since the first day of your training as a tall, skinny lad, it's been my duty, like it's your duty to protect Dunakin."

"That does not extend to Grace," Keir said, his teeth set. He didn't like to be at odds with the only person he considered a friend, but he didn't need Brodie meddling.

Brodie frowned. "If she affects the great and mighty warlord who protects Dunakin and Clan Mackinnon, my guidance, and if needed, interference, certainly does extend to the Englishwoman."

Keir frowned back at Brodie. "That does not include trying to get under her skirts," Keir said. "She's innocent and doesn't need the likes of ye panting around her."

"Innocent?" Brodie's brows rose to his hairline. "Even after last night?"

"Because some bastard banged on the door," Keir said through his locked teeth.

Brodie glanced toward the rocks where Grace had

retreated. "And she didn't know ye were taking her to Dunakin, with or without her permission." He shook his head, raising a finger to scratch his ear. "I guess I don't need to worry about her sweetening up to ye and turning your attention from your duty, do I?"

"She hates us both for taking her," Keir said, dropping his fist. Out of the corner of his eye, he watched Grace sneaking in a wide path around them. She'd risk the wild woods rather than continuing with him.

Brodie chuckled. "I'd say she hates ye quite a bit more than me."

Keir turned, his gaze connecting with Grace's, making her freeze, half hidden behind a tree. After a moment, she dropped her skirts with a huff as if realizing the futility in her escape attempt.

Keir watched her march back toward the horses. "I had no choice but to take her to Skye. 'Tis the duty of the Devil."

Brodie's grin faded with a slow, knowing nod. He placed his hand on Keir's shoulder. "Aye, my friend. I know."

• • •

Grace focused on the horse's gait while her rage simmered under her skin. She continued to run through escape plans, but with wolves, snow, and damnably fast Highlanders about, all plans would end in disaster. The bitterness accompanying that realization helped her sit straight for hours, holding herself apart from Keir.

She loathed him, yet the way his parted thighs rubbed her, her backside pressed intimately against him, only reminded her of the passionate rhythm they'd set last evening. Damn her traitorously wanton thoughts. *I hate him. He lied to me. God, carry him to Hell.*

"He isn't favoring his leg," Keir said. Grace glared at his

hand where it rested easily on his thigh, the reins in his strong fingers. "Your poultice took care of any taint, but we shouldn't make him ride into the night. It's been a long day."

The rumble of his voice behind her made Grace squeeze her eyes shut for a moment. A long day, indeed. She'd tossed without sleep the night before and had been taken by force, riding all day with rigid anger. Anger at Keir, but also anger at herself for ignoring her earlier concern that he'd take her when she told him that Mairi was too difficult to reach.

"Cogadh was fortunate that a talented healer was near," Keir said.

She snorted softly. "I suppose if I hadn't been so bloody talented, I wouldn't be riding to Skye right now." But the poor horse had nothing to do with his master's betrayal and lies. She leaned forward toward Little Warrior's ears and stroked his neck. "I'm glad I was able to help you…Little Warrior," she said, purposely adding the horse's name so Keir wouldn't think she extended the sentiment to him.

She should have left Keir bleeding in the snow and stolen his horse. The furious thought pinched inside Grace, making her feel worse. She'd never have left a person to die like that, even if he hadn't risked his life to save her from the wolves.

"It all unfolds as it should," Keir murmured.

She turned in her seat to stare into his face, ignoring his rugged jawline and the deep brown of his eyes. "So, I am taken away from an ailing man left alone in Kilchoan and a woman who needs help on Barra giving birth? God didn't want me stolen. That was you, Keir Mackinnon."

His gaze bored into her own stare. "It had nothing to do with what I want, Grace. It is the duty of the Devil of Dunakin to follow the chief's orders and protect the clan."

"Did your chief order you to kiss me?" she whispered, leaning in to prevent eavesdropping. "Touch me? Taste me?" She felt her face growing red but pushed on. "Was it your duty to seduce me into coming with you?" Damn, but he bloody well had. She'd been ready to offer to see his nephew this morning, but she'd never admit it now.

Keir grasped her hand, pulling it to lay flat on his chest. She could feel his heartbeat thud against her palm through his shirt. "On the souls of those I've lost, I swear to ye, Grace Ellington, nothing that happened between us last eve had anything to do with duty. No matter what comes of this, know this to be true."

Grace's pulse seemed to flip about as she watched him closely. "What did it have to do with, then?"

His voice was low, nearly a whisper. It rumbled with his Scots accent like his words last night when they were wrapped together. "Just a woman and a man, alone, without fear, without judgment or duty. Only heat and a willingness to give pleasure."

Grace swallowed past the squeeze in her throat, reminded of the words she'd spoken. Keir's gaze still held that heat now. Was he telling her the truth? Would he dare to swear on the soul of his mother with lies? It didn't matter. He'd tricked her, and she would hate him forever now. Though he probably didn't care. Grace broke the connection by turning to stare out over Little Warrior's head. "What will become of me once I help your nephew?"

The horse took several steps before Keir answered. "I will take ye to Kisimul Castle or Aros, as ye wish."

Grace caught Brodie's glance, but he didn't say anything. "Is this another lie, to get me to cooperate?" she asked.

The forest was quiet as the sun lowered, filtering down through the jutting trees. "When ye have seen and helped Lachlan, I will see ye to your destination, unless I am dead," Keir said, signaling for them to stop in a small clearing at the base of a hill.

"Is that a possibility?" Grace asked, trying to keep her

voice light, as if she didn't much care if he lived or died.

Brodie laughed. "Not likely that anyone could best the Devil of Dunakin, but if he's unable, I will take care of ye."

"I don't wish to be taken care of by any man," Grace said, frowning over Brodie's choice of words. Did Brodie Mackinnon like to cause trouble or was he just obtuse?

"Lo, lass," Brodie said, rubbing a hand down his short beard. "It would be safer if a man took care of ye, especially up in the wilds of the Highlands."

"Grace has my protection," Keir said, and Grace could feel the power behind his words, almost as if they were an oath. They sent a little thrill through her body. *Foolish body*.

"I can protect myself," she said, looking down at Keir as he dismounted.

He didn't smile or say anything, but the look in his eyes was amused. "What?" she asked. Reaching up, he lifted her down. "What?" she repeated, her voice terse when she realized that she hadn't demanded to climb down on her own. She could have at least kicked him in the chest.

"And what will ye do if another pack of wolves decides that ye smell like their next meal?" Keir asked, dragging the saddle off the horse's back.

Grace tipped her chin higher and looked beyond to the white-blanketed meadow, surrounded by snow-clad evergreens. The limbs hung low as if bowing to them in greeting. Grace crossed her arms. "To foster courage, one must envision dangers and form a plan to know what to do if the danger occurs. I had no plan before. Now I do."

"Which is?" Keir asked. Brodie led his horse toward them as if wanting to join in the ridiculous conversation. She ignored him.

"I will stand tall and growl back, to start with," she said.

"That didn't work well for me," Keir said, making Brodie chuckle.

"I will climb a tree and throw my dirk at the leader."

"First, the tree must be low enough to climb, but not so low that the wolf can climb after ye," Brodie said and pulled the saddle from the back of his own horse.

"And ye need further practice with your *sgian dubh*," Keir said.

Grace pursed her lips. "The wind snatched my dagger from its path during the storm. Otherwise I would have hit the wolf instead of you."

"Ye hit Keir with a dagger?" Brodie asked, laughing out loud. "'Twas quite a difficult rescue, eh?"

Grace would have nodded but was certain both men thought the rescue was difficult for Keir, not her, even though *she* was the one who'd covered them with cut evergreens and blankets to keep them alive. "My earlier warning stands," she said, looking pointedly at them. "When not buffeted by gale winds, I throw quite well," she said. "Gavin has been training me to aim with mortal consequences."

"Who is Gavin?" Keir asked, his voice stripped of mirth.

"A mighty Maclean warrior," Grace said, exaggerating. Gavin was strong, but she had no idea if Tor, the Maclean chief, considered him mighty.

"Why is he teaching ye to throw a dagger?" Keir asked.

"He wants to protect me, too," she said and rubbed a gloved hand across her lips to dispel the grimace. Good God, she was tired of this talk. "Just because a woman lacks courage doesn't mean all the men around her must swear to protect her," she said, throwing her words over her shoulder as she walked away.

"He has sworn to protect ye?" Keir asked, leaving his horse to follow her across the clearing.

"He thinks ye lack courage?" Brodie called, his voice full of surprise.

"Yes, and yes," Grace said, turning. She frowned at the

little leap her heart did to see Keir was close. *I loathe him*, she reminded herself, narrowing her eyes.

"Why?" Keir and Brodie asked at the same time.

She looked past Keir to Brodie. "Why what?"

"Why has he sworn to protect ye?" Keir asked first. "Which, by the way, he hasn't come close to upholding his oath, letting ye journey alone to Barra and be nearly eaten by a pack of wolves."

Brodie coughed in his hand and spit on the ground near his horse's hoof. "And a lass who willingly rides with the Devil of Dunakin isn't lacking courage. This Gavin sounds like a dolt."

"Gavin is not a dolt," she answered. "He's quite nice. And I'm not willingly riding with Keir." She scrunched her nose at him as if he smelled foul.

"Why has he sworn?" Keir asked again.

Grace stretched her sore back, reaching high. "He wants to wed me, so he can take care of me."

Keir walked past her, and she realized he held a rolled tarp. He flicked it open, shaking it wide to drape over the thick, horizontal branch of a tree. Even though he didn't look at her, his words carried. "Ye need more than nice, Grace. Ye have too much passion in ye for a weak dolt."

Grace refused to look at him and watched Brodie clear a spot, arranging stones in a circle for a fire. "Whether ye are riding willingly or not, ye are one brave lass," Brodie called, glancing over his shoulder with a nod. "The Devil of Dunakin is the meanest, most brutal warrior in all the Highlands. Even his own men tremble under his scrutiny."

Grace walked away from Keir, gathering twigs that had dried in the sun. "Well, that's foolish. A leader shouldn't rule his men with fear and brutality."

"It has worked for generations within the Mackinnon clan," Brodie said, shrugging. "The Devil of Dunakin rules the warriors with ferocity and strict adherence to clan law and duty." He leaned in, hitting the flint to catch a spark on a small piece of wool between his thumbs.

Grace glanced over at Keir where he pulled taut the corners of the tent. He'd thrown off his outer covering, and his massive biceps strained against the fabric of his shirt as he forced sticks into the frozen ground to act as tent stakes. Grim frowns, savage markings on his skin, and powerful muscles might frighten some who didn't know Keir, but the man was far from cruel. Maybe if she reminded him of that, he'd realize abducting her was dishonorable. "Does saving wolf pups by not slaughtering their parents, fall under strict adherence to clan law?" she asked. "A brutal, cruel show of force?"

He straightened to his full height. "And the favor earned me more scars and three days of fever."

And my respect, she admitted silently. That must be the reason she'd let him trick her so easily. Grace sniffed and watched a clump of snow fall from high up in a tree where a large bird had landed. "You pulled through, and those pups have a chance of surviving the winter. Intelligence and thoughtfulness, reasonable judgment to accompany strength and strategic prowess. That is what earns a leader the respect of his warriors. Not brutality and fear."

"And how many warriors have ye led, Grace Ellington?" Keir asked, brushing his hands together.

She met his sharp gaze. "And how many warriors would die to keep you safe when they fear you, Keir Mackinnon?"

"One," Brodie called over. "'Tis my duty."

Grace snorted, bringing over the small gathering of twigs for the fire. "Foolish men. Always ready to kill rather than find a civil way to proceed."

"Some men would rather fight than have a pointless conversation," Keir said.

"Good Lord," Grace said. "I think I'd rather not ride with

you."

"Well, ye aren't allowed to ride with me," Brodie said. "So, I guess ye'll be running behind Cogadh."

Grace looked between them. "Why am I not allowed to ride with you?" she asked.

Brodie scratched the side of his head and glanced toward Keir. "Uh…'tis a rule. All stolen lasses must ride with the Devil of Dunakin." He shrugged. "It's an old rule, ancient Mackinnon law."

Grace squinted her eyes at Brodie in blatant suspicion, but he turned away. "There are more bannocks, dried fish, and a few apple fritters," he said, leaving her to retrieve a sack from his horse.

Grace inspected the crude tent Keir had suspended. She'd need something to protect her from the frozen ground. She used her *sgian dubh* to saw through the limb of an evergreen across the clearing. Her muscles had strengthened since coming to the Highlands. Perhaps she could survive if she escaped into the woods.

"What are ye doing?" Brodie asked, walking over to stare at her growing pile of branches.

"Cutting branches to dry before the fire to sleep upon," she said.

"Clever," he said.

"It helped keep the snow from freezing Keir and me in the blizzard. I rolled him over and stuffed the branches under him when he was unconscious. Although those boughs were wet. If I dry these out by the fire, they should work even better." She stopped to rest, hands on her hips.

Brodie's mouth dropped open. "Ye knocked Keir out when ye hit him with your dagger?" He sounded completely astounded.

"Nay," Keir called from the other side of the fire, where he checked his horse's hock, rubbing the muscles in the animal's leg.

"The wolves then? They rendered ye unconscious, and Cogadh trampled them to keep ye from being further eaten?" Brodie asked. He bent to gather the load of cut boughs, shaking them to shed the snow.

"I fell on him," Grace said and picked up the last two boughs to follow Brodie to the fire.

"Her limb knocked me in the head," Keir said. "After the wolves decided the taste of my leg wasn't worth the wrath of my horse."

"And ye cut branches in a frozen tempest and tucked them around to keep the blizzard from freezing ye two solid?" Brodie asked, his brows high.

"Yes, I did," Grace said with a slight rise to her chin.

He shook his head. "Clever lass," Brodie said. "Clever and brave."

His words made Grace feel lighter. Someone thought she had courage. It didn't matter that he was an annoying arse. He was also a warrior.

"I had to lie on top of Keir to keep us warm," she said. "And when he woke, he thought I was an angel." She bent at the waist to prop her boughs over a log at the edge of the fire.

She expected a humorous comment from Brodie and possible embarrassment from Keir, although she couldn't imagine him blushing over anything. But there was only silence. Straightening, she spotted Keir spitting one of the rabbits they'd caught. Brodie stood frozen, staring at him with a hardened, dark surprise etched on his features.

"An angel?" Brodie said, the two words spat out as an accusation.

"I'd been struck on the head," Keir said, his glance going to Brodie. He shrugged his broad shoulders. "It means nothing."

Grace's gaze moved back and forth between them,

Brodie stiff, his hands fisted and Keir ignoring him. She let out a small, dark laugh, meant to be threatening. "And I am definitely not an angel."

Thawing slowly, Brodie turned on his heel, disappearing in the thickening shadows of the woods.

Chapter Ten

Grace stood, watching Keir set the spit between two thick branches they'd erected on the edges of the fire to hold the rabbit. The breeze teased the undulating flames, and they crackled in the silence that came with the falling night. "Brodie doesn't like angels?" she asked, glancing where the man had walked.

"It's foolish," Keir said and stirred the burning bits of plank he'd taken from the barn.

"Foolish?"

He shook his head. "'Tis an old legend that says the very last Devil of Dunakin will die after an angel pierces his heart."

She stared at him, his powerful frame looking even larger in the shadows. "You said 'finally' when you saw me." Finally? As if he'd been waiting for the angel of death. "Do you want to die, Keir?"

His eyes appeared black in the firelight as his gaze connected with hers. "I do not fear death, but I would not walk willingly into it, either. Nay, Grace. 'Twas only a word, spoken by a waking man who'd taken a blow to the head.

Nothing more."

"Brodie thinks there is more to it," she said.

"Brodie gets grim when he thinks I might relinquish my position in the clan."

"Why?"

Keir turned the rabbits slowly on the spit, checking one of the props. "Because if I die, he might be ordered to be the Devil of Dunakin."

"Which he doesn't want to be?" she asked, watching the night breeze tug at Keir's loose hair.

Keir looked over his shoulder, one side of his mouth tipping upward in a dark grin. "Brodie is much happier being the merciful squire to the murdering executioner."

"Murdering executioner?" she asked, her eyes opening wide.

"'Tis mostly tales."

"Except for the crosses on your skin."

His gaze turned back on the browning rabbit. "I am a warrior, Grace, and efficient at doing my duty."

"And who gave you this duty?" she asked, sitting on a log where the heat could reach her.

He stood, brushing his hands. "Aonghus Mackinnon."

"Your father?"

Keir sat on the log next to Grace, staring at the fire. "He was the chief of the Mackinnons before my brother. I was the second son born, and therefore the one trained and raised to protect, while my brother was raised to lead. Rab is now the chief, since Aonghus Mackinnon's death ten years ago."

"He wanted you to be a murdering executioner?"

"He wanted what most fathers want, for their sons to be strong and dutiful."

She watched him for a long moment, his body stiff, saying more than words could, that he didn't want to talk about his abilities or his father. Grace crossed her feet at the ankles, letting the flames warm the soles of her boots. "My father didn't have much to do with me, but my mother raised me to be a lady." Her heart hurt at the memory of losing her to illness several years before.

Grace exhaled through her nose. "And the skills of a wellborn lady are fairly useless here in the wilds of Scotland."

"Cutting boughs to keep ye warm in a blizzard isn't something taught to wellborn ladies in England?" he asked, a bit of light coming back into his voice.

A chuckle broke from her before she could stop it. Because she was a prisoner, and prisoners didn't spend their time laughing with their jailors, no matter how horrible the jailor's childhood was. "No. Luckily for you and me, I happened to ask Thomas about surviving a blizzard on the way to Kilchoan." Her voice dropped. "I hope he is faring well without me."

Keir leaned his elbows on his knees. "He is under shelter, warm, and cared for by a maid. He is better than most in this world. He will heal, and I will take ye to Kisimul and then Aros."

"How can I believe a man who steals away a woman against her will?" She crossed her arms. *He's a scoundrel. I hate him.* She clenched her teeth to fan her softening fury. She was not so weak as to look past such an assault on her freedom.

He stood, looking down at her, his hand resting on the hilt of his sword. "I keep my word, Grace. As long as I have breath, I will see ye home."

As long as he had breath? As long as he wasn't dead? Did the man always assume that he would die early? She studied him. His broad shoulders and powerful arms, along with the constant training, made him invincible. Yet, the brutality of his youth and the dark duty thrust upon him made Keir more than a Highland warrior. It made him flawed, fine cracks of vulnerability that Grace was certain he refused to acknowledge. But she saw them, and they made him…more. More human. More complex, and definitely more tempting. *Damn.*

A tendril of heat flowed inside her, like sap thawing in the spring, as she watched him turning the rabbit. They were alone in the darkness. Every time she thought of what he'd done to her, the words she'd let pour from her lips, she felt her skin flush. But all that had occurred before he had thrown her over his shoulder and whisked her away. She forced her gaze back to the undulating flames.

The crunch of Brodie's footfalls broke through the thick silence. "I marked the perimeter," Brodie said, his face more relaxed than when he'd stormed away.

"Marked?" Grace asked, though her mind continued to whirl around Keir's dark duty.

"He pissed around," Keir said.

Brodie puffed out his chest, stretching his back. "It keeps the animals away."

He strode to the bag he'd taken from his saddle and rummaged through it. He carried out wrapped bannocks, two bladders of ale, cheese, and several fritters drizzled with honey. Having barely eaten throughout the day, Grace's mouth watered. "We will have a feast tonight?" she asked. "Surely we need to ration for the journey."

"I have another full sack," Brodie said. "And we should make it to Mallaig by tomorrow night or the next morning, where there is a well-stocked tavern."

"Brodie always makes sure we have plenty of food," Keir said, cutting into the rabbit to check for doneness. "If made to choose, I think he'd bring tarts on campaign over his sword."

"Make fun, Keir, but a gnawing stomach is no way to travel or battle. The Devil of Dunakin must be well fed to keep his strength." Brodie took a long haul from his bladder.

Grace stood to help Keir turn the rabbit over the flames. "And you must keep full of ale to mark the perimeter against animals."

Brodie chuckled. "Most certainly."

They ate the hot pieces of rabbit with the other food, saving the fritters for last. "It might be the fact that I've barely eaten this week," Grace said, "but I don't think I've tasted anything this tempting before. I have a sweet tooth and long to taste anything wrapped in pastry." She licked some of the honey off her fingers. "Like Keir."

Brodie coughed into his fist. "Keir wrapped in pastry? Now that would be a sight."

"No," Grace said, feeling her cheeks warm. "Keir likes to taste sweet things."

Brodie's wide eyes shifted between them, his brows raised. "Ye two discussed Keir's appetite for sweetness? Back at the cabin? Perhaps while chasing that mouse about?"

Ballocks, the man's mind was filthy. Although, Grace's whispers back in the cabin had been anything but pure. Could Brodie know that Keir had said that he wanted to taste her? Keir wouldn't have shared something so...intimate. "I had a tart," she answered, "and gave him some before he succumbed to fever." Grace looked away, feigning a yawn. "It's been a long day. Shall we take turns sleeping, in case Brodie's markings don't keep the wolves away?"

"We will handle that, lass," Brodie said. "Ye can sleep on your warmed boughs in the tent."

Grace carried three evergreen branches inside with her. It would still be cold, even with a blanket. She laid down her load, spreading them out the length of her body, and straightened halfway, ducking back out. Her backside collided with someone, and she jerked upright. "Oh," she said. Keir stood there, holding two more boughs. It took her a moment to inhale. "I was coming to find a blanket."

He moved around her to stoop under the tent, and she followed him to the ground where he knelt to snap out a blanket. "If ye are cold, ye can sleep by the fire," he said, his back to her.

"Are you and Brodie sleeping there?" she asked, her voice small.

He pivoted on his toes, still crouched before her. They were only inches apart. "We will take turns sleeping and guarding while we keep the fire going."

Grace searched his stony gaze in the darkness. "Guarding against animals or guarding me from escaping?" she asked.

"Ye will die if ye head off into the woods on your own," he said, his voice rough in warning.

Grace stared back without blinking. "I am not afraid of death, either, Keir." Let him make of her false boast what he will. Maybe he'd lose sleep over the worry that she'd try to escape, even though she was too tired to even consider it tonight. Biting back her usual polite "good night" she turned away from him and settled onto the boughs.

...

The sky was heavy with gray clouds, heralding more snow. Keir held Grace before him on Cogadh as they rode at an easy gait between tall, bare oaks, Brodie up ahead. The woods were silent, as if the birds felt an oncoming storm or...

Brodie stopped his horse before several large boulders that flanked a narrow pass farther on. He raised an arm, which meant "stop, caution," and pointed to the ground without turning in his seat.

Keir leaned into Grace's ear. "'Tis an ambush." She sat up taller, nearly hitting his chin with her head as she turned to look at him, her eyes wide. "Stay behind my targe."

Keir brought his shield from its mount on the back hip

of his horse. Round and made of thick black leather, it would guard Grace against arrows. He yanked the Devil of Dunakin's black leather mask off the back of the shield, quickly donning it before he set the targe before Grace. Sensing the unease, Cogadh's ears flicked, waiting for danger to present itself.

Grace bent her knees, pulling her legs up under the shield. Smart lass. Keir adjusted his mask, the black leather with silver spikes and demonic wings on the sides. After a decade of wear, it fit the contours of his face perfectly. If he'd have had time, he'd have taken off his shirt to show the swirls of pigment that marked him as the legendary warrior, but the mask would have to do.

Keir brought Cogadh up to Brodie, the two of them side by side with their claymores drawn. "*Caraid no nàmhaid?*" Keir's voice boomed out in Gaelic, making Grace bump against his chest. "Friend or foe?" he repeated in English.

Grace leaned her head to the right, peeking out around the edge of the targe. Keir pressed his hand against her forehead to push her back behind as five men, draped in furs, emerged. They were on foot and held crude weapons: three short swords, a wooden pike, and a pitchfork. "Who raises arms against the Devil of Dunakin?"

Keir felt Grace turn to look at him, but it couldn't be helped. Her gasp at his appearance sat like a boulder in his gut, but he ignored it and shifted to his familiar role. Brodie sat his charger, his own sword out and ready if the fools attacked. There were only five of them, easy work if he rode alone, but he had Grace before him. Brodie knew, without orders, that he'd have to do most of the fighting while Keir protected the lass. Brodie gave him a nod, an anticipatory grin on his face. Aye, the man loved to war.

"They'd be bloody goats charging into a wolf's den to challenge the Devil of Dunakin," Brodie said and looked back out at the men. "Or do ye not recognize the harbinger of your own foolhardy deaths? Do ye wish to forfeit your heads to sit upon Mackinnon spikes?"

The man in the middle wore a fur hat that looked odd with his poorer wrapping. Thieves, no doubt. "Drop your moneys, and we will let ye pass," he said, though his eyes stared out widely as he took in the devil's symbol etched into the leather front of Keir's targe. Were they still far enough south that his name and symbol didn't bring avoidance? A pity for the doomed group.

"We do not bow to the demands of thieves," Keir said over Grace's ducked head. "Be gone, and leave unscathed, or I will paint the snow red with your blood."

"God's teeth," Grace whispered and curled forward, grabbing tighter to the saddle horn.

Several of the thieves glanced at one another, but the leader kept his gaze straight. "Do your worst, Devil. I'd sell me own soul to feed my family."

Mo chreach. Keir exhaled long and caught Brodie's questioning gaze. He wouldn't attack without Keir's command. And a man desperate to feed his kin was not the greedy cods that deserved their heads on spikes. Yet, they couldn't threaten innocent travelers without recourse, either.

Keir reached for the tops of his boots, grasping the four daggers he kept sheathed there. "Hold onto my shield, lass," he whispered, his gaze directly on his targets.

"Oh God," Grace said, ducking farther as her slender hands replaced his around the inside handle.

"Ye've been warned," Keir said, and waited for the leader to raise his sword, his friends following. But instead of spurring Cogadh forward, Keir whipped each of his dirks through the air with a sharp snap of his wrist. And one, two, three, four, all the dirks embedded into the tops of the men's right shoulders. One heartbeat behind him, Brodie hit the fifth thief in the same shoulder and the leader in both thighs.

All five men yelled in pain, the leader dropping to the snow.

Keir pressed inward on Cogadh's flanks, and his mighty war horse broke easily through the line of injured bandits. "Brodie!" he yelled and signaled to him to drop a sack of coins amidst the men as he plowed through, sending them flying to escape Cogadh's hooves. The horses, fueled with battle frenzy, tore through the snow, their stout hooves finding purchase.

"Did you kill them?" Grace asked, grasping his middle to twist, looking behind him where he was certain she could see that they were not mortally wounded.

"Of course he did," Brodie called over the heavy plodding and huffing of the galloping horses. "The Devil of Dunakin shows no mercy."

Through the cutouts of his black mask, Keir could see Grace staring up at him, confusion on her features, but he returned his gaze to the path. He had no wish to see her judgment.

Another mile churned away under hooves, and Keir signaled for them to slow to a fast walk. Yanking up the back edge of his mask, he peeled the leather shroud away, clipping it easily to Cogadh's saddle with his targe.

Grace sat against his chest, her face forward, where the wind tugged tendrils of hair from her hood. They rode in silence for another mile before her words drifted back to him. "You didn't kill them, yet Brodie would have the world think you did." She stared ahead. "The mask, the title, and the tales work to make you sound like a monster when you are not."

Her words coiled inside him, relief that she understood something of him that he could not admit, mixed with regret—neither of which changed anything about Keir's life. He was the protector of Dunakin, and he always would be. He'd sworn the oath as a young man, and believed in fulfilling his duty to keep the Mackinnon clan safe.

"My reputation alone can save people. The mask, title,

and tales frighten them away before they come to harm. 'Tis a mercy," he said. "Else I'd be covered head to toe in black crosses."

Grace kept her face forward. "It sounds lonely."

His gut hardened at the edge of pity in her voice. "The Devil of Dunakin is surrounded by warriors and family, revered and feared. There is no room for loneliness in the press of duty."

"I'm not talking about the monster in the black mask," Grace said. "I'm talking about Keir Mackinnon."

Keir stared forward over her head. The snowy path wound between large winter-bare oaks. A small bird flitted from branch to branch, hopping higher until it could break free into heavy, gray sky. "They are one and the same, lass. I was raised to be the Devil of Dunakin, and I will die as the Devil of Dunakin."

Chapter Eleven

"You have a sister and a brother," Grace said from her seat on Little Warrior. They'd camped a second night. Grace had once again slept alone in the tent, or rather tried to sleep inside the tent with evergreens under her and thoughts of Keir rolling around her traitorous mind. They'd risen at dawn and had ridden all day across the snowy landscape toward Mallaig. "And a nephew who is ill, and a grandmother, your father's mother, who is still alive." She should learn all the players in this dreadful adventure so she could make her plans for escape.

"Aye," Keir answered.

"Fiona Mackinnon," Brodie called from where he rode several yards to the side. "Now, she's a strong woman."

"Physically or mentally?" Grace asked.

"Both. She was a warrior in her youth," Keir said.

Grace twisted in her seat to see Keir. The breeze teased his loose hair around a strong jaw that held a week's growth of hair. "She battled?"

"With perfect aim," Brodie said.

"After her husband died, she would ride into battle with her son. She was talented with the bow, staying in the rear and picking off the enemy from the back of her horse. She was quite fierce," Keir said.

"Still is, just more with her tongue now than with her arrows," Brodie added with a chuckle.

"And your sister, Odara, isn't married?"

"She goes by Dara," Keir said. "And no, she hasn't met a man strong enough to lure her to the pulpit."

"If this new fellow works out, she might wed. He's a warrior from the south who's become friends with Rabbie," Brodie said. "Has lots of scars and a crooked nose. He might be strong enough to handle her."

"Dara's been working to heal Lachlan, but nothing seems to be helping," Keir said.

Grace worried at her bottom lip and took mental stock of what herbs remained in her satchel. She'd used most of the feverfew, garlic bulbs, and honey for Keir and his horse. Despite her fury with Keir and his brother's orders, the boy deserved her healing talents. "Since you've demanded my help, I will need more medicines. Does he have a fever?"

"At times he feels hot, flushed, but it was the weakness that first took hold of him. He began sleeping for great lengths of time, and when awake, he complains he can't lift his limbs." Keir's voice had taken on the heaviness of concern.

"What has he been treated with?" Grace asked, wishing she had Ava with her to confer.

"He's been bled and given blessed water with rosemary. That seemed to revive him for a bit. Sometimes he vomits. My sister never leaves his side, but she is not a healer."

"There are no healers on the Isle of Skye?" she asked, finding that hard to believe. Skye was larger than Mull from what she remembered of her studies back in England.

"Our clan is renowned for our warring, lass," Brodie said.

"Not our healing. Healers can be found within the other clans on the isle but none whom we could trust not to kill Rabbie's heir."

"And yet you trust me? I could be as malicious. An unknown woman who is furious that she's been stolen from her original journey."

"Furious?" Brodie asked, his face breaking into a grin. "I've seen frolicking kittens more furious than ye, lass."

She frowned at him, narrowing her eyes. But guilt tightened her stomach, not anger. She was a terrible prisoner. Bitterly, she considered ordering Brodie to drink a purgative as a preventative to some made-up illness with which she sensed he was coming down.

Keir spoke behind her, his tone even. "Regardless of your mood, Grace Ellington, ye are a kind woman. Your character would not allow ye to harm a child."

"And," Brodie called over, "ye don't know Rab well enough to kill his offspring."

"God's teeth, who would hate a man enough to want to kill his child?" Grace caught the glance between the two men from the corner of her eye.

"Any opposition to a king with an heir," Keir said.

"Humph," Grace said, though she knew it was true. England's King Henry had been overly worried that his Princess Mary would be murdered by assassins or die from illness like his son, Henry, who had died soon after birth. It was still whispered that Queen Catherine had been poisoned, thus causing her son to die. "Well, your brother is not a king," she said.

"In our clan, he may as well be," Brodie said. "He is the chief, and the clan moves according to his say." Brodie's face hardened with his words, making Grace's stomach tighten. She wasn't sure she wanted to meet Keir's brother.

"You said his wife died in childbirth," Grace said, listening to the regular plodding of the horses.

"Aye," Keir said.

"Was it long ago?"

"Two years now. We buried Bradana with her newborn bairn," Keir said, his voice flat. Neither Highlander said anything more. Grace remembered the larger cross with a tiny one next to it, etched over Keir's heart. They were both ornately drawn with intertwining lines.

The horses walked swiftly, their hooves breaking the crisp surface of the deep snow. Evergreens stood, draped with white, while oaks and birch trees looked like gray skeletons, their bony arms reaching to the sky. As the sun began to slide behind the branches, the smell of woodsmoke tinged the breeze.

"Mallaig is up ahead," Brodie said.

"We will gather your supplies, lass, and pay the ferryman to take us across tonight," Keir said.

She was tired, but she knew that every minute counted with an ill child. "We need to go straightaway to an apothecary to purchase feverfew, garlic bulbs, any fruits available…"

Keir shifted behind her, reaching for something. "My grandmother tends an herb garden for the family since Bradana died. There is garlic, as well as rosemary, still alive in the winter. We have fall apples and cabbages."

Grace nodded while watching a path appear between the trees. Without examining the boy, she really didn't know what would be needed. Perhaps the cure would be easy, and Keir would keep his promise to return her to her journey. But she'd keep vigilant and learn as much as she could about her captors. As soon as Lachlan improved, if there was any hint of Keir breaking his promise, she would find a way to leave on her own.

They followed where other hoofprints muddied the snow. Keir shifted again, making Grace turn. She blinked. "What happened to your shirt?" she asked. He sat behind her naked from the waist up. Dark markings wound about his thick arm, and the crosses could be seen running down one side to disappear under the draped sash that came up from the kilt. He wore black leather gauntlets and a severe expression.

He didn't answer. Brodie cleared his throat. "We are coming into sometimes hostile territory. The Devil of Dunakin isn't affected by cold, and the markings remind people who he is."

Grace looked between Brodie and Keir. "Well, that's the most ridiculous thing I've ever heard. You'll freeze."

Without bending his head, his gaze shifted to Grace. There was a warmth in his eyes despite the angular hardness of his features. "I am used to riding bare, even in the winter. Cold doesn't affect me."

"Bloody hell, you are human. Of course, cold affects you," she said, turning to face front and rocking side to side to inch backward into his chest, silently giving him some of her heat. She leaned there, the feel of his mostly bare torso and chest against her back. "Absolutely foolhardy," she murmured with as much seething as she could muster.

Mallaig seemed to be about the size of Kilchoan. Grace took note of a humble chapel, tavern, smithy, boatyard, bakery, butcher, and several rows of thatch-roofed cottages with smoke wafting from propped openings along the edges of the dwellings. Perhaps she could find help among these people. Were they God-fearing and kind or Devil-fearing and loyal to the Mackinnons?

"I'll find the ferryman," Brodie said and veered toward the tavern.

Keir guided Little Warrior to the right. "The apothecary sits at the edge of town."

Grace didn't answer. She was too busy watching a child scurry back from the road as they passed, his eyes as round as full moons. As they trotted past a woman sweeping her stoop, she looked up, her eyes widening like the boy's, and slid the sign of the cross before her bosom. Several men at the smithy, who were covering the open fires for the night, stopped to stare at them. One man nodded solemnly toward Keir, but Grace saw another make the sign of the cross as if Satan himself passed. Ahead, two ladies, who were talking out front, hurried into the house, and an elderly woman snatched up a little girl, practically running to get her inside.

"God's teeth," Grace murmured. "Do they think you eat children?"

"Most likely."

She twisted to see if he was jesting, but he stared ahead, the same hard scowl in place.

"But you don't," she said with angry confidence, turning back to frown outward. Were they all foolish, cowardly people who would be too afraid to help her? "They probably don't want their children thinking it's normal to ride out in winter without a shirt."

He remained silent, guiding his horse to stop before a small cottage with a wooden sign over the door. A mortar and pestle was painted in burgundy upon it. "Come in with me," she said, thinking to get him somewhere warm. The breeze had picked up, and she was cold even with her layers. "I worry who might be in there." Although, she shouldn't care one whit if he sickened and died from his own foolishness.

"The woman is Maude MacDonald. She is old and harmless," he said, dismounting. With a grip around her waist, he lifted her down onto the snowy ground.

"I will be in after I check Cogadh's hock."

It seemed he wished to freeze, so she settled her satchel on her shoulder, turning toward the door. With a short knock, she pressed inward. The room was warm and held a pungent, mixed odor of herbs and medicines.

A woman peeked out from a back room. She nodded at Grace but wore a wary expression. *"Co thu?"*

Grace smiled. "I am Grace Ellington. I was told I could find some herbal medicines here. That you are Maude MacDonald." Could Maude help her escape?

"Ye have coin?" the woman asked, stepping into the room, her eyes dipping to Grace's bag.

"Yes," she said and pulled out a leather pouch, which jingled as several gold and silver pieces rubbed together. Coins could make some people very brave.

The woman waved her to the shelves that lined the back wall. Jars, filled with dried herbs, sat in orderly fashion. "You have quite a bounty," Grace said sweetly. Her smile was reported to be her best weapon, and she used it whenever dealing with grumpy patients or apothecary crones who looked like they'd rather shoo her out the door than help her.

"What is it ye need?" Maude asked, her accent thick.

Grace studied the old woman. She seemed to live alone, but if she had a horse to sell, Grace might have a chance. "I'm not completely certain. Feverfew, one garlic cluster, burdock, roseroot, self-heal with goldenrod, and tormentil. If you have them."

"Ye know the ways of medicines?" she asked, her frown smoothing into an assessing neutral look.

"Yes," Grace said, helping the woman move a ladder to reach a clay jar on an upper shelf. "My sister is a wonderful healer. She and her husband's mother have taught me much."

"The husband, he is a Scot?"

"Yes. Ava and I have left England. We live with the Macleans of Aros on the Isle of Mull."

Maude seemed to weigh her words, finally giving her a nod. She waved Grace toward a series of clay pots on a lower shelf. "Pick ye out a garlic while I scoop the feverfew."

"I am fortunate to have found you," Grace said, glancing

around, but Keir was still freezing his ballocks off outside. "I was wondering if you might also have a horse for sale."

Maude narrowed her eyes. "For the right amount of coin, I could possibly find ye a horse. What are ye needing it for, lass?" Maude asked, just as the door behind Grace opened. Keir stepped inside, his height and broad shoulders filling the space. Being confined within four walls reminded Grace how large he was.

Grace didn't answer as she watched the woman's face pale. Maude leaned back, knocking a jar from her shelf to shatter on the floor.

"Oh," Grace said, rushing to help, but the woman stood there staring at Keir. "Are you well?" Grace asked, studying her fear-filled face, which told her that she absolutely wouldn't be helping Grace if it meant going against Keir.

Keir said something in Gaelic, his deep voice without warmth. Grace frowned at him. He must know he was frightening the old woman, but considering his comments when riding into Mallaig, scaring her was probably his intent.

Grace smiled reassuringly as she picked up the broken pottery to set the shards on the shelf. She patted the woman's arm and leaned in to her ear. "He isn't as fierce as he looks."

The woman turned her head to Grace, her expression full of worry. "God be with ye, lass."

Keir said something else, and Maude began throwing herbs and a few other clay pots into a linen. Grace added her garlic cluster, and Maude gathered the cloth, tying it at the top. "How much does it cost?" Grace asked, looking to Keir for him to pay. After all, it was his nephew.

"Nothing," Maude said. "A tribute to the Devil of Dunakin."

Grace looked back and forth between the woman and Keir. He nodded, and Maude's shoulders relaxed. Grace huffed softly. "We are paying," Grace said and pulled two shillings out of her own bag. She wouldn't steal from the woman, especially if she could be a future ally. As she placed them on the table, the woman's eyes went wide. "A fair coin for your medicines," Grace said, but Maude shook her head.

Grace jumped as Keir's hand slapped down on the wooden top over the coins, and slid them back. He grabbed the bag Maude had fastened and nodded to her. "Thank ye," he said. "I will be sure to let Rab know ye wish his son good health with your gift."

Maude's mouth fell open, and she nodded quickly. "Aye, that I do."

He looped his arm through Grace's and guided her out the front door. "Thank you," she called, but as soon as the door shut, she rounded on Keir. "The woman needs that money."

"She needs to feel like I will protect her more," he said, tucking the shillings into the palm of her hand. He curled her fingers around them and then produced a much richer sovereign from the leather pouch he wore at his waist, dropping it on the woman's front stoop. "Let her feel lucky to find it while still procuring my favor."

Grace stood there, her lips parted, staring at the gold coin on the lip of Maude's doorway. "Wouldn't you protect her anyway?" she asked, following Keir to where he secured the wrapped herbs into a bag tied to his horse.

"Aye," Keir said, "but it gives her ease to know I will do so not from the kindness of my heart, since she's certain that the Devil of Dunakin has no heart." He lifted her into the saddle, where Grace flipped her leg over to straddle the horse, tucking her skirts around her. Keir climbed on behind. As he leaned forward to take the reins, questions swarmed inside Grace's mind, but she kept her mouth firmly shut. The boulder of anxiousness, which Grace tried to deny, cracked further open as she thought about the woman's palpable fear. Who exactly was Keir Mackinnon, the Devil of Dunakin? She must keep her attention focused on finding a way out of this mess.

Chapter Twelve

The boat creaked as the oarsmen rowed the stout vessel across the channel. The moon crept out from the clouds, only to retreat again as if frightened. Grace understood. Surrounded by grim men, tossing among the dark, choppy waves, she felt rather like hiding, although the only place that seemed safe was with Keir. Yet she was hating him for tricking her, leading her on in her belief that he cared for her. Her face felt hot in the biting wind as she replayed her naïvety back at the cabin.

She glanced at the four stout oarsmen, whom the ferryman had gathered, and almost laughed. Obviously fearful, they wouldn't look directly at Keir. Even if they appeared trustworthy, which they did not, none of them would come to her aid. Keir's ability to withstand the cold and his dark, swirling marks and fierce face gave him an unnatural essence. He was also larger in height and brawn than all of them. Bloody hell, if he put on his leather mask, they'd probably foul themselves.

The hulking shape of the Isle of Skye lay in shadows, but the men knew the way and eventually pulled the pitching ferry against a dock where several warriors stood, swords in hand. They yelled something out in Gaelic, which Brodie answered in the same booming voice. Keir lifted Grace onto his horse but left her on the ferry to walk forward with Brodie. If they were still on the mainland, she'd be tempted to wield Little Warrior around and charge away, but on the island she had no idea which way to go to find sanctuary.

Keir walked up to the men guarding the shore. He didn't even have his sword out, but they all took a step back as he advanced. One by one, they lowered their weapons. Brodie offered some words that sounded like a demand, and each man bowed his head, and Keir sauntered back to retrieve her.

He lifted himself easily into the seat behind her. "Kinsmen?" she whispered.

"Defeated foes," he answered near her ear. He wrapped an arm securely about her middle, and with barely a warning, the horse surged forward off the ferry, making Grace gulp in a quick breath of salty sea air. She clasped the saddle horn as they rode straight toward the gathered men, making them leap out of the way of Little Warrior's thundering hooves. Horse and riders tore up the shore, diving into the darkness of the forest, Brodie bringing up the rear.

After long minutes of dodging trees along the narrowest of paths, Keir slowed his horse. "Was that necessary?" Grace asked.

"Aye," Keir said. He twisted behind and yanked his heavy wrapping out of one sack, pulling it around himself.

"Thank you," she said.

"For what?"

"For regaining your mind and putting some covering on. Watching others suffer makes me suffer."

"I wasn't suffering."

"Humph. Of course you were. Or does the Devil of Dunakin not suffer?"

Keir didn't answer, and she looked behind her. Shadows and moonlight slanted across his face as they rode under leaf-bare trees. His eyes were obsidian, filled with night, and his lips, which she knew to be warm and tender, pinched together in determination. Gone was the man from the snowy cabin where they'd spent five days. Gone was the man who had kissed her with gentleness, playfulness, and molten passion.

Tugging at her glove, she shucked it and raised her naked fingers to his bearded jaw. She stroked upward to his cheek, and he glanced down at her. "You do suffer. We all do. It is not a weakness. Suffering can make one stronger."

The hint of a smile tugged at the corner of his mouth. "How do ye think I became the Devil of Dunakin, lass? The strongest warrior in the Highlands?"

His gaze turned outward again, and after a long moment, she turned to face front. The forest thinned until they crossed a snowy moor where the horses ran as if sensing home. "Is this Mackinnon land?" she asked when they slowed to enter more forest.

"Nay," Brodie said from his seat a few yards away. "MacDonald. That's who met us at the shore. It is the closest shore to Mallaig, though, so we land there and ride the rest of the way to Mackinnon land. Until we reach it, we must be on guard."

"How do you know when you're on Mackinnon land in the dark?" she asked, looking around suspiciously at shadows, all of which now seemed sinister. Could MacDonalds of Skye be hiding to ambush them like the thieves?

"Oh, ye'll know, lass," Brodie said, his usual light tone coming out hard.

Curiosity made her sit higher in the seat, waiting to see something that would mark the boundary. "Is it much farther?" She was nervous and could use the privy if presented with one. She blamed both on the darkness and Keir's fierce transformation since Mallaig.

"We open up onto a moor after this forest," Keir said. "It sits before the village that leads up to Dunakin Castle."

Through the forest, Grace could see the flash of firelight. "I see torches," she said. Perhaps Mackinnons guarded the boundaries.

Keir slowed his horse within the trees and threw off his fur wrappings. He pulled them around to the front of Grace. She opened her mouth to tell him once again how foolish it was to go without clothing in winter when she felt his warm breath touch the side of her face.

"Grace," he said, a hint of the Keir she'd known in the cabin in his tone. "Ye will want to hide under my cloak as we cross."

A prickle of dread skittered across her back, and she almost ducked under without asking. Grace inhaled, finding bravery in the fact that she sat before the fiercest warrior in the Highlands, half godlike and half devil. "I am stronger than you think."

"Granted," he whispered, "but ye may want to close your eyes." He straightened in the saddle, and Grace looked out over his horse's head. Little Warrior must know they were almost home, but instead of relaxing, the horse's ears flicked as if he sensed danger. Keir clicked his tongue, and they rode forward, building speed as they neared the edge of the woods. Grace could see torches set in a curve fifty yards back from the tree line. They burned upward into the sky from some type of brackets, but what caught at Grace's inhale was the roundish objects hovering before them.

Keir pressed them into a gallop as they neared the line of fires. Despite the speed, time froze as Grace clung to the saddle horn, her legs clutching to hold her steady. She blinked, trying to draw breath until the stench filled her nose, and she gagged. *Good Lord and Mother Mary*. Her gaze swung around as they rode between the torches where human heads sat on spikes jutting out from the torch shafts. A line of them stared outward, guarding the perimeter. Dozens of torches, and from what Grace could see, each one had a ragged, decaying head attached to it, stabbed up through the neck.

Her body grew numb, and nausea bubbled in her stomach. Only Keir's arm around her middle kept her firmly in the seat. He said something about taking longer breaths, but Grace could focus only on the images of impaled heads, their eyes black as if crows had already pecked them clean, their mouths frozen open in grotesque grimaces, showing their last moments of anguish. Arms tingling and her breath coming so fast her throat hurt, Grace let the blessing of darkness close in until the images dissolved into oblivion.

...

Keir halted Cogadh in the bailey. They'd been spotted riding across the moor, and Liam had raised the portcullis for Brodie and him to ride through. Holding Grace against one shoulder, Keir dismounted, pulling her off into his arms. *Damnation*. If she'd shut her eyes or gone under the cloak, she'd be awake right now, asking him more questions he couldn't answer instead of looking… Keir leaned over her until he could ascertain that breath issued from her parted lips. Och, those beautiful, soft lips. He looked away, knowing that they were probably lost to him forever.

The front doors of the keep banged open, the space filling with firelight from the great hall inside. Brodie dismounted to walk across to meet Rab next to Keir.

"Ye've returned sooner than I'd expected," Keir's brother, Rab, said. His dark hair stood out in disarray, and his shirt sat about his waist untucked and stained. He'd been considered handsome before, but too much grief had beaten against him when Bradana died.

"I hurried to bring help for Lachlan," Keir said.

"What did ye do to her?" Rab asked.

"She saw the heads," Brodie answered, leading the way into the empty hall.

Rab chuckled. "They are a beautiful sight, ain't they."

"I will be back after I lay her down to recover," Keir said and headed for the stairs that curved around on themselves, leading to two more floors above. The wolf bite ached slightly at the climb, but it barely registered. Aye, the lass was a talented healer.

At the very top, he walked along the dark, cold corridor to his bedroom, pushing the door open with his boot. Pitch black met him, but he knew his way. Laying her down gently on the furs across the large down-filled tick, he went to the hearth, throwing in kindling and peat he kept ready along with a flint. Within minutes he had a small, growing fire splashing light about the stark room.

Standing, he touched the small portrait of his mother that sat on the mantel, as he always did when returning home. He looked over to the lass laid out on the bed. What would Margaret Mackinnon think of Grace? Despite fainting from the sight of bodiless heads, Grace Ellington was brave, even if she didn't know it. For one, she stood up to him, the only woman, the only person besides Aonghus Mackinnon, who ever had. She'd worked to keep them alive and had healed him in the cabin instead of abandoning him, which also showed how kind she was. Kind and brave and beautiful like…an angel. Perhaps Brodie was right, and she was dangerous to the Devil. The thought brought a lightness to his chest.

He grabbed a fresh shirt from the chest at the end of the bed and stepped around to Grace. He raised the fur on the bed up to her chin. It was best for her to sleep off the blow, because she might be up all night with Lachlan. And if she woke with him still there, she'd have questions about the heads, his family, and the Devil, questions for which he had no good answers.

Shutting the door, he signaled to one of the maids down the hall, who walked toward him like a woman condemned. "There's a lass in my room," Keir said. He thought the maid's name was Peigi, a girl from the village. "She has fainted. Sit with her and keep her calm when she wakes."

Peigi nodded and swallowed, probably wondering what he'd done to make Grace faint. "See that she receives food and ale, and a bath if she wishes. I will be up later."

"Aye, sir." She hurried past him and pushed into his room.

Keir frowned as he pulled on the fresh shirt. Normally, he ignored the fear he raised in everyone around him, but since Grace had disliked the reaction, the maid's scurrying irritated him.

Mo chreach. He was the Devil of Dunakin. The only things that mattered were his ability to induce fear and his strength to fight for his clan. Grace knew nothing of his life here, his place and duty, and she most likely never would. She'd help Lachlan, and he'd take her safely home.

Keir strode into the great hall below, where Rab sat with Brodie and Dara's new suitor, the tiresome and scarred Normond MacInnes.

"Where is she?" MacInnes demanded.

"She's resting from the journey," Keir said, glancing at Brodie. His friend shook his head, telling Keir what he already knew. Brodie wouldn't say a word about Grace, or the journey, without him present.

"I want her brought to my chambers," MacInnes said, turning to Rab. "Mairi Maclean MacInnes and I have a matter to discuss."

Rab had the alertness to frown over the request, although he looked pale with circles under his eyes. Normally by now his brother was drunk past caring, but they'd arrived before he'd downed too much whisky. "What matter would ye discuss with a beautiful lass alone, when ye've just asked my sister to wed?"

MacInnes ran a dirty hand up through his cropped wheat-colored hair, his mouth twisting under his badly crooked nose. "'Tis personal, and I would see it done before I pledge my life to your sister."

Keir narrowed his eyes at the man's tone, knowing he wouldn't let the bastard near Grace. How could Dara wish to wed this man? "I did not bring Mairi Maclean here," he said, watching MacInnes closely.

"What?" The word burst from his twisted mouth, followed by a line of foul cursing. "Where is Mairi?"

"Who did ye bring?" Rab asked, his face growing red. He leaned back in his seat as if the chair held him up. Maybe he had been drinking. "Ye were tasked with finding the Maclean healer. 'Twas your duty."

"I know my duty," Keir said softly, his hands curling into fists. "I made a choice to help Lachlan instead of helping this bastard seek some sort of revenge on a lass," he said, looking to MacInnes. "And I have reason to believe Mairi Maclean isn't a healer like you said."

The man moved forward, drawing his sword. With two powerful steps, Keir walked right up to him, his arm already cocked, and slammed his fist into his face. Normond howled, dropping his sword. It clattered to the floorboards as blood gushed from his nose. Maybe the new break would straighten it. "Don't draw your weapon in our keep," Keir said, standing over him. "Unless ye wish to feel more pain."

Rab crossed his arms over his chest. "Who is the woman ye brought?"

Kicking MacInnes's sword away, Keir turned to his brother. "Grace Ellington, of Aros Castle on Mull. She is a talented healer and saved me from a tainted wolf bite." He lifted his plaid to show the still-pink puncture wounds on his thigh. "And Mairi Maclean is wed to the chief of the MacNeils of Barra and about to birth her first child."

Behind him MacInnes swore, spitting into the rushes strewn about the floor.

"Lachlan doesn't have the time it would take for me to lay siege to Kisimul Castle to claim her. The castle has never been breached, and the woman would likely give birth on the way here."

Rab nodded, tugging gently on his beard. MacInnes stood, a bloody cloth to his face. "Mairi can heal," MacInnes said, his voice altered by the plugging of his nose. He jabbed a grimy finger toward Keir as he yelled. "If Rab's boy dies, 'tis your bloody fault for not bringing Mairi." The man scooped up his sword and continued out of the keep into the bailey.

"Rab," Keir said. "Tell me ye didn't agree to him wedding Dara?" His sister was a warrior herself, and was attracted only to strength, but the type of strength Normond MacInnes displayed was sloppy and petulant.

Rab shrugged. "Dara came to me. Said she wanted to marry him. I gave her my blessing."

"*Mhac na galla.*" Brodie cursed low, his arms crossed to mimic Keir's brother.

Rab swung around toward him, eyes wild. "If he will make Dara happy, I don't care what he is." He ran a hand through his dark hair, raising his shoulders to rotate them up and behind. "I have enough trouble to worry over." Keir watched for signs that he'd have to talk his brother calm. It seemed Rab lost his sense more easily these days, lashing out with rage and suspicion until Keir could talk him into reason. But Rab shook his head as if clearing it.

"How is the lad?" Brodie asked.

Rab rubbed hands down his face to clasp his neck firmly,

like he might want to break it. "Not well. Dara sits with him and brings him all his meals, trying to persuade him to eat. Though he didn't touch food today."

"*Och*, Rabbie," Keir said. He laid his hand on his brother's shoulder. "Let Grace see if she can help him."

Rab's face lifted into a smile. "I would reward ye for your journey, brother. I can send for three fair lasses to bathe ye. A night of heavy swiving will make up for the wolf bite and renew the Devil of Dunakin."

"I'm too tired to deal with three frightened women," Keir said.

Rab shook his head, his grin turning into a leer. "I took a turn with Jane, Malcolm's widow, and told her ye were vigorous and kind when between a lass's legs. She said she'd like to find out for herself, and I'm sure she can entice two curious friends who like a little danger."

"Nay," Keir said.

Brodie smiled broadly. "Send her my way. I can be vigorous and kind, too." He took a swig of ale from a tankard that had been set on the table by another housemaid who scurried away. Keir watched her go, wondering what she'd say to all her friends about Rab suggesting they take turns with Malcolm's widow.

Rab squinted at him and looked toward the stairs. "Nay? Perhaps ye crave a different flavor tonight?" He turned to Keir. "I was rather hoping ye hadn't claimed her. Despite her weak constitution, Grace Ellington looks delicious."

His words tightened within Keir's gut, even though his brother didn't look like he could stay upright, let alone swive. "She's in my bed," Keir said, with the inflection that she was going to stay there. "Ye wouldn't like her anyway, Rab. She's a *Sassenach*."

"Ellington does sound English," Rab said, frowning. "And yet ye trust her to treat my son?"

"Her sister is wed to Tor Maclean, the chief of Aros on Mull. She has an English tongue but a Scottish heart."

"A Scottish heart?" Rab said and laughed. "A Scottish lass wouldn't have fainted from seeing severed heads."

Brodie's eyebrows shot up. "Perhaps we should ride Jane out there right now and see how she fares."

"Dara wouldn't faint," Rab said.

"Dara's a trained warrior," Keir said. "Grace has probably never seen a severed head, let alone forty of them, half-rotted, their eyes plucked out."

Rab tugged his beard, which had grown scraggly. He used to keep it neat, along with his dress, but much had changed, his mind tainted with bitterness. Brushing off Brodie's suggestion and Keir's defense, he looked back to the steps. "Rouse her, and bring her to Lachlan's room. See what she can do as our new healer."

Keir's mouth tightened. "She is here only to cure Lachlan. After that I will return her to Aros."

Rab shook his head. "We will need her here."

"I gave her my word as the Devil of Dunakin," Keir said.

"Bloody hell, Keir," Rab yelled, yanking the hair near his temples, the gesture making him look unsound. He breathed deeply through his teeth, like a wild beast. After a long moment, he collected himself and stared hard at Keir. "*If* she cures my son, ye can take her home. If she cannot, and my son dies, your oath to her is broken, and she will remain at Dunakin to atone for her failure."

Keir glanced toward Brodie, who gave the smallest shake of his head. He would get Grace off Skye if the worst happened, and Keir would deal with his brother. "I will see if she's awake after I bathe," Keir said. He'd give the lass a little more time to refresh before sending her into the sickroom.

Rab raised his arm to curve over his head, making Keir wonder if he was, in fact, drunk. "I'm going back to bed. Wake me if anything of consequence happens." He sauntered off to climb the stairs. Would he dare to visit Grace in Keir's room? Nay. Despite Rab being the chief, he, too, held a certain fear of the Devil of Dunakin, which Keir reinforced each time he brought Rab the head of another enemy.

Brodie walked with Keir to the soldiers' quarters in silence. There wasn't anything to say. It was Brodie's turn to do his duty to further Keir's reputation. His friend would be the one to tell the men about the thieves and how Keir had slayed them, how their mighty Devil fought off a pack of wolves and abducted a *Sassenach* to save Lachlan. The stories would become another part of the legend surrounding Dunakin's Devil, the fiercest, most unforgiving demon to climb up from Hell.

Chapter Thirteen

If she hadn't been able to lay a solid oak board across the door, Grace would never have succumbed to the lure of the warm bath. But the mouselike maid had left, telling her to lower the bar to keep from being disturbed, even though Grace was ensconced in the lair of the Devil of Dunakin. The maid hadn't said "lair," but her wide eyes and pitying glances told Grace that "lair" was exactly what she was thinking. Did she know that her home was surrounded by rotting heads? It might explain her scurrying.

"Ballocks," Grace whispered and raised her arms to scrub with the fragrant soap Peigi had brought. Keir was the only thing in this place that didn't make her want to run away screaming. That was obviously the reason she wished to know where he was.

Grace looked about the sparsely furnished room that she'd explored before her bath. She felt Keir's presence in the black plaids and folded, bleached shirts stacked in a wooden chest at the end of the bed. They held his essence when she inhaled near them. Not that she was sniffing his clothes. Well, yes, she was sniffing his clothes. A woman had to use all her senses to gather information, especially when waking in a castle surrounded by heads on spikes. *Spikes. God's teeth.*

The only adornment in the room was a small portrait of a woman on the mantel who seemed to have Keir's eyes. The bed was huge, sturdy, and draped in blankets and furs. It was the kind of bed a warrior like Keir would find comfortable. All these parts, combined with the maid's pitying glances, reassured Grace that she was in the only safe room in Dunakin Castle. She held her breath, dunking way down to wash the soap from her scalp before leaving the now filthy water.

Grace squeezed her sopping hair and rose, wrapping up in one of two bath linens Peigi had left. She sat on a wooden stool before the built-up fire and ran fingers through the wet tresses. Good Lord, what had she gotten herself into? Ava would never believe the tale of wolves, thieves, the apothecary woman, and heads on spikes. And then there was Keir Mackinnon, a fierce warrior of mountainous strength with a conscience that kept him from slaughtering a family of wolves, killing a band of starving thieves, and stealing herbs from a frightened, old woman.

Grace let the heat from the flames prickle against her face and watched them dance. "What a horrible, bloody life you must live," she whispered. She'd realized, when they'd arrived at Mallaig, that the Devil of Dunakin Castle was more than a boastful name. It was a position within the Mackinnon clan, a role Keir must play, building up the legend of the vicious warrior without compassion or mercy.

"And I should hate you." Or at least attempt to escape, though she had no idea how to escape an island in winter and a castle surrounded by severed heads. She sighed and turned slowly before the flames, warming each part of her. Her hair dried in wavy curls as she spread the heavy tresses, her mind tumbling around plans that ranged from futile to ludicrous. The floorboards were freezing, and Grace hopped quickly over them to don the borrowed smock Peigi had left. Grace looked at the ratty, muddied gown she'd taken off. It was hopelessly ruined after days of surviving and traveling, and her small trunk was back in Kilchoan. She huffed and took her wool stockings to the bath to wash, hanging them over a chair before the fire. Opening Keir's trunk, she pulled out one of his shirts, throwing it on over her smock. It reached below her knees.

"It will have to do for tonight."

Bam! Bam! Bam! "Keir!"

Grace jumped, a hand pressed to her heart, spinning toward the door as a woman's angry voice cut through the thick wood. She yelled several heated phrases in Gaelic, which Grace couldn't understand, except for the curse words, Keir's name, and possibly something about a broken nose. Whomever she was, she was as mad as a swatted hornet and felt she had instant access to Keir despite the lateness of the hour.

"He's not here right now," Grace called. She frowned, walking to stand a foot from the door.

There was a pause. "Who the bloody hell are ye?" the woman asked in English. "And where is Keir?"

"I am Grace Ellington, lately of Aros Castle on the Isle of Mull. And you are…?"

"Ye are a *Sassenach*," she said, as if it were an accusation.

"Yes, I am English. And who are you?" Grace said, punctuating each word with her clipped tone.

"He doesn't bring Mairi Maclean, but he brings a *Sassenach. Mo chreach*!"

Grace's hands fisted in the loose fabric of Keir's shirt, her face growing red. "Well, it is obvious you are a loud muck-spout, but what the bloody damn hell is your name?"

"Open this goddamned door!" the woman yelled.

Grace crossed her arms over her chest. The woman could swear that Maclean warriors from Aros were surging over the moor to rescue her, and Grace still wouldn't open the door. "No."

"Ye are a coward," the woman said.

"Firstly, you haven't told me who you are. Secondly, it's the middle of the night, and lastly, this castle of horrors is surrounded by decaying heads on spikes. You see cowardice. I see bloody common sense."

"I cut off one of those heads," the woman said, her voice full of pride.

"A fourth reason I'm not opening this door." The woman was either a murderer or a female warrior. A warrior? "Are you Dara Mackinnon, Keir's sister?" Grace asked, laying her palms on the thick barrier.

Heavy footfalls neared the room, and the woman switched back to Gaelic as she yelled at someone. Grace pressed her ear against the door when a man answered. "Keir?" she whispered.

"He deserved it, Dara," Keir said. "Ye should not wed him."

"'Tis none of your bloody business. He's a mighty warrior," she answered.

"So he says," Keir replied. "But he didn't anticipate my punch, and he seemed entirely too interested in Mairi Maclean to be faithful to ye."

Dara answered in Gaelic and traipsed off down the corridor. "Grace?" Keir called.

Without hesitation, Grace lifted the bar, letting it fall slowly to the ground to lean against the wall. She pulled the curved iron handle, swinging the door inward. Keir filled the doorframe, darkness behind him, broken by a splash of light from a candle he held. It illuminated his face, his beard trimmed neatly, hair damp. He wore a clean shirt, and she was close enough to him to smell pine soap. "You bathed," was all Grace could think to say.

His gaze slid along her hair and down her form. "As did ye." He reached in to catch one of the curls that twisted over her shoulder. He dropped the lock and studied her. "Are ye well?"

Oh, right. The fainting. She swallowed. "Why are there heads on spikes around Dunakin?"

"'Tis complicated." Keir glanced behind her, reminding Grace that this was his room, after all. She moved aside and motioned for him to come in. They'd slept in the same cabin alone for days, so ushering him into his own room seemed no more scandalous. And if she wanted to figure out a plan for escape she should gather as much information as she could.

"Your sister seems…confident," Grace said, watching Keir walk to the fire to add more peat, stirring it with an iron poker. Captured within four walls, he seemed too large, like a wild animal that should have the moors over which to run free.

"She's…unhappy." He stood, turning toward her, which made Grace's heart skip a bit faster. "She would rather be a warrior than a wife but feels trapped in doing her duty. It has made her choose foolishly."

Grace suddenly felt pity for the groom. She nodded, clasping her hands before her. "You broke someone's nose?"

"Ye are wearing one of my shirts?"

Grace looked down, forgetting her question. "Yes." She met his gaze, feeling her cheeks warm. "Peigi left a fresh smock, but my gown is in tatters." She indicated the once lovely traveling costume. "I was cold, so I put this on. I will need a new costume in the morning." She tipped up her chin. "Or do you keep your prisoners barely clothed?"

"While at Dunakin, ye are free to roam, but it would be safest for ye to stay on castle grounds, and in my room. No one would dare to enter my room." His head tipped slightly to the side as he studied her. "And I think ye look quite bonny in my shirt."

Keir's gaze pulled at Grace. The tone of his voice plucked forward the memories of their brief evening together. And here they were, alone in his room, half clothed and clean from their baths. Heat trickled through her, making her skin feel extra sensitive where the linen feathered across her naked form. Freshly washed, she wondered how good his skin would taste. Had he thought about their intimate time together at all? God's teeth. It didn't matter. There would be nothing between them now. She needed to gain control over her wanton thoughts and flying pulse.

A door closed farther down the corridor, giving Grace the mental shake she needed. *He is not to be trusted*. She pursed her lips. "How is your nephew?"

"Lachlan is still alive, though even weaker from what my brother says. If I find ye a robe, could ye come see him now?"

"Certainly," Grace said, rushing toward the small table where she'd dumped out her meager pile of possessions to find her comb. The herbs were wrapped in a cloth there.

Keir disappeared, returning within minutes. "This was my mother's. It is old but warm."

"Thank you," Grace said as he held it open for her. She frowned. One didn't thank a captor. Keir's hands slid along her waist as he wrapped the tie around front. Turning, she realized he still stood close. She swallowed hard and dropped her gaze to the hollow of his throat, her heart beating wildly as if they were lovers. She stepped back and sniffed. "Whatever may have started between us in the cabin ended the moment you threw me over your shoulder." There, the words were out. Ice water on the smoldering that continued to plague her. "I just want to make that clear."

"As ye wish," he answered, piquing her irritation.

"I didn't say that was what I wished," she said, narrowing her eyes as she lifted them. "You did. If there was anything at all, you ruined it when you lied and showed that you have no integrity by abducting an innocent woman." She turned to stride to the fire as if she wore a court gown instead of an old robe over a man's shirt. Luckily, he couldn't see her shaky knees. For everything about Keir Mackinnon drew her in when he was like this. Gentle. Agreeable. Too handsome for her to keep her wits about her.

His stare was intense, snaring her as solidly as a serpent catching a bird with its gaze. "My actions are not always my own, Grace," he said. "I've explained that."

"Of course they are," she said, throwing one arm out. "You can choose to not follow an order."

"But I will not choose to let my young nephew die without trying to save him." His voice was low. The fire crackled in the grate next to her as they stared at each other.

Wouldn't she do the same to save little Hazel, her niece? She inhaled deeply and released it. "Before I help, I want to know why we are surrounded by the dead and decaying."

He picked up the candle that he'd set on a small table by his bed. "They are defeated enemies. Their presence deters others from attacking Dunakin."

"You have enemies who must be frightened with such horror?"

He grabbed up her herbs in the cloth. "Skye is divided between three powerful clans, any of which would benefit from ruling the entire isle. We have an uneasy peace, which was broken a month ago by the clan meeting us at the shore. Those are MacDonald heads, which may be reclaimed by their clan if they have the courage to come and take them. So far, they have not."

"It's barbaric," Grace said, following him to the door.

Keir looked down at her. "Have ye been to London, lass?"

Grace's lips pinched tight. "I know, King Henry displays heads of traitors on London Bridge. That doesn't make it any less barbaric."

Keir walked out the door. "Aye, but it's effective. Come. Lachlan's room is on the second floor, near my brother's."

Grace kept close to Keir as they made their way along the shadow-filled corridor and down the stairs. All seemed quiet, Dara having retreated to wherever banshees withdraw when they aren't screaming. "Your sister said she cut off one of those heads." Grace slid her hand along the rough wall to help her balance on the narrow steps.

"She did. 'Twas the raging son of a MacDonald chief who thought she'd be an easy target, since she was a woman. She's quite proud of the kill."

Grace stared at Keir's back, silently shaking her head. Lord, she'd come very far from Somerset Estate in York. "She's like no woman I've ever known or even heard of."

Keir turned to her as they walked down the second-floor corridor. "Have ye heard of *Jeanne d'Arc*?" He said the woman warrior's name in a perfect French accent.

In the candlelight, Grace watched Keir's eyebrow rise slightly, giving him an almost teasing appearance. She frowned. "You are annoyingly educated."

He exhaled long as they stopped outside a door. Pressing the handle, he pushed into the door, releasing a wafting of stagnant, hot air. Grace coughed into her fist. "What is that stench?"

"The boy lost his bowels," a woman said from the other side of the bed where a small form in the middle looked merely like a wrinkle in the blanket. "I had to change everything."

"*Seanmhair*," Keir said. "This is Grace. She's a healer. Grace, this is Fiona Mackinnon, my grandmother."

Keir's grandmother nodded, her face tired and bleak. "I hope ye be skillful, lass." She shook her head, a long gray braid hanging down the back. "The lad's taken a turn toward death."

Grace tried to inhale through only her mouth and walked across the small room to the shuttered windows. "We need some fresh air, first of all. I've found that excessive heat doesn't help the ill." Nor did the overwhelming stink of dung.

"Ye seem too young to be an adequate healer," Fiona said, following behind Grace.

Grace cracked the shutters, letting in a tendril of cool outside air, but Fiona slapped it shut. Grace turned to the old woman, remembering that Keir had said Fiona had been a warrior and knew very little of medicine. Grace kept her smile neutral. "And you seem too old *not* to be an adequate healer."

Fiona frowned at her. "I was a warrior."

Grace raised one eyebrow, her temper worn as thin as wet parchment. "Which does nothing right now for your great-grandson." Still meeting the woman's fierce stare, Grace pushed the shutter back open. "Keir, open the second window an inch to allow adequate circulation. Then bank the fire to keep the room warm enough."

Keir moved without hesitation, making his grandmother's frown turn his way, but she remained silent.

"I would like to see Lachlan," Grace said, waiting for Fiona's permission. After a pause, she nodded, leading Grace over. "More light, please."

Keir moved around the room, lighting five oil lamps, bringing them to sit on tables near the bed. The room was small with scattered furnishings: a trunk, wardrobe press, privacy screen, and several small tables. A few books splayed knocked over on the hearth mantel, and a stick horse leaned against the wall with a wooden sword. Curtains around the bed were tied to four posters.

Grace sat in a chair on the boy's right side, leaning over

him. If she didn't see the slight rise of his chest, she would have guessed he was dead. *Good Lord in Heaven, guide me to help this child.* She wished her sister, Ava, were here, or Joan, Ava's mother-in-law. Both were truly gifted healers. Grace inhaled slowly. She was this child's only hope.

She touched his head, stroking up gently through his hair. Some of the light-colored strands came away, covering her fingers like spider webs. "He's losing his hair?"

"It started today," Fiona said, sitting on the other side. "But no fever."

"But he's wet, damp," Grace said.

She nodded. "He sweats. I can't keep enough fluid in the boy. He sweats it out or vomits it up."

Keir stood braced at the foot of the bed like a sentinel ready to slay whatever demon Grace found to be killing the boy.

"You've been trying to give him food?" she asked. "Has he eaten anything?"

"Mostly broth. Dara brings it up from the kitchens three times a day and sits with the lad while I rest and check on my livestock," she said.

"The two of you have done well to keep him alive," Grace said. She took the boy's limp hand from under the blanket. It was thin, skeletal. She flipped it over and stared at the skin on his palm. "Has he always had these freckles or flecks?" She held his hand to the light to show where small dark circles spotted all over his skin.

Fiona picked up his other hand, turning it this way and that in the light. "Nay. This is new." She met Grace's gaze, her eyes large. Worry and guilt mingled there, as if she condemned herself for him getting worse under her watch. "I will ask Dara if she noticed them this afternoon or morning." Fiona hurried out the door.

Keir sat opposite Grace in a chair and studied his nephew's

hand. Lachlan's little hand looked like a thin piece of linen in Keir's large palm. "Ye know what this is?" he asked.

"Perhaps," she said, not wanting to cause more alarm. She leaned over the boy, his small face closed in heavy sleep. She pinched his lips gently, making his mouth pucker, and inhaled his breath. A garlicky smell wafted out on a shallow exhale. "Check his feet for the same spots," she said.

Keir yanked up the tucked blanket. "Aye, not as many, but there are spots here, too."

Grace checked Lachlan's nearly lifeless body, where more brown spots marked him. She took his hand again, inspecting his fingernails. "White ridges across the nails, spots on hands and feet, hair loss, diarrhea, sweating…"

"Ye've seen this disease before?" Keir asked.

Grace met his gaze. "He's not infected with disease, Keir." She shook her head. "He's being poisoned."

Chapter Fourteen

"Poison?" The word shot through Keir like a battle cry. "How? What poison?"

Grace sniffed Lachlan's breath again and took his pulse. "I saw it once at Aros. A woman came from Oban to see Joan Maclean, because she was weak and had spots. Her breath smelled of garlic even though she said she hadn't eaten any. She was weak but without fever, was losing some of her hair, and sweated terribly. And the white ridges on her fingernails looked the same as Lachlan's. The woman's brother had experienced the same symptoms and had died. Joan said it was from arsenic poisoning, probably in their well."

"But no one else here has these symptoms," Keir said, already knowing the answer to his unasked question.

Grace met his gaze firmly. "Someone must be adding it to his food or drink. Has been for a while if he's had slowly worsening symptoms."

"The lad would have said something," he argued, feeling the fury within him gather like an advancing storm. He grabbed onto one of the four posters, squeezing the hard wood.

Grace shook her head. "It is odorless and tasteless. Joan told me it was the weapon of kings. They used it to kill off anyone threatening their reign."

"*Gòrach pìos de cac.*" He swore, the words coming from the tight, nauseous boulder sitting in his gut. "The only people near the lad's food are kin and the cook. Rab, Dara, *Seanmhair.*"

Grace walked closer. "You don't know that for certain, since you haven't been home, and when you were, you didn't know to be guarding him." She laid her hand on his arm, her touch suddenly an anchor in the churning of his fury. "Why would someone want to kill your nephew?"

Fiona walked back in with Dara on her heels. "I thought the spots were nothing. They were faint this morning." Dara stopped, her worried expression hardening as she spotted Grace. "Ye must be the coward hiding behind Keir's door."

"Not now, Dara," Keir said, barely holding on to the violence within him.

Grace squeezed his arm, and he glanced down at her. She gave a small shake of her head and looked to the two women inspecting Lachlan's limp hands. "I'm fairly sure I know the sickness."

"Can we help him?" Fiona asked, her eyes alert, determined, like Keir had seen in the faces of warriors on a battlefield. If steel could fight Lachlan's illness, his *seanmhair* would surely take up her dusty sword.

"I believe so," Grace said. "But we will have to watch him closely. I will supervise all he has to drink and eat. He will need more chicken broth, fresh ale or water—"

"Which I will get from the falls inland," Keir said. Grace nodded.

"Once Lachlan is conscious, he needs to eat mashed apples, fresh fish, eggs, and oats. If you have any fresh lemons, that would be of help. And garlic should be infused in the broth."

Dara frowned but didn't say anything. Fiona nodded after each item.

"What is it called? This sickness," Dara asked, her arms crossed before her.

"Spotting sickness," Grace said confidently. She met Dara's stare without wavering.

"I haven't heard of it," Dara said.

Keir studied his sister. Was she suspicious of the name because she knew it was poison and not a disease? Dara had always been obstinate, wishing to be a warrior like their *seanmhair* rather than a lady. But what motive would she have for poisoning Rab's son? Her own nephew?

Grace shrugged. "Have you read many physician texts or helped to heal more than a hundred people during the last year and a half?" She didn't wait for Dara's answer, but went instead to the pitcher of water on the table next to Lachlan's bed. She carried it behind the privacy screen, the sound of her pouring it in the jakes obvious. She walked back around, handing it to Keir. "Let's start with fresh water in a new pitcher. And I need a pallet brought in, so I can sleep next to the boy."

"I will stay by him," Keir said. No one would get near his small nephew without him there to watch.

Grace smiled, but it wasn't her genuine smile. "Let me. Women heal while men kill." She rolled her eyes. "Men and Dara, I suppose."

Dara cursed in Gaelic. Grace ignored her. "I would also like to give him a sponge bath, wipe his skin with warm, clean water."

"I will get that as well," Keir said. Before going to the door, he walked up to Dara. Leaning in, he spoke in Gaelic, his words succinct. "Do not threaten the healer in any way, or expect the wrath of the Devil." His sister was brave, obstinate, and easily annoyed, but she wasn't a fool.

"Then hurry back, brother." She turned toward the lifeless form of their nephew.

With a quick glance at Grace, who shooed him with her hand, he strode out the door into the dim corridor. Would Dara poison Rab's son? Keir wouldn't become chief if something were to happen to Rab. The position of the Devil of Dunakin wasn't something he could give up. He had been raised to be the executioner, the brutal leader of the warriors and vicious protector of the clan. Did Dara believe she could fill the seat of chief if Lachlan and Rab died? It would be an impossible feat for any woman except one who had the support of the Devil of Dunakin. But she was a fool to think he would back her if she killed Lachlan, unless she sought to make it look like the boy had succumbed to a disease. Would she then kill off Rab?

Keir traipsed down the hall toward the steps and looked to his brother's door. He hated that room, the chief's room, and rarely went inside. After the death of his parents ten years ago, it would always smell of fresh blood to him.

He paused before it. Had Rab already given up on his son? He should be in Lachlan's room to see what the healer might think. About to turn away, a noise inside made him lean toward it. Retching?

"Rabbie?" Keir called and knocked. More retching.

Bam! Bam! "Rabbie, let me in."

Keir had been concerned with Grace's swoon earlier, but now that he thought about it, his brother had seemed pale and blotchy merely an hour ago, leaving the hall in his haste to return to bed.

Rab's voice was terse, as if annoyed by his own sickness. "Best not to come in, Keir. Seems I've caught what Lachlan has."

"If ye don't open this door, I will kick it in," Keir warned, feeling his muscles tense. Maybe his brother was too weak to lift the bar. "Stand away."

"Shite, Keir, I'm coming," Rab said. Seconds later, the bar scraped along the inside of the door.

As soon as it hit the floor, Keir pushed inside. Rab stood there, his shoulders bent as he leaned his hands on his knees. Keir grabbed him under the arms, catching him before he fell.

"*Mo chreach*. I said I've got what Lachlan has, Keir."

Keir ignored his weak outburst and set him on the bed, grabbing his hands. "Spots. Sard it," he murmured. "When did the spots start?"

"This morning." Rab coughed. "Get me some ale." He gestured to the pitcher near the window.

"Rabbie," Keir said and waited until his brother looked at him. "Don't drink or eat anything in here. Grace looked at Lachlan. He's got spots all over him now. Rab, she says it's poison, arsenic poison."

"Bloody hell," Rab whispered, his face pinching. "Why hasn't anyone recognized it?"

"Lachlan started with the spots today, ye too." Keir's hands fisted at his sides. "Are ye two the only ones sick?"

Rab nodded, opening his mouth to draw in a labored breath. "As far as I've heard."

"Then someone is poisoning Lachlan and now ye, too."

Rab grabbed his stomach, hurrying behind the privacy screen to retch. His voice came weak but with determination. "I want their heads, Keir. And their bowels. The Devil will find them and slaughter them."

• • •

Grace dozed on the hay-filled pallet that Keir had dragged to lay beside Lachlan's bed. When he'd come back with freshly boiled water and weak ale from a newly tapped barrel, he'd sent both his sister and grandmother to their beds. He'd helped Grace wash his nephew down and drizzle untainted ale into his mouth. He barely stirred but managed to swallow. Now Keir sat near the fire, staring into the flames.

"You should sleep, too," Grace said, her words thick with exhaustion.

"I will sleep when I'm dead," he said.

Grace rolled her eyes, although she knew he couldn't see her. "That is such a foolish male thing to say."

"I *am* male," he answered. "And the fact that someone has been poisoning my nephew and brother, right before me without notice, certainly paints me the fool."

She pushed up on an elbow, watching him poke the fire. "Small amounts of arsenic imitate a long, drawn-out illness. It's very difficult to detect until the later stages when the spots appear." She sighed when he didn't respond. "You won't be good to anyone if you're falling asleep in your pottage tomorrow. If there's an assassin about, I need you alert."

His face turned, his dark eyes meeting her. "We should keep the treason a secret. I've warned Rab not to say anything. I'm to spread about that he has a mild illness. The assassin will know what it truly is and will try to complete his evil deed."

"Come sit with me," Grace said and sat with her back against the rock wall. He set another square of peat into the flames and walked over, lowering his large frame slowly as if he might ache. He leaned next to her, his shoulder brushing her arm.

She kept her voice low. "That is why I told Dara and Fiona that it was called Spotting Sickness. We must watch anyone who comes close to either Lachlan's or Rab's food or drink." Grace could see Keir's jaw clenching. "You are worried it is Dara?" she asked in a whisper.

"She's had access to both, especially Lachlan. Or perhaps

Seanmhair."

"Your grandmother?" Grace tried to keep the disbelief from her hushed tone. "I don't see it in her, Keir."

He crossed his arms over his chest and raised one hand to rake through his hair. "She's Aonghus Mackinnon's mother. Madness runs in the family." He stared out at the side of Lachlan's bed.

"Aonghus was mad?" she asked, feeling the brittleness of Keir's underlying pain in the way he held himself.

"Aye, he was mad when…he died. *Seanmhair* raised him."

"He died ten years ago?"

"Aye," he answered.

Grace thought back to the concerned elderly woman and shook her head. "She is too worried about Lachlan. My instincts tell me her fear for him is genuine, Keir." She patted his leg under the blanket. "I have very good instincts when it comes to people."

He looked down at his lap where her hand rested beneath. Grace yanked it back to her side. *Blasted.* With the treason and worry, and for her, the horror of a ring of heads around the bloody castle, she was having a difficult time remembering her anger. Sitting so close, the threads of their passion drew her. Maybe it was her fear that eroded her fury at Keir. He was the only one at Dunakin whom she somewhat trusted.

She looked toward the bed, her pulse picking up when she felt his leg shift against hers. "What do your instincts say about me?" he asked, his voice a soft burble of Scots accent, pulling her gaze back. Question and doubt filled the deep shadows and lines of his face. "Am I mad, too? Brutal and cruel as the Devil of Dunakin?"

"Mad, brutal, and cruel? No," she answered without hesitation.

A wry smile touched his lips, lips she knew tasted like wild passion and heat. "Then I'm sorry to say, Grace Ellington, I don't believe your instincts."

He didn't move, yet his rigid posture softened, the firelight behind him making the details of his expression difficult to read in the shadow. "Ye must sleep," he said.

Grace's skin tingled at his nearness. She wet her lips and watched as his gaze dropped to them.

"I…" she started and swallowed. "Yes, we must sleep, in order to work together to find this fiend."

He looked away. "Lie back. I will watch the night."

"God's teeth, Keir. The night will watch itself." She pinched her lips tight to give him a glare. "The door is barred, and if anyone tries to enter, you will no doubt jump directly out of sleep to slice them to bits and claim their heads to decorate your hall for next Christmastide."

His rigid jaw relaxed enough to allow a thin smile. "Ye have a way with words, lass."

He'd said the same thing over her passion-evoked rambling in the cabin. Grace felt her cheeks warm but kept his gaze. "Words are powerful," she said. "Spoken with passion and truth, they can bend hearts and persuade others to act."

Keir pulled the covers up slightly and pressed against her shoulder until she tumbled over, her head meeting the pillow. "I'm speaking with truth when I say ye must sleep," he said.

She snorted and pulled his arm until he followed her to lie between her back and the wall. She yawned. "If I wake to find you up and black-eyed from exhaustion, you'll hear some powerful, loud words from me."

"I am warned," he said.

Her back facing him, she could still feel his heat. It seemed to radiate out from him, warming her, inviting the heaviness of peace that was necessary for sleep. She tried not to move, knowing that if she shifted her backside she'd likely brush against him. The thought made her restless, but exhaustion won out over smothered, ignored lust, and Grace fell asleep.

The lust, however, followed her into her dreams.

Keir's hands stroked down over her breasts, making Grace's gown fade away like magic, exposing her to his sight. He smiled, holding her close but not kissing her. Waiting. The magic word that would spur him into action, gloriously erotic and tantalizing action, sat on her tongue. Grace opened her lips to say "more" but nothing came out. She breathed out a huff, pinching her lips together to make the M sound, but only a whisper released, too quiet to hear despite her screaming the full word in her head. She tried again, and a whimper escaped.

Keir's mouth hardened as he stared at her, his brows coming down until he glared. His mouth opened in a grimace, showing his teeth. "Nay," he yelled.

Keir's voice jerked Grace out of her dream, and she bolted upright, the word finally breaking free. "More," she said on an exhale and looked around. *Where am I?* Blinking in the darkness, the gray tones of dawn filtering through the window's glass panes, the details of her circumstances rushed back to her. Wolves, snowstorm, Keir, a kiss, the cabin, Keir in the cabin, Brodie, the journey to Skye, heads on spikes… poison.

"Nay," Keir rasped behind her, making her twist to see him. He lay on his back, his fists held tight on the pallet. He mumbled words in Gaelic, his head turning side to side.

"Keir," Grace whispered. Was he ill? She reached to touch his forehead and gasped as his hand shot up, encircling her throat.

Chapter Fifteen

Keir stood before the man who had been his father, Aonghus Mackinnon. The old warrior's face was exceedingly red, looking almost purple with his fury. "Let go, Keir," *he said, spittle shooting out through his clenched teeth as Keir held his bulging neck.*

"Nay, ye can't do this," *Keir said, his other fist locked around the hilt of his sword.*

"I must, since ye are too much of a coward to do your duty. I thought ye were ready to be the Devil of Dunakin, delivering justice to traitors. I've already done half your job. Now finish it."

Keir wouldn't turn to look, knowing what lay behind him. "Ye are mad," *Keir said, feeling his hatred for the man surface like vomit up his throat. He released him, and Aonghus rubbed his neck.*

"Ye are weak," *Aonghus said.* "I am your chief first and the father who raised ye second, and both of me have ordered your obedience." *He reached for his own sword.* "Ye do your duty, or you're no son of mine."

When Keir didn't move, Aonghus cursed. "Bastard. I will finish it."

"Nay!" Keir grabbed his father's wrist.

"Keir?" A woman's voice came from the lump on the floor behind him, a voice that couldn't be. "Keir," she said again, beckoning him, but if he turned he'd be forced to see...

"Move aside, coward," Aonghus shoved Keir, raising his sword.

"Nay!" Keir yelled, and in one swift motion that he'd practiced for hours daily, he stepped back, swinging his claymore with muscle and power, the finely sharpened blade whistling through the air until it struck. Aonghus Mackinnon's head thudded to the floorboards, spattering blood across the wood grain.

Keir's eyes opened, the fogged mist of the nightmare crisping to reveal an angel's face. Grace, her hands up around her neck and unguarded fear in her face.

"Keir?" she whispered. "You were dreaming."

"Grace. Did I... What did I do?"

She shook her head. "Nothing really. I startled you, I think. You reached for my throat but let go as soon as you touched me."

He flexed his gripped fingers. "Good God, I am sorry," he said. "'Twas a bad dream."

"Horrific dream, from the way you looked," Grace said, lowering her hands. Her throat looked slightly red but not bruised, not like the broken, mottled throat in his memory. Relief hit him hard, and he closed his eyes, his palm covering his nose and forehead.

"Were you in battle?" she asked.

He pulled his knees up to sit, running hands over his face. If only he could sponge away memories as easily as sweat and grime. "Aye, it was a battle." With one man, a madman drunk with power and bitter rage and determined to spill blood.

Grace touched his shoulder, running a light hand down his arm. "Did you win?"

He turned his face to meet her searching gaze. "I don't know."

A gentle knocking pulled their attention to the door. Keir expanded out of his seat, ignoring the aches of sleeping on the lumpy mattress. His eyes rested on the shallow inhale and exhale of Lachlan before he finished walking to the door, where he raised the bar, swinging it open.

His *seanmhair* stood there in the dark hall, holding a bowl. "I brought the broth Grace mentioned would be good for Lachlan."

Keir stepped aside to let her in, watching as she set it down and began inspecting the boy. Grace stood to help, taking the boy's pulse. She looked to Fiona. "Still weak," she said.

Fiona nodded. "Let us try to get some broth into him."

Keir put himself between his *seanmhair* and nephew. "Try the soup first," he said. "I wouldn't want it to be too hot and burn the boy."

Fiona looked confused. "'Tis fine."

"I see steam rising from the surface," Grace said. "Please try it."

Fiona shrugged, tipping the bowl to her lips. A heartbeat before she drank, Grace let out a gasp as she tripped before her, hitting the bowl out of the woman's hands to splash on the floor, the bowl clattering.

"Clumsy girl," *Seanmhair* said, frowning viciously at Grace.

"Goodness," Grace said, bending to pick up the bowl and place a square of linen over the mess. "I'm certainly not living up to my name this morn."

Seanmhair mumbled unkind words in Gaelic, but the knot in Keir's gut, at the thought of her guilt, relaxed. She wouldn't have nearly tasted the broth if she'd put arsenic in it. Would she?

He glanced at Grace. Even with bits of her hair sticking out from the quick braid she'd fashioned last night and the light imprint of her pillow crease on her cheek, she was lovely, especially now when she smiled despite *Seanmhair's* rebuke. This evidence backed up her instincts about her being innocent.

Seanmhair propped her hands on her hips. "Ye can go fetch some more for him."

"I am sorry," Grace said. "I will get more and some bread for us." She nodded to Keir as she grabbed the bowl.

"I will remain here," Keir said and crossed his arms.

"Don't ye have discipline to hand out?" Fiona asked. "I hear there's a lad who stole some bread. He's in the stocks outside the bailey."

"I'll see to it soon," he murmured. Could no one deliver justice when he was gone? It was as if the town hungered to see the Devil of Dunakin in brutal action. And why was one of Dunakin's lads stealing bread in the first place? The harvest had been plentiful.

He ground his teeth. It didn't matter if the boy had stolen the bread or not. If Rab had passed judgment, Keir had a duty to uphold. Like every Devil of Dunakin in the history of the clan, his duty was to strike fear into everyone and anyone who didn't adhere to the strict dictates of Mackinnon law. No exceptions.

• • •

Grace followed the steps downward until they opened into the great hall. Would Ava ever believe she was walking the dark halls of a strange castle alone, a castle surrounded by bloody heads on spikes? "Damnation," she whispered, the curse strengthening her courage. If Keir didn't take her home, how could she ever hope to escape if she was too frightened to find the kitchens on her own?

The low light from the yet-to-be revived fire cast shadows, and just enough illumination for her to see an archway at the back. The kitchens were usually housed in a separate building with the risk of fire and, since the arch seemed the only other exit, she swallowed past her fear and walked briskly toward it. Grace followed a back corridor that was barely lit by tallow candles in sconces, most of them flickering out at the end of their wicks. Slippered feet moving briskly, she kept her ears alert. She took a deep breath of the damp, dark air to steady her pounding pulse. "Courage," she whispered and rounded a corner, gasping as she smacked, face first, into a wall.

"Ballocks," she said, her hands flying up, and she realized it wasn't a wall but a man. A large man, hidden in the shadows.

She jumped back. "Oh sir, excuse me."

He said something in Gaelic and held his rush light before him. He had a full beard, closely cropped light-colored hair, and a puckered scar slanted across his forehead to continue down his cheek. Dark circles surrounded each of his eyes, indicating a recently broken nose. Was this Dara's suitor?

His gaze slid down her body, and she remembered she wasn't properly dressed in her robe over Keir's long shirt. "Lo, lass, who are ye?" His rough voice and perusal sent a shiver down Grace's spine, the hairs on the back of her neck standing on end.

Grace's fear screamed so loud in her head, that she could hardly remember her name. She was alone in a pitch-black corridor with an unknown warrior of questionable honor. If he was Dara's suitor, his leer indicated he wouldn't be very loyal to her.

Grace's mouth opened as her mind churned. "I...I am Keir Mackinnon's...woman." The words popped out of her mouth before she could truly think them through, for Brodie's advice about it being safer to belong to a man in the wilds of Scotland seemed valid at that moment.

The look on the man's face slowly turned from lecherous to lethal. Damn Brodie and his bloody bad advice. "Where is that bastard?" the man asked.

Grace pointed behind her. "Right back that way. He'll be along any moment."

The man narrowed his gaze at her. "Ye speak with the tongue of a *Sassenach*."

"Oh, yes, I am originally from England, but have since changed my loyalties to all Scottish causes." She smiled confidently. Could the man see her lips quiver with the effort? He didn't say anything, just stared, making her mouth open again. She shrugged. "All the good bloody causes that kill English, I support them." She must stop talking. "If you'll excuse me, I was on my way to the kitchens for the Devil Keir, who's right behind me, and very hungry."

He rubbed his jaw, his tongue pushing out the side of his cheek. Grace stepped to the side when he didn't move and walked on.

"Devil's woman," he called, making Grace's heart thump.

Stopping, her muscles tensed, and her hands grabbed her robe, lifting it slightly for an easier escape. She looked back over her shoulder. "Yes?"

"Tell Keir I'm looking forward to working with him after I marry his sister."

"I…I will," Grace said and hurried forward. She didn't even know the man's name, but Keir would. Dara must be the bravest woman alive to wed a warrior like that, bravest or most foolish. Grace's instincts told her that Dara's groom didn't own an ounce of compassion or kindness.

She reached the end of the dark hallway and pushed through the door out into the dawn. The freezing air bit against her hot cheeks, refreshing her. She took a moment to lean back against the wall and peered up into the gray sky. Snowflakes floated down, adding to the few inches of snow covering what she supposed was the kitchen garden enclosed by a tall wall. Several stone benches were placed along what she imagined was a pathway when not draped in white, icy crystals.

Inhaling, Grace continued down the covered cobblestone path to another building. The aroma flagged it as the bakehouse. Tangy, yeasty, and mouth-watering, the smell was a welcome balm to her frayed nerves. She stepped inside to find three maids working along a wooden table, while one portly woman withdrew buns from a fire-lit kiln.

"Good morning," Grace said, and the three women, who didn't appear old enough to be called women, looked up, curious. One of them was Peigi. Grace smiled at her, and she nodded, eyes growing wide. "I'm searching for more warm broth."

The portly woman frowned and slaked a condemning expression over her. "What be an English lass doing at Dunakin?"

Grace forced her annoyance into a sweet smile. "I was brought by Keir Mackinnon to help his nephew. I am Grace Ellington, currently of Aros Castle on the Isle of Mull. He sent me to fetch young Lachlan some more broth and some bread and ale for our breakfast."

Peigi whispered into the ear of the girl next to her, and they both stared at Grace with a look that could only be described as aghast. The portly woman came closer, her face softening. "Och, lass." Her gaze scanned Grace. "Ye look none the worse for wear."

"Wear? Oh, the journey was…difficult, but I've had some sleep. I should be right again with some food and proper clothing."

The baker studied her. "He didn't bruise ye?" she asked

and lifted Grace's arm, studying her wrists. The woman *tsk*ed. "I have a poultice for bruises. Any cuts or burns?"

Grace's smile soured. "Keir would not harm an innocent woman." She turned at the whispering behind her and saw that all three girls had their heads together.

The woman murmured something in Gaelic, which brought Grace's gaze back to her.

"I am Nora MacDonald," the woman said. "The head cook here at Dunakin."

MacDonald? Good Lord, did the woman know any of the MacDonalds stuck to the torches along the edge of the moor? Grace dipped in a shallow curtsy.

"Aros, ye say?" Nora asked, tipping her head to the side. "Do ye happen to know Alyce? She's my sister and the head cook at Aros."

Whereas Alyce's face was usually tight with a jolly smile, Nora seemed to be the opposite. "Oh yes," Grace said. "I've been working with her in the kitchens at Aros. She's taught me to make tarts."

A chuckle broke from Nora's tight lips, making her cheeks swell like rosy apples, and Grace could finally see the resemblance. "Alyce can't resist a sweet," Nora said. "She's been perfecting her tarts since she was a wee lass."

"I'm very fortunate that she's taught me, though I will never have her skill."

The woman wiped her sweaty forehead with the corner of her apron. "I miss her. She married and moved with her man's family down there. She doesn't come home."

Grace swallowed a bubble of dark laughter. The bloody heads of possible kin surrounding "home" might be the reason. She looked around at the neat kitchen. "Perhaps I could help here when I'm not tending to Lachlan."

"Aye, if Alyce welcomes ye around her tarts, ye're welcome here."

Grace held her smile. "Thank you." She glanced at the three girls. "Do you have more people in your kitchens to help?"

"Nay, only us four." She frowned. "And they spend most of their time whispering."

Grace walked toward the blackened pot over the fire. "Could I dish out some more broth for Lachlan? I spilled the first bowl."

The woman's face paled. "In front of the Devil?"

"Uh, yes, though I don't call him Devil."

"Did he beat ye?" Nora ducked before Grace's face, grabbing her chin to tip it toward the bright light of the fire as if a bruise could have been hiding before.

"No. Of course not." She twisted her face until the woman released her. "May I ladle out another portion for him?"

"Aye," Nora said and shook her head as if confused by Keir's benevolence. Did everyone here think Keir was a monster? What did Brodie tell them? That he ate kittens and raped every woman he came across?

Nora pointed a flour-encrusted finger toward several stacks of wooden bowls. "Take one belonging to the lad. It has his initials carved in the side."

Grace walked over. "He has his own bowls?"

"Aye, they were made for him. The far stack. Plates and bowls from the finest oak. Beautiful workmanship."

"Are the other stacks for anyone else?" she asked, picking up one of the smooth bowls to examine.

"The middle stack is for the chief, and the third one is for anyone."

Grace peered at the smooth wood grain where there seemed to be a fine dusting in the very bottom. Running a finger to pick some up, she sniffed it, careful not to touch it to her nose or lips. Odorless. "Did someone give them the bowls?"

"Aye, at Christmastide. 'Twas an anonymous gift," she said with a shrug of her wide shoulders.

"They were made here at Dunakin?"

"Not certain, but there is a platemaker in the village. Several grateful folks probably commissioned them."

"I would think they'd have taken credit for the gift," Grace said, selecting one of the bowls that did not have an *LM* carved into the side. There was no residue in the bottom. She checked Rab's bowl, too, since Keir said he was exhibiting the same symptoms. Sure enough, there was a fine coating on the bottom.

Grace pursed her lips as anger curdled within her. With each plate she studied, all of them dusted, her stomach coiled tighter until she felt sick. The bowls confirmed that this was definitely no accident. She spooned out some more broth into the clean bowl meant for someone other than the chief or his son, setting a napkin over the top.

Nora gave her two flasks of weak barley ale and set three oat bannocks, from a common plate, on top of the napkin. "There will be more closer to noon," she said, "and perhaps some tarts tonight."

"Thank you, and I'll be sure to return to help you someday soon."

"Aye, but take care of wee Master Lachlan first."

Grace stepped out of the warm bakehouse into the chill and let her smile fade. Whoever had the dishes made was most likely poisoning them. By labeling *LM* or *RM*, the assassin could feed them each a little bit of arsenic without even being near them, making it look like father and son were slowly succumbing to an illness.

She opened the back door to the castle cautiously while balancing the bowl and bannocks. The dark hall was empty, and Grace released the breath she'd been holding. With brisk, even steps she hurried to climb the winding stairway, reaching the top with her heart pounding and breath coming hard.

"Afraid of the dark, are ye?" Dara said where she stood with Fiona outside Lachlan's door.

Grace tipped her chin higher. "I hurried back with the fresh broth."

"Aye, clumsy and a coward," Dara said.

Grace, her spine straight as a needle, stepped before the woman who seemed to guard the door. "Pray tell, Dara, have I done something to offend you? Spoken ill of you to your clan? Revealed your sins to your priest? Pissed in your morning pottage? Because your bitter pettiness is making you a very ugly young woman."

Dara's eyes opened the slightest amount, but enough to tell Grace that she was surprised. Fiona grinned but kept quiet. "If you have no answer, or even if you do, move aside. Now."

"Why ye little—"

But Fiona cut her off by sliding before her flushed granddaughter to rap on the door. She spoke in Gaelic, saying Grace's name. The door swung inward, and Grace made certain to step carefully so as not to trip if Dara decided to retaliate. But the sight of Keir, his face a lethal warning, made his sister step back.

Grace walked past Keir, and caught only a glimpse of another large man near the hearth before she realized that Lachlan's eyes were open. She hurried over, a smile on her face. "Hello," she said. The boy didn't seem likely to muster even a small grin. "I am Grace, and I'm here to help you grow strong again."

Behind her, she heard the door shut, and she set the bowl on the table next to the bed. "Do you think you can eat?"

The boy's eyes, cast in sunken shadows, glanced to the man near the hearth. Grace followed the gaze, and the man stood up slowly as if he ached. "And you are Chief Mackinnon?"

"Aye," he said. "How do ye know the broth and ale are safe?"

She cast her eyes between the boy and his father, and then to Keir. "The lad knows now that he's being poisoned," Keir said, his voice soft.

Grace turned back to father and son. "I spoke to your head cook, Nora. It seems a set of bowls and plates were given at Christmastide to the chief and his son, each with initials engraved on them."

"Aye," Rab said, his brows drawing together.

"I checked the stack of bowls for each of you in the kitchen, and there is a fine dusting of powder in the bottom of each. My guess is that the plates and bowls are poisoned. Whatever gets put in them picks up the arsenic, and you two ingest it. This bowl was from a stack that anyone could use, and looked clean. I also wiped it out before I spooned the soup into it. I took the flasks from a common basket and filled them from a common butt of weak ale."

She sat on the edge of the bed and uncovered the broth, setting the bannocks on the napkin next to it. "The faster we push untainted foods, herbs, and ale into you both, the sooner you will feel better. Hopefully, there will be no long-term effects, but that's something I cannot predict."

Rab rattled off a long line of Gaelic words, some of which Grace knew to be offensive swear words.

"I agree," she said. "To poison a child." She shook her head.

"And a chief," Rab added. "'Tis treason." He nodded to Lachlan, who let Grace spoon broth between his lips.

"The bloody damned dishes," Rab said, and rubbed his hand down his pale face. He sat back in the chair by the fire. "I don't even know who gave them to us."

"I will talk with Hamish, the platemaker in the village," Keir said. "He will tell me who had him make the dishes as a gift."

Grace continued to spoon the broth into the weak boy. "And the kitchen should be watched. Whoever poisoned the dishes might return to dust them some more."

"Anyone entering the kitchens is suspect," Keir said.

Grace broke off a bit of bannock and gave it to Lachlan. "Nora said that only she and the three girls work in there."

"Did ye tell her she was serving poisoned food?" Rab asked, slowly chewing a bannock that Keir handed him.

"No." Grace watched the boy swallow and glanced at the chief. "We should keep that a secret, or the assassin might stop, which will make him harder to catch."

"I want this traitor dead, Keir," Rab said, his teeth bared. "I want him forced to eat his own poison before ye disembowel and behead him."

"God's teeth," Grace said, frowning. "There is a child in the room."

"A child who must learn to judge and dole out punishment before he becomes chief," Rab said.

"I've known a number of Scottish chiefs," Grace said. "And none have ruled by brutality."

"People only truly understand fear," Rab said.

"I completely disagree," Grace said.

Rab looked to Keir. "She's an uppity bit of fleece."

Grace stood. "And I'm no bit of fleece. I am a healer, a good one. I am saving your son's life, and maybe yours, if you behave."

Rab smiled at her. "Aye, see, even the healer sows fear to persuade me to comply."

Grace felt her face warm. Ignoring the Mackinnon chief, she looked to Keir where he stood frowning, his arms crossed. "I will need coriander, the leaves in boiled water, and the seeds to crush. Also, fresh fish and cooked eggs will help sop up the arsenic already in their bodies. And plenty of fresh ale or water to wash the poison out."

"And one of the three of us must be with Lachlan at all times," Keir said.

Rab waved his hand toward the door. "I will sit and eat with the boy. Ye have punishment to hand out, Keir." He grinned at Grace. "And if he doesn't kill the lad, ye will have someone else to heal."

Chapter Sixteen

Keir followed Grace out into the vacant corridor, shutting the door. She rounded on him. "You aren't really going to kill a boy, are you?" Both of her eyebrows rose high. She poked him hard in the chest. "Keir Mackinnon, don't you dare kill a child."

"He's fifteen, considered a man and old enough to know not to steal."

"What did he steal? The bloody jewels from the Scottish crown? The king's horse? A galleon perhaps?"

Keir frowned deeply at her. "My room is one floor up. There should be a clean gown for ye laid out by the maid." Damnation. He didn't want Grace to think he was… What? The Devil? That was exactly what he was. He raised his fingers to her cheek, marveling in the fact that she didn't flinch away from him. Maybe it was her bravery to stand up to him, question his heart, that made him lean close, revealing a secret he never had before.

"The lad will be saved," he whispered by her ear and turned away, not wanting to see his self-loathing reflected on her angel's face. Keir stepped down the winding stairs, walking into the great hall where Fiona and Dara had retreated to eat at the table. Brodie poked at the growing hearth fire.

Dara frowned at him. "I don't like her."

"That doesn't concern me," Keir said, grabbing a dark roll. He used his knife to slather on butter from a crock.

"Even *Seanmhair* hasn't heard of Spotting Sickness," Dara said. "She may not know what she's talking about. She's not Mairi Maclean."

Keir centered a hard gaze on his sister. Could she be the one who was dusting the bowls in the kitchen? She'd always liked to spend time in there to sample Nora's creations. "I find it odd that ye would rather have me bring a woman here whom your betrothed wants."

She set her clay mug down with a hard tap. "He doesn't *want* her. She's a talented healer, is all."

Brodie chuckled, walking over to grab a roll.

"What?" Dara snapped.

Brodie shrugged. "Your groom tents out the front of his kilt every time he talks about Mairi Maclean. I'd say he'd like a bit of her healing balm, if she be the one stroking it on."

Dara's aim was true as she threw her roll at Brodie's head, hitting him with a *thunk* right between the eyes. "*Dùin do ghob*," she yelled, stressing each word of the foul phrase.

Seanmhair grinned, shaking her head. Nothing shocked the old woman.

"I don't know why ye'd want to marry the arsehole, Dara," Keir said, gaining a glare from her.

"He's a fierce warrior, Keir," she said. "The scars he wears proves it."

"There's more to a fierce warrior than the evidence of battles," Keir said. "It could mean he's a terrible warrior, lucky to be still alive."

Dara huffed, rolling her eyes. "He's the only one around

here who is strong enough to wed me."

"I'm strong enough to wed ye," Brodie said and grinned.

She made a pretend retching sound. "Someone I haven't spent my life thinking of as a brother."

Keir touched her shoulder, making her look up to him. Dara really was bonny when her face wasn't pinched with annoyance. She had their mother's expressive eyes and thick brown hair. "Ye don't have to wed him, or anyone, until ye meet someone ye truly fancy. There are others in this big world."

"None of which come to Skye." She turned back to her plate where he saw her touch the edge, sliding her finger along the rim. Was she double-checking that she didn't have one of Lachlan or Rab's poisoned plates? The suspicion coiled like a snake in his gut.

Brodie came up to him. "Ye heard about Rachel's lad out in the stocks?"

Keir walked toward the double doors. "Aye, for stealing bread."

Brodie's frown turned fierce. "Idiot." He lowered his voice. "And Rab, in one of his fits, proclaimed he should be flogged until he passes out or dies. He was to be held there until ye arrived to see it done."

"How long?"

"Only a day, and his mother's been feeding him. Wrapped him in blankets last night. A group is gathered out there since they saw ye ride into town last night."

Keir nodded. "Give me a space and then come out."

"Aye." Brodie's face relaxed, and he handed him his black mask. "Make it good."

Keir turned away, but paused to glance back at his friend. "If Grace comes down, stop her from seeing."

Brodie looked to the still-vacant stairs. "Even if she doesn't see the Devil in action, she'll hear about it."

"Seeing is worse," he murmured and headed into the entryway chamber where he removed his shirt. After years of snow baths and showing he was impervious to cold, it hardly bothered him anymore. It was a discomfort that seemed a warranted punishment for the fear he was about to sow.

He grabbed the lash that hung inside the door, the braided leather handle rubbed soft by generations of Dunakin Devils holding it. Long black leather strips hung from it, several peppered with sharp metal teeth to bite into skin. Keir stepped outside the double doors.

At the top of the keep stairs, he braced his legs, crossing his arms over his bare chest where his ancient markings stood out like swirling serpents over his biceps. Several of his warriors looked up, bowing their heads in greeting and respect. He was their feared leader, the one who pulled them through battles when they were vastly outnumbered. His reputation alone evened the odds by striking fear in their enemies before the fighting began. It was a strategy, sharpened over the centuries, until the Devil of Dunakin and his fierce fighting men had become legend. The Devil was usually the second son of the chief or the son of the Devil of Dunakin himself, which was why Keir had never sought to sire a child. He wouldn't raise a son to be the monster that he'd been trained to be.

Keir inhaled, filling his lungs, and let out a fierce yell. "Where is the thief?" His men pointed toward the gates, and he walked down each step, snapping the lash, the ends cracking in the air. Power radiated from each of his steps, his boots crunching on the pebbles in the heavy silence. Villagers lined the short path to the stocks beyond the gate. Tears sat in some eyes, tears he ignored. To acknowledge them would show he could be swayed from his purpose. Several older women held the boy's mother back as if she would lose her mind and throw herself on the Devil.

"Please," Rachel said. "Have mercy. He's just a boy."

"He's old enough to hold a sword, he's old enough to know that no one is above the law," Keir said, his words breaking through the gray morning. He stared at the streaked face of Niall Mackinnon. The boy had at least some bravery to hold his gaze for a moment before dropping it back to the dirt. "Niall Mackinnon, your chief has found ye guilty of thievery and has sentenced ye to be lashed until ye either pass out or die where ye stand."

"Nay," Rachel cried, but the ladies dragged her back when Keir's gaze swung around to her. They obviously thought she would be next to feel the lash. Bloody hell, he hated this.

Gritting his teeth, Keir stepped up to the stocks. "Tie him to the lashing pole." Two of his warriors came forward and lifted the heavy yoke of the stock that had held Niall all night through the freezing temperatures. He remembered how that felt, the aches in the back from bending. He remembered the humiliation when his father's men had dragged him to that same pole, tying him to receive his beating. But instead of the lash, Aonghus Mackinnon had punched him in the gut and nose until he bled and vomited. Grooming him to be the next Devil of Dunakin had saved Keir's skin from deep lash scars that would be evidence, later on, of his weakness. The internal scars were the same, however.

The crowd stood silent, faces grave, as Niall was tied and his shirt stripped to hang around his hips. Keir saw Normond MacInnes standing off to the side, watching. Perhaps the brutal show would make him pause if he ever tried to lift a hand against Dara. Keir flicked the lash out, making it snap like lightning. Several people jumped, and Rachel wailed until one of her friends, desperate to save her, threw a hand over her mouth.

A burst of movement near the gate caught Keir's attention. *Bloody damnation.* Grace. She pushed into the crowd. Brodie ran out the gate two steps after her, but she'd managed to weave between people, dodging toward the front. He turned away from her. It was too late for them anyway, not that he could ever earn the affection of a woman like Grace, gentle, intelligent, and strong. He snapped the whip again, regret turning to fury.

"Prepare to feel the results of your thievery, Niall Mackinnon!" he yelled, bringing the whip down to hit the ground next to the lad.

Brodie marched forward. "Ho there, Devil of Dunakin," he called out and bowed his head low until Keir turned to him. "I would not interrupt your duty, but Rab has commanded ye come to him."

"I am delivering justice in his name," Keir said, raising his hand. Everyone around him seemed to hold their breath, not knowing the outcome he had already planned with Brodie, like all the beatings of children and minor offenses his cruel brother insisted upon. There were a few worthy offenses in grown clan members that Keir did deliver with brutal strength, but if Rachel had paid attention, she'd know that Niall would not feel Keir's spiked lash.

"Forgive me, powerful Devil of Dunakin," Brodie said. "But Rab demands your presence now."

"*Mo chreach*," he cursed and slammed the handle of the lash into Brodie's hand. "Finish his sentence and cut him down. If he lives, he will learn never to steal again."

"Aye, sir," Brodie said, lowering his eyes as if the sight of Keir was frightening to him as well.

Keir turned, his boots grinding in the pebbles beneath his heels as he hiked toward the gate. Would Grace follow him? He whipped off the black mask, clenching it in his hand. Nay, not after witnessing the truth of his foulness.

• • •

A brisk wind sent snowflakes swirling down from the clouds to prick against Grace's hot cheeks. She blinked against the tears threatening to spill from her eyes as she watched Keir stalk off, his hair in disarray from yanking off the hellish black mask. His skin, bared to show he was immune to the cold, showed his markings, the crosses of those he'd killed pocked across his back. She'd touched them all, yet now he seemed untouchable.

"Are ye the Maclean lass he brought back?" a woman next to Grace asked in a near whisper. "To heal wee Lachlan?"

Grace cleared her throat. "Yes, though I am not the one he sought, but I'm a healer, too."

The woman passed the sign of the cross over her chest. "I will pray for ye, milady."

Grace felt a hollow flutter in her chest. "Thank you, however I'm sure Lachlan could use your prayers more than I."

"So, brave," the woman said, shaking her head. She leaned closer to Grace's ear. "Prepare yerself, lass. If he hasn't raped ye yet, he will. He's a true devil. Even killed his own mother."

Grace's breath balled up inside her for several heartbeats. Killed his own mother? She didn't believe it for a moment.

"Please, Brodie," the woman who must be the boy's mother, called across the circle of villagers. She shook her head. The ladies who had held her in Keir's presence released her to run over to Brodie, falling on her knees. "He's a stupid, hungry boy."

Brodie looked out at the gathered crowd while holding the lash. His voice boomed as loudly as his face was dark with anger. "A hungry boy, son of a valiant warrior killed in battle, and none of ye brought them bread or meat?" His gaze scanned the crowd, and Grace watched as many of them shifted, looking down at the dirt beneath them.

Brodie snapped the whip, and several people flinched.

"We are a clan, all of us. The only time one family should be hungry is if we are *all* hungry. We had a good harvest, and the only way the Mackinnon clan can remain strong is if we all partake in it." He folded the flail, pointing the heavy handle around the circle as he pivoted on one heel. "If one is forced to steal bread, ye are all guilty of the same. Each of ye should stand in the stocks and feel the strike of the Devil of Dunakin."

The weight of his stare fell heavily on each person in the crowd. After several long moments, he moved around to stand in front of the boy. "Ye will stay within your mother's house for a week and keep your shirt on whenever out, until spring. I will tell the Devil that I delivered three lashes before ye fell unconscious and were carried home by several villagers." He looked out, and two men stepped forward. Brodie nodded, and with his dagger, cut the boy loose. His mother wrapped Niall in a hug.

"Thank ye, sir Brodie," she called, tears coursing down her cheeks.

Brodie nodded and turned, traipsing away from the crowd. The woman next to Grace squeezed her hand. "What is yer name, lass?"

"Grace," she answered numbly.

"The ladies will offer prayers to Saint Mary to keep ye brave and alive."

Grace had no idea how to reply. Her mouth opened. "Thank you?" she said, but it sounded like a question. She turned away before the woman could say anything else and saw Brodie striding along the outside of the great castle wall. He walked with purpose, the lash still in his fist. Grace followed at a distance, glancing over her shoulder, but no one followed.

Brodie ducked into a low, thatched barn. Grace hurried toward it and circled behind where it butted up against a copse of trees near the river, concealing her from anyone walking by. The gurgle of the water made her heart thump faster, but she focused on the building before her. The chinks of daub between the hewn planks were loose, and she searched until she found a missing chunk.

Peering in, she saw Brodie and Keir. Keir had donned a shirt and took the flask Brodie handed him. "Thank ye," Keir said.

Brodie slapped a palm down on his shoulder. "It was earned. The boy was scared enough to piss himself."

Keir frowned. "And ye couldn't keep Grace out of it."

Her breath stopped altogether. He hadn't wanted her to witness his abuse. She blinked, her eyelashes touching the outside of the barn.

"The woman is slippery," Brodie said. "When I told her she must stay inside, she excused herself to the privy, but that's not where she was going. Dara saw her sneaking out."

Brodie pointed to something Keir held wrapped in cloth. "Bread for Rachel and Niall?"

"Aye. I didn't know they were short on food," Keir said.

"Rachel's too proud to go to Rab for more, and Niall is growing so fast, I don't think she can keep him fed. I shamed the villagers for letting them get hungry when others are not."

Keir nodded. "Good. And bring Niall to training," Keir said. "He's old enough and will receive two hearty meals a day up at the castle."

Brodie nodded. "I told him to act like he was healing for a week. If anyone comes to tell Rab—"

"I'll intercept," Keir said, "and scare the piss out of them for trying to curry favor. Make sure Rachel's given a few chickens for eggs, and teach Niall how to set traps for rabbits. Even with the others helping them now, the lad needs to learn to feed himself. Without a father to teach him, I am responsible."

"Actually, as chief, Rab is responsible," Brodie said. Grace couldn't see his face, but his tone was solemn. Keir's face was hard, his brows low.

"What would have happened if we hadn't come back for weeks?" Brodie asked. "A perfectly good lad would die, bent over in those damn stocks." He shook his head. "Rab's gone mad since Bradana died, Keir. Perhaps it is time for ye to replace him."

Grace's eyes opened wider, and she pulled away to readjust over the open chink in the daub. Could Brodie want Rab and his son out of the chief's seat? Enough to poison them?

"'Tis treason," Keir said.

"Or is it liberation from a tyrant who forces ye to do his dirty work?" Brodie asked, his voice low.

Keir stared back for a long moment. "Are ye poisoning my brother and nephew?"

Brodie took a step back as if Keir had struck him. He shook his head. "How could ye ask if I'd poison Lachlan? Nay, Keir, I am not."

Keir's shoulders slumped forward, and he set his hands on his knees, propping himself up. "I know, but I had to ask."

"Now if it was just Rab…" Brodie said and chuckled, breaking the tension Grace could feel permeating the low barn, the ewes clustered at the far end, barely paying the two men any attention.

"Well now, what do we have here?" A man's voice made Grace fall forward, her forehead thumping the side of the barn. She turned to see the man from the dark corridor this morning standing there. "Peeping at some sheep, *Sassenach*?" The words were teasing, but the leer that tightened his face once again stiffened the hairs on the back of Grace's neck. His gaze stripped her bare, making Grace cross her arms over her breasts.

She stepped away, sliding back along the edge of the barn until only a few trees separated her from the river. "I was happening by and wondered what animals dwelled within," she whispered, the man's large frame trapping her against a tree flanking the water. "I need to…go," she said.

"Ah now, not so fast, lass. I hear ye're from Aros." His grin turned dark. "I have an acquaintance with the chief there, Torquil Maclean. I've heard that ye are sister to his wife."

Between the man before her, who held himself in a very predatory fashion, and the sound of water behind her, Grace's panic reared up with paralyzing strength. She stood there, unable to yank her *sgian dubh* from the inside of her pocket. Her lips parted to gather more air to feed her fleeing heart.

As if sensing his menacing power over her, the man stepped closer. A wicked grin darkened his features, making it clear that he enjoyed frightening her. "If ye survive Dunakin, lass, perhaps ye could take a message back to your bloody chief."

Riding over the pounding in Grace's ears, a voice made the evil man pivot, hand to the hilt of his sword. "Normond MacInnes, your ragged head will be atop a pike by nightfall if ye don't step back. Now." Keir. Relief flooded Grace, making her sag against the tree.

Normond MacInnes? Her eyes widened as she stared at the back of the stranger's head. *God's teeth*. She'd found the man that the chiefs of Barra, Mull, and Islay Isles all wanted dead, the man who'd disappeared after stalking and trying to rape her friend, Mairi Maclean.

Chapter Seventeen

"Pull your weapon," Keir said, his gaze centered on Normond MacInnes's eyes. "And Dara won't be wedding a dead man."

"Sard off, Keir," MacInnes said, turning to stride past him away from the riverbank. Keir watched him go and shifted his gaze to Grace. Her face was flushed. "He didn't touch ye, did he?"

She shook her head. "That is…Normond MacInnes?"

"Aye," he said and glanced at the wall where she stood. "Ye were spying on me."

Grace threw up both of her hands as if wishing to freeze time in its place. She glanced behind him at the wall and back at Keir. "Yes, but I need to tell you about that man."

"What did ye hear?" he asked, much more interested in that than the fool who he was convinced wouldn't stay loyal to his sister.

"That man is evil. Tor Maclean, the chief of the Macleans, and Cullen Duffie, who is the chief of the MacDonalds of Islay, as well as Mairi's new husband, the chief of Barra Isle…" She held up a finger for each chief and pointed them in the direction Normond had gone. "They all want him dead for terrorizing and trying to rape Mairi Maclean. She was his stepmother, and he trapped her at Kilchoan when his father died. Is he the one who sent you to find her to heal Lachlan?" She shook her head. "You can't let him marry your sister. Throw him in Dunakin's dungeon."

Keir frowned, stepping closer. He had distrusted Dara's suitor from the moment he arrived, a lone traveler who'd left his clan to fight for any army. But it was more than that. It was the glint in the man's eyes and obvious hatred of anyone questioning him. "Stay away from him," he said. "I will talk with Rab and Dara."

Grace opened her lovely lips to say something else, but he beat her to it. "What did ye hear through the wall?"

Her mouth shut, and he watched as the lovely flush came back to her cheeks. She tipped her chin higher, but stared directly at him. "A captive must use one's resources to survive by learning the truth."

"Sometimes the truth is ugly," he said, his words low in warning.

She looked heavenward before centering a glare at him. "Or the truth is much less ugly than what is played out before a quaking crowd." She huffed. "Keir, you are forced to play the part of the Devil, but you aren't in your heart. You don't need to follow Rab's brutal orders to beat a boy or steal away a woman."

He studied her. "Ye would leave now, then, after seeing how sick Lachlan is?"

They stood in silence, and he watched her gaze rise to the trees.

"I... Blast, Keir." She shook her head. "I will help him, but that doesn't change the fact that I'm a prisoner here and that you are one big brutal lie."

Two men walked by, spotted Keir, and changed directions.

"Come," he said and stepped forward, taking Grace's arm. He didn't need her to spout secrets here in the open.

"Where are we going?" she asked as he partly dragged her behind him. "To another pretend whipping? Or maybe an authentic head spiking festivity?"

"Keep your words inside ye, lass," he said and led her to the bailey, steering her to the stable where Cogadh was housed. Once inside, he released her.

"I don't understand you," she said and flung her arm toward the closed door. "All those people out there are terrified of you. I met a woman in the crowd who is having the whole town pray for me because she knows you will be raping me sometime soon." She paused, but he kept moving, throwing a saddle on Cogadh and tightening the girth straps. "Doesn't that bother you?" Grace asked, her voice demanding.

"They've been taught to fear the Devil of Dunakin. It is what has always kept order here, for generations."

Before she could ask more, he lifted her up in the saddle. "If ye keep your lovely mouth shut until we are away, I will answer questions."

Grace pinched her lips shut with a *humph* as he opened the stable door and mounted behind her. He clicked to send Cogadh into a fast walk out of the bailey and into a canter through the streets of the town. Let the staring villagers think he was taking Grace away for dastardly sins. *The worse they think of ye, the better.* Aonghus Mackinnon's words threaded through him, words he'd heard from the moment he left his mother's apron strings.

He stared ahead over the blue hood Grace wore. "Close your eyes," he said as they drew closer to the ring of heads encircling the moor around Dunakin.

"Perhaps they are only stuffed sacks made to look like heads," she said. "I don't know what is real around here."

He leaned closer to her ear, trying to ignore the scent of

flowers that had grown stronger since she'd bathed. "I have no wish to hold ye unconscious throughout the rest of the ride. Inhale the taint on the breeze to know they are real, and shut your eyes."

In case she spitefully ignored his prediction, he kept his arms snug around her waist, pressing the softness of her curves into him. They flew through the grotesque barrier, and he slowed Cogadh to enter the sparse stand of trees where he followed a thin path. Grace remained silent, and they broke out of the small woods to canter up a snow-covered hill. Spindly tufts of dead grass shot up from the white, and Cogadh's hooves churned as they rose upward to ride between two jutting boulders. He felt Grace shiver in his arms and opened the sash from his kilt to drape before her, blocking the wind.

Up ahead, a few low myrtle trees flanked a stream. Cogadh followed it, picking his way around the edges of ice cut away by the flow of clear water. The breeze blew fresh air in, free of woodsmoke and the tang of death that ringed Dunakin.

Farther up, where the stream turned to the north, he spotted the edge of the cabin. Squat and secure, the thatching was still fresh from the fall when he'd climbed above to mend the few leaks. The walls still looked clean, swept by wind and snow. He pulled Cogadh to a stop before the small barn and jumped down.

His hands grasped Grace around the waist, pulling her toward him, guiding her down to the ground. She didn't look at him but stepped away, crossing her arms. "Ye can go inside. I'll stable Cogadh and be right in."

Grace walked to the porch and tentatively pushed against the door. It swung inward, and she stood there trying to see into the dimness. Keir exhaled long, his breath fogging in the cold. Why had he brought her here? Brodie was the only other person alive who knew of this place, hidden on the border between Mackinnon and Macleod land. He walked Cogadh into the stable and took off his saddle. Grabbing a bucket, he strode out to get some water from the stream and saw Grace leaning against the open cabin door. Her gaze followed him to the stream and back, but she didn't say a word. She was angry, probably hated him enough not to talk. *Bloody hell.*

He filled the small trough inside and stuffed some hay into the iron feeding grate. "If she slits my throat," he said, drawing his horse's gaze, "she's your new master." Cogadh snorted.

Keir washed his hands and trudged to the door. "It's safe," he said.

"I no longer enter places when I don't know what is inside. I learned my lesson from the wolves."

The old door creaked as Keir pushed it to walk in. There was a table and two chairs, a large bed, a swept hearth, cupboard and trunk, a willow broom in the corner, and dry kindling. Exactly how he'd left it. He went straight to the hearth and pulled flint and steel from his leather pouch. He snapped them together while holding a charred piece of fabric, which caught the spark. He added a small piece of milkweed fleece to it, blowing on it softly until the flames caught. Laying it in the cold hearth, he fed it twigs and then larger pieces of kindling until the fire grew strong enough to leave.

Grace stood inside the door. "Your country home?" she asked.

He gave a small, cold smile. "'Tis a place we can be alone."

She moved forward, circling the room to stop before the fire. Splaying out her fingers, she warmed her hands. "It's kept up. Who lives here?"

"No one. It belonged to Graham MacLeod at one time, but only I come here now." He grabbed a chair to sit.

"You keep it up?" She waved her hand at the floor and the roof overhead.

"Aye."

She narrowed her eyes. "Why?"

"It's the only place on the Isle of Skye where I do not need to be the Devil of Dunakin."

Grace took a big breath and let it out. She sat in the other chair, facing him. "What is going on here? This whole farce where you must act cruel and vicious?"

He crossed his arms over his chest. "It has been done within our clan for generations. I was raised to be nothing but cruel and vicious and warlike like every other Devil of Dunakin. Aonghus Mackinnon was the chief, and I was his second son. Therefore, I was instructed on ways to make men quake, women cross themselves, and children hide. The Devil's reputation can often be enough to prevent attack."

"Why then are there heads around Dunakin?" she asked.

He shrugged. "Sometimes we still get attacked. We win, and Rab orders the show of strength as a warning to others. Like your good King Henry on London Bridge."

She shook her head. "But your own people are afraid of you, like you are some murdering, raping monster. Even though you aren't."

"Ye've seen all the men I've killed etched on my skin. I am a killer, Grace. It is all I've been taught to be."

"In battle, to protect yourself and your clan. That is different. The fact that you honor those killed by placing their cross on your skin shows your heart doesn't ignore cruelty and human loss." She leaned forward. "You saved that boy today, planning for Brodie to stop you, meeting Brodie with bread for the boy and his mother, instructing him to invite Niall to train with the young warriors. A cold-hearted monster wouldn't do that. Why must you play the Devil?"

"It is who I am, what I've been trained to be." How many times did he have to say that before it sank in to her? "I know nothing else."

"Maybe you've been taught nothing else, but you surely *know* something else or that boy would be bleeding or dead." She leaned forward. "You mention your father teaching you to fight and scare people, but what of your mother?"

Margaret Mackinnon. The thought of his kind mother brought both shame and a sweet comfort. She had smelled of freshly baked bread from spending time in the bakehouse, kneading and braiding her beautiful creations. Aonghus would ridicule her for working with the servants, but Keir's mother had been kind and looked beyond simple status among people. And…she had been hiding. Her rough, loud husband didn't enter the kitchens where the warmth and delicious aroma embraced her all day.

He realized he was staring at the swirls of wood grain on the table when Grace bent her head low to reach his gaze. "Keir, what did your mother teach you about?" she asked.

"Secrets," he said, pushing away the dark memories that crept in whenever he thought of Margaret Mackinnon. "She taught me to keep secrets."

Grace stared at him for a long moment. She shook her head. "About being kind? How to trick people into thinking you're horrid when your heart is good. Those secrets?"

Anger and dishonor curdled in his stomach. He shoved back his chair, scraping the wood floor, and stood. He leaned his knuckles on the table to peer down at Grace. "My heart is not good. Ye need to know that."

She narrowed her eyes back up at him, unafraid. "If you are trying to convince me of your cruelty, why didn't you want me to see you beat that boy today?" Her fingers curled into the edge of the table. "Why, Keir?" She stood up, to lean forward. "You even whispered to me that the boy would be fine before you headed out. Why bother to give me comfort when you want me to believe you to be a vicious, murdering monster?"

"Dammit! I don't know." He pulled back, walking around to grab her upper arms, holding her there where he knew she couldn't disappear, leaving him alone like he'd been his whole life. And yet she should stay away from him and his black soul.

Grace, her lovely angel face, tipped up so her eyes could pierce him. But the anger that had narrowed them, softened. A gentle smile touched her lips as one eyebrow arched delicately. "Well," she said. "I don't believe any of your devil act, Keir Mackinnon. It is all lies. You are honorable and kind. Traits that were born to you, innate parts of you like your wavy hair and deeply dark brown eyes. You were taught to be a devil, but you are not one in your soul." Her words finished soft like a breath of a whisper, words that pulled at his heart, a heart that he had thought died years ago in Aonghus Mackinnon's bloodstained room.

He should turn away from her, have Brodie take her home before Rab could order the Devil to harm her, but no one had ever looked past his mask before. No one had dared. Only Brodie knew the secret, his trusted friend from boyhood, who'd sworn to help him. Keir stood still, frozen on a precipice, unsure whether to walk away or…

Grace lifted her fingers to his face, running one along his hairline and down his temple, past his ear to his jaw. "You were born a man, not a devil. Remember, I have excellent instincts when it comes to people, and I'm a coward. If your heart was as dark as you say, I'd be running away."

She lifted her hands to his shoulders, sliding them up until he could feel her fingers behind his neck. Standing on her toes, Grace brought her face to his and pressed her lips to his mouth. He didn't move, didn't breathe; the feel of her softness was like a chisel against the brittle shield he held around himself. As she backed up, she tugged softly at her bottom lip, her lashes opening as she focused in on his gaze.

And Keir's discipline snapped.

Chapter Eighteen

Grace sucked in a small gasp as Keir pulled her to his hard form, his mouth lowering to capture her lips.

The dam on her passion that had begun to crack with their argument broke, flooding her with sensation, molten fire that weakened her legs. Keir's thick arms wrapped around her, holding her to kiss her soundly.

His hands lifted under her backside, pressing the *V* of her legs against his hardness, which she could feel even through the many layers separating them. She should fight him, remind him of his sins in taking her against her will, but the memory of their evening together in another cabin turned traitor against her resolve. Was this another cruel ruse? The fire leaping between them felt too real to be deception.

He broke away to kiss a hot trail down her neck, his hold moving her slightly up and down against him. "Bloody hell, Keir," she said, with a breathy whisper soaked in desire. "Is this all another lie?"

Keir lifted his head from her skin to meet her gaze. He breathed in through his nose and gave a slight shake of his head. "When I touch you…'tis the only time I am real."

His words, spoken with such emotion, cleaved the anger inside her. "Blast. No matter how much I want to be furious at you…" The man had tricked her, taken her against her will, carried her to this damned castle surrounded by death. She should hate him, but she couldn't. Not when he'd shown her some of his heart. She wrapped her hands over his shoulder. "I want to despise you, but instead I fear that I want…more." Her stomach fluttered, making heat flow downward.

"Och," he whispered, as if her words were almost painful to him. "Despise me, lass, but whatever ye do, do not fear me." His eyes held the heaviness of regret and want.

She shook her head. "I don't fear you, Keir." She rose onto her toes. "Give me more."

His hands dove into her hair, raking away the small hood, the pins scattering to plink against the wood at their feet. Grace tipped her face to his, seeking his mouth. Slanting to deepen the kiss, she clung to his shoulders, her nails scratching against the linen of his shirt until she reached the edge of his kilt. She tugged the shirt out, desperate to feel the heat of his skin under her palms, his muscles thick and rolling.

"More," she moaned against his kiss as she slid palms over his skin. He radiated heat, his strong fingers working to unlace the back of her gown, and she realized her cape was already pooled at her feet.

He kissed her ear. "More what, lass?" he asked, inhaling along her neck as her bodice slipped downward exposing her thinly covered breasts.

"More of this." With the heat still rushing through her, Grace lowered one shoulder and then the other until her ample breasts spilled forth to sit upon her lowered smock. Feeling wicked, she slid hands under each one, plumping them up and pinching her own nipples.

"Aye, Grace," Keir said, the awe in his tone fueling her

brazenness so that she continued to pull and tease herself. Keir rubbed his large hand over his obvious arousal.

She came forward, her mouth going dry as she slid her hands underneath his tented kilt, reaching for him. He was thick and hot and long like she remembered. It caused her to ache anew. "Huge and heavy," she said, bringing out a smile on Keir's mouth. Oh, how she wanted to kiss it again. With Keir there was no shame, no worry that he would think her improper or too delicate for passion.

He bent his head to trail kisses down her chest until he captured her nipple between his lips. Hot and wet, he surrounded it, teasing her. "Good God," Grace breathed, feathering her fingers through his hair as he loved first one breast and then the other. She shifted restlessly against him. "Damn all these layers," she said as he stroked down over her covered backside. "I want to feel your hot skin sliding along mine."

He growled low in the back of his throat as he trailed back up her neck. "I love what comes from your sweet lips, lass."

She breathed shallowly at the sensual tickles he delivered. "What comes out of these lips often creates trouble." He nuzzled the skin of her collarbone, making her head swim. "At times, I wish I could capture the words I say and suck them inward." Sensation, hot and rushing, filled her. "Yes, Keir," she purred as he palmed her breasts while kissing up the side of her neck. "Capture and suck," she murmured, her mind flowing with the heat.

Keir stopped, glancing up at her. She blinked at the intensity etched in the planes of his face. "What?" she whispered.

He shook his head. "Aye, lass, I love the words that come from those lips. Capture and suck all ye want, but don't stop talking."

Keir covered her mouth with his. She held herself to him

by gripping his biceps, which hardened and flexed under his shirt. "You need to become naked," she whispered.

"I heartily agree." He backed up to remove the sash from his shoulder. Grabbing his untucked shirt, he raised it in a fluid motion, pulling it off over his head.

Grace's tongue turned dry as week-old toast as she took in the fullness of his arms, the broadness of his shoulders and ripples of muscle in his chest and stomach. She wet her lips. "Good God," she said, stepping forward to lay her hands on all that masculine beauty. She let them trail down to find the slight indent on each of his sides at the edge of his low-slung plaid. "Michelangelo should have sculpted you."

Keir chuckled with teasing happiness, the sound so foreign that Grace stared until he bent to kiss her. She barely noticed the release of the ties of her costume until Keir clasped her waist and lifted her up toward the ceiling. Breaking their kiss, she looked down to see him liberate her from her stiff farthingale, kirtle, and petticoat simply by lifting her out of them, as if she weighed as little as a child. She stood in her lowered smock, exposed from her navel upward.

"Much better," he said, drawing her against him. He stroked down her form, his hands gliding over her buttocks covered only by the thin smock. "All beautiful, soft curves."

Without the layers between them, Grace felt his heavy member strain for liberation within the wool kilt. She trailed her fingernails along the skin of his shoulders and down his sides to the wrap. "Your turn, Keir Mackinnon," she said. She tugged on the end of the heavy belt that kept the layers in place.

Keir's hand closed around her wrist. "Grace," he said, one hand grabbing the back of his neck as he looked up for a moment at the heavy beams of the ceiling, the playfulness vanishing from his face.

"What?" she asked, her stomach contracting. Had he

been ordered to stay away from her? Or worse, did he just not want her?

With one finger, he gently raised the neckline of her smock, blocking his view of her breasts. "Grace." He wrapped his arms around her, cradling her against the heat of his massive chest. "I didn't bring ye here to seduce ye, to take your innocence. 'Twould not be honorable."

The tightness in Grace's stomach relaxed. She looked up at him, but he stared out over her head. "I hadn't planned to steal away your innocence, either, Keir. But here we are, mostly undressed." She rubbed hands down his strong arms. "And I'm not putting those layers back on until you…do more."

She nodded, her face set. For Grace had decided well before his betrayal, when she'd tended the man who'd taken a wolf bite without dooming the pups back in the den, that if given the chance, he was the adventure she wished to give in to.

He looked down at her, his brows pinched. "I have no innocence."

She tipped her head. "Innocence can be a damned nuisance at times."

A slow grin grew on his mouth, and he narrowed his eyes. "I should have expected ye to peek through a barn wall to eavesdrop on me, since ye've done it before," he said, reminding her of the confession she'd made about spying on the couple in the barn at Somerset.

The mere memory of moaning and wicked words, the undulating, mouths and hands everywhere, made Grace's core boil. "Yes, I suppose you should have expected it," she said, her words a breathy whisper.

Keir's hand slid down her spine and back up, the feel of it gentle and luring. "Tell me again, lass. Were the maid and groom wild against each other?"

She nodded, a clenching feeling adding to the ache in the *V* of her shifting legs. "There was much thrashing and rolling about, moaning and…tasting each other."

"Like I planned to taste ye before," he whispered, the smile replaced by an intensity that left Grace breathless.

Her nipples pearled under her smock, and she lowered the linen again, drawing Keir's gaze down. "She tasted him before he mounted her."

"And ye watched and listened the whole time."

"Yes," she said, drawing out the word as she once again scooped slowly under each breast. "Just spying on them made me ache with want." He watched her pinch her own nipples. "Do you like to watch me touch myself, Keir?" she whispered.

"Good God, aye," he said. "And bloody hell, keep talking."

She ignored the blush creeping up her neck and smiled mischievously. "Words can paint a wicked picture."

He reached forward to heft one of her breasts, stepping to pull her against him. "Aye." He kissed her, moving his hand to stroke the side of her head. "But ye are certain, Grace? We should stop now if ye aren't, because once swept up in the heat that I'm planning to kindle in ye, there will be no going back."

His words made her stomach quiver. "'Tis my choice, and I choose you, Keir Mackinnon. Make me burn, and moan, and thrash about."

"Och, lass, I intend to." Keir reached down, tugging the ties holding his boots and toeing them off. He stood tall and met Grace's gaze as he loosened the belt holding up his plaid, and the whole wrap dropped with a *thunk* to the cabin floor.

For a moment, she couldn't breathe. Broad shoulders tapered down his muscled chest, narrowing at his waist and hips to display his full, powerful arousal. Even without a stitch of clothing, he looked completely at ease and invincible.

Slowly, she stepped around him, trailing her fingers along

the skin of his waist. His head turned to follow her with his gaze. The dark serpentine markings around his thick biceps flowed over his shoulder to drape the side of his back down to his full, taut buttocks, while the legion of small crosses stood in rows over the other side. Her gaze raked his chest to the intricate crosses over his heart, but she let her focus slowly fall in perusal down his frame, rippled with underlying muscle. His arousal stood proud against his abdomen, and although she'd touched it before, she hadn't seen it in all its large proportions.

Keir pulled her in, and she felt its hot length between them. "Your eyes are very round, lass," he said as his hands swept up under her hair, raking through the tresses to stroke her head.

She stared into his handsome face, focusing on the bits of gold in his dark brown eyes. "You are large and hard, and I am small and soft. You are experienced, and I am a maiden. You are a brave warrior, and I am a coward. It all adds up to very round eyes, Keir."

He leaned in, kissing the tip of her nose. "I have yet to see this coward ye speak of, Grace Ellington." He stroked her hair. "I see a courageous lass who speaks her mind." He rubbed the pad of this thumb over her bottom lip. The only sound was the low crackle of the fire in the hearth. "A beautiful woman who decides what she wants and pursues it."

The world outside the cabin no longer existed. The only place that mattered was the narrow space between their bodies. Grace set her hands on his shoulders and gazed into his deep brown eyes. "And I want you. Absolutely and completely."

Before another thump of her heart, Keir's arms surrounded her, his mouth pressing against her lips. All sense within Grace shattered, and she met his kiss with a ravenous one of her own, rising on her toes to thrust herself against him. She slanted her head and opened her mouth, tasting him as he tasted her. His hands pressed against her back as she slid her palms down his arms and up his chest, her thumbs tweaking against his nipples. The cool air of the room broke along her legs and backside as Keir lifted her smock, rucking it up until he broke the kiss to pull it off over her head. They were both naked.

Hands slaked over skin, and Grace rubbed against him, her stomach teasing his rigid length. He said something in Gaelic, guttural words that sounded like a growl, causing more excitement to flood into Grace. She felt years of ladylike training give way to animal instinct. Scratching her nails down his spine, she squeezed his tight buttocks, his groan making her bold. She reached around front to grasp him, wrapping around his hardness to stroke him up and down. Soft skin over steel, she marveled in the power that a simple appendage could exude. God help her, she wanted it inside her, wanted Keir inside her.

Grace's nipples pearled, and Keir broke free of her mouth to trail hot, wet kisses down to one. Plumping the other with his palm, he swirled his tongue around the nipple of her other breast. When he grazed it with his teeth and sucked hard on it, Grace moaned deeply as she felt the tug reach down to her aching core. Her hand lifted to hold his head to her breasts, reveling in the feel of hot, wet heat on her sensitive skin. "That feels wickedly good," she said, running her fingers through his hair to his scalp.

He kissed back up her chest and neck to her ear, holding her close against his hot body. His lips grazed her earlobe. "Ye've moaned. Now for the burning and thrashing."

His deep voice and the erotic promise in his words melted through Grace, making her shift against him, her core seeking his hardness. "I want you in me, Keir."

He growled back in answer, pulling her in for his fingers to dive between the globes of her backside, searching for her hot woman's opening. She arched back, spreading more for him. Teasing along the outside, she moaned, rearing against his hand until he entered, strong fingers working up inside her. "Oh God," she said, her words breathy.

"Och, lass, ye are so hot and wet." He kissed her mouth, playing within the kiss to match the thrust of his fingers below. Breathing and slanting, tasting and exploring, she kissed him with wild abandon, succumbing completely to sensation.

"No," she said when he withdrew, but he lifted her, carrying her with swift intent toward the large bed against the wall. Setting her down, he lay next to her, his face over hers to kiss as his hands slid back down her side and waist. Her legs parted on their own as he sought her heat again, but this time from the front, his fingers deftly plucking at the nub Grace had explored herself. "Yes, Keir, right there," she said, thrusting her pelvis higher into his hand as he played, rubbing outside while also delving within.

"Open your eyes," he said, and she blinked, gazing at him above her, his arms leading down to work her flesh as he watched her thrust and squirm on the blanket. Seeing him watch her sent another wave of heat, and Grace lifted her hands to her breasts, squeezing them together upward as she plucked her own nipples. Keir stared, his features tight and intense before he lowered his mouth down to suckle again.

"Oh God, Keir, I'm going to burst with want," Grace said, finding a rhythm against his hand. The ache inside her was building, and she panted.

He raised his gaze to her. "Aye, lass, we will."

Lowering to the other breast, his teeth tugged at her nipple as his fingers worked against her flesh below, faster, until Grace felt the ache build so high she couldn't hold on any longer. Hands fisted in the blankets, she opened her mouth, tipping her head back to arch her neck. "Oh God, Keir!" she yelled, the noise of her passion, released upon the world, throwing her over the crest.

With the waves still flooding within her, Keir climbed atop. Her legs were already spread wide, giving him complete access to her body. Poised above her, Grace met his stare. "Yes," Grace said, wrapping her arms around his back as his hardness pressed against her wet, throbbing entrance.

"See me, Grace. See who claims ye completely," he said, grasping her face. "*Mo ghaol*," he said and slammed forward, impaling her. The sting of his entry almost dissolved as soon as it broke through her. Braced on his forearms, he leaned in, kissing her as he held his body still.

"Keir," she moaned against his lips, thrusting her pelvis against his. "More."

Backing up, he pressed forward again, rubbing her most intimate and sensitive places. "Yes, more," she said.

"I would not hurt ye," he said, and she could see the strain in his features.

"I've ridden astride since I could walk. The sting is gone." She reached behind to slap her palm against his backside and thrust upward. "I said more."

He growled, his arms braced around her face as he looked down. "Bloody beautiful," he said, and his lips pulled back, showing his teeth as he rose and plunged back into her with a guttural groan.

Grace met it with a growl. "Bloody hell, yes," she yelled, thrusting to meet him as they picked up a rhythm that fed the flames within her. "Hard and deep, Keir. Mark me as yours from the inside out."

Her words shredded any remaining limits between them, and they strained together, their bodies slapping against each other as the bed shook and scraped the floor. The aching wave rose, breaking once more over Grace. "Keir," she moaned.

Keir met her call with a fierce growl, his voice filling the cabin as he, too, exploded. "*Tha thu a 'mhèinn!*"

Grace's body convulsed as his heat flooded within her. Shivers of sensation coursed up and down her, melting her muscles and prickling her skin as they continued to rock together, their rhythm slowing as the waves of intense pleasure receded like a slowly lowering tide.

Breaths ragged, Keir drew her with him as they rolled, intertwined, to the side. With a stretch, he reached over Grace to work the edge of the blanket up over her back and shoulders. She buried her face in his chest as it rose and fell rapidly. She inhaled their combined scents, mixed with the tang of their love. They said nothing, just held each other, as the muted sunlight fell in the window, and a wind blew around the corners of the snug cabin.

In Keir's arms, completely sated, warm and safe, the flame of joy grew inside Grace. No wonder Ava preferred to love her husband rather than get a long night's sleep. No wonder the maid had risked being caught when meeting the groom in the stables at Somerset, people sang tributes to love, and rogues sought out willing women. God's teeth! She'd definitely been willing.

She tipped her gaze up to search Keir's eyes. "I can see why people would want to do that every day."

He kissed her gently and chuckled, running a hand down her back under the blanket. "If they did, there'd be more bairns about."

A baby? Of course, she knew that a baby could come of this, but that certainly hadn't been in her mind at the start.

Keir sat up. "The fire's waned." He stood, letting the blanket slide off him, and padded barefoot to add one square of peat. They must not be staying long enough to require more. She raised up on her elbow, watching the fluid motions of someone in complete control of his muscles, like a predatory creature, as he stalked back. Naked and proud and impervious to the chill in the room, he grinned down at her, his finger teasing her breast that had broken free of the blanket. "What's churning in that bonny head of yours?"

Grace watched him closely, her question sitting like a bubble in her mouth. She tilted her head to the side, feeling her long hair fall over her naked shoulder. "Just...have you ever thought to marry?"

Chapter Nineteen

Marry?

The word tightened through Keir. Turning away, he lifted his plaid from the floor, stepping into it.

"I'm not asking you to marry me, Keir," Grace said, sitting up on the bed with the blanket wrapped over her bountiful breasts. "I only want to know if you've ever thought about it."

"The Devil of Dunakin doesn't wed."

"Why not?" A frown pinched her angel-like features, her blue eyes serious. Did she hope to one day marry him?

"It is rarely done," he said, his words short to cut off the conversation. He threw his shirt back on and avoided her gaze.

Grace dragged the blanket behind her as she walked to where he'd lifted her from her many layers. "Oh," she said, nodding, her brows raised high over her bright blue eyes. "Because to keep up the ruse, you'd have to beat her every night." She tapped her lip with one finger. "And how could you ever be faithful to a wife when the Devil must spend his days raping the women in every village you storm through?

If you think about it, that's a lot of work, all that swiving. You would hardly have anything left for a wife."

"Grace," he said, warning in his voice. "Those are stories, bred by gossips and spun by Brodie to grow the legend."

Grace dropped the blanket, reaching for her discarded smock. As her breasts hung with their fullness, Keir almost forgot what they were talking about. Och, she was beautiful. She threw the thin, white gown over her head, tugging it into place. Without a word, she moved to the pooled layers of her costume, climbing into the middle.

She sighed. "I know the stories aren't true, but as long as everyone believes them, no one will come close to you."

"'Tis how it should be." He'd been told from the start, as a scrawny lad with freckles across his nose, that one day he would frighten away everyone. He had been given no other option.

"What happens to Keir Mackinnon?" she asked, pausing in her dressing, her eyes sad.

The pity he glimpsed there hardened his jaw. "He protects his clan and dies."

"What a terrible and boring life," she said, crossing her arms under her breasts. The skirts still sat around her hips, undone. Her hair wound around her shoulders in wild curls. She looked unbound and free.

When he didn't respond, she continued. "I doubt you dance, and you hardly laugh. You will never get to hold a small boy who has your beautiful brown eyes or drink fine whisky at your daughter's wedding. As the damn Devil, you will never know the pleasure of rolling dice with friends over wassail or laughing at the antics of the Abbot of Unreason at Christmastide. The Devil of Dunakin can't know love—"

"Enough," he said, the churning in his gut turned to rock, hardened by the mix of pity in her tone and his own regret, which he thought he'd buried ten years ago, the day he'd held his mother for the last time. The day he'd fully become the Devil of Dunakin.

"I thought you liked the words that came from my mouth," she said, meeting his gaze directly. How could Grace Ellington have ever thought herself a coward? She didn't seem to care that he'd slaughtered hundreds, that his lethal look had been known to make men piss in fear. Yet, here, alone, Grace wielded a sharper blade than any he had ever carried before. Truth. Even he, Keir Mackinnon, the infamous Devil of Dunakin, struggled not to look away from her gaze.

"It is time to return to Dunakin," he said finally and pivoted on his boot heel to stride out the door. Welcoming the chill of the winter air, Keir walked briskly to the single stable to re-saddle Cogadh. His horse looked at him with intelligent eyes, as if asking what was amiss, but Keir didn't need to answer. That was one reason he liked animals. They didn't require explanations and didn't pry into issues that had been locked away.

Keir patted Cogadh as he buckled the girth straps, securing the saddle on his back. What had he been thinking, bedding a virgin, an honest, pure-hearted woman? The Devil of Dunakin must be separate, alone, not tied to a soft, beautiful creature who made him question his duty. *Bloody hell.* He'd add the act of ruining a virgin to the list of his sins, which would surely fly him to Hell. After all, wasn't that where a devil was destined to spend eternity?

He led Cogadh outside where Grace waited in the doorway. "I've stirred the fire apart," she said. "And fixed the bed."

He could tell by the color in her cheeks and the tilt of her lips that she was angry. *Sard it.* Leaving his horse, he walked up to her. "Grace."

She turned bright blue eyes up to him, and he could see a slight sheen there as if tears had welled up. "Och, lass." He pulled her into his chest, hugging her. "I have no answers for ye, and I'm sorry if ye regret this afternoon."

She pulled back, her face serious. "I have no regrets." She laid her palm flat on his chest over his heart. "Do you?"

Hadn't he been damning himself moments ago for taking her, making her writhe and burn with passion? He exhaled, shaking his head. "Nay. I will cherish the memory, but I regret putting those tears in your eyes."

She blinked but didn't deny them.

He released an exhale. "Ye have to know, Grace, that I hurt all the people who come close to me. I am not just a man. I carry the devil's name and his duty."

Her lips pursed tight but then opened. "And you have to know, Keir, that I will always speak my mind when I think someone about whom I care is headed toward pain and sorrow."

Her words coursed through him, but he squelched the small flame of happiness they sprouted. "Ye should not care for me."

She gathered her skirts to climb upon the horse and narrowed her eyes at him. "Too late."

• • •

Grace watched the weathered, gray stone of Dunakin's wall grow crisper as Little Warrior carried them closer to the open, toothed portcullis.

A shiver trailed through her at the feel of riding into the gaping maw of a monster. Only Keir's strength at her back kept her sitting straight, eyes forward and gaze steady. The ride back through the perimeter of heads had reeked of death. Even closing off the sight didn't stop her mind from conjuring the horrific images behind her eyelids.

The villagers had retreated as they rode slowly between

the thatched houses. With each closing door, Grace's emotions twisted with anger and sadness. Keir didn't flinch at the obvious shunning, the villagers' fear making them abandon any type of loyalty to him. If Keir ever met a foe more powerful than himself, no one would come to his aid. Perhaps Brodie, but none of his clan. It didn't matter if the Devil of Dunakin had been a Mackinnon guardian for generations, fear would cause his people to leave him to the wolves.

She leaned into the warmth he gave off, enjoying these last moments of closeness they might have before he became the damned Devil again. They had become lovers this afternoon, but she had no idea what that meant or if it would continue. In England, she would be considered ruined. At Aros, she might be thought of as weak and wanton to crave the touch of her captor. But was she truly a prisoner now? She'd agreed to see Lachlan through his illness, and she would stay to see justice uncover the assassin.

And what about Keir? Could she leave him here, embroiled in his clan's fear and disloyalty? Suddenly, everything that had been straightforward—her attempted plans for escape, her hate for her captor—had been blurred by the passion they'd just shared.

Lifting her down, Keir squeezed her hand, bending toward her ear. "Only Brodie knows of the poisoning. I asked him to watch both Rab and Lachlan today if we were away."

They climbed the few steps into the keep where Dara and Fiona sat at the center table. Keir's sister stood, scowling at them both. "Where have ye been?"

"Has something happened to Lachlan?" Grace asked, breaking away from Keir to head toward the steps.

"Nay, but now Rab looks ill," Fiona said. "This Spotting Sickness is spreading. Brodie has been up with them. He sent us away." She frowned. "Here. Take this up if ye are allowed in." She handed Keir a wooden plate that held bread, cheese, and a cooked egg.

"Ye said eggs could help," Fiona said, looking at Grace.

"Yes, thank you."

Grace and Keir climbed the dark stairs silently and stopped before a sconce outside Lachlan's door. "Is there a fine powder on the plate or on the food?" she asked.

"I can't see for certain in this light." Keir knocked.

"Aye?" The voice sounded like Brodie.

"It's Keir."

"And Grace."

The bar scraped down the door on the other side, and Brodie opened it. The room smelled of human sickness. "Make sure the shutters are cracked to let in fresh air," Grace said as she passed to Lachlan. The boy's eyes were open, but he still seemed weak. She smiled as she sat on the chair by his bed. "Awake is good. Have you taken in anything? Broth or ale?"

"Some," he whispered. Relief at the simple word filled Grace, changing her forced smile into a real one. The boy's mind wasn't muddled from the poison.

She stroked his cool forehead. "Always make certain that one of us, in this room, has inspected your food or drink before you take it in."

He gave a little nod, and Grace patted his arm, looking to a pale Rab. He sat in a chair near the fire. "You have a strong boy."

"We are a solid lot," he said.

"Who is doing this?" Brodie asked, his voice soft as he checked the hall outside the door. It remained empty. "And why?"

Grace pulled her wild hair to the side and hoped no one noticed the tangles. "I have my theories."

"Which are?" Rab asked and sipped at a flask.

She glanced at Keir and then his brother. "You have a

visitor. Normond MacInnes."

Rab's lips pulled back as if he'd tasted something bad and wished to spit. "He's more than a visitor. He's betrothed to Dara and soon to be a member of our clan."

Grace stood. "He's also the bastard who is being hunted by four powerful clans, south of here, for terrorizing and nearly raping Mairi Maclean, the woman whom he convinced you to retrieve."

"Shite," Brodie said. "Ye know him?"

"I've never met him in the flesh before Dunakin, but I know his name, and he fits the description. Also, he cornered me today, and my instincts tell me he's not to be trusted."

Rab rubbed his beard, tugging.

Grace continued. "Even if Normond MacInnes isn't behind the poisoning, he should be held for the chiefs of Mull, Barra, and Islay, as well as the new chief of the MacInnes. If he becomes part of your clan, you will have four powerful clans against the Mackinnons."

Rab leaned back in his chair and nodded toward Keir. "I care not, for the Devil of Dunakin guards our clan."

"One man against four clans is hardly a defense," Grace said. "Even if he is a devil."

Keir stood as if carved from stone, his expression flat.

"And when the English decide that Skye is worth fighting for," Grace said, "you will want allies, not enemies among the clans."

Rab cursed under his breath and said something in Gaelic. "We will watch MacInnes, but I will not throw Dara's betrothed into my dungeon until I've heard his explanations and we've caught the bloody culprit."

"How shall we flush the traitor out?" Brodie asked.

She studied the white powder under the egg. "Considering the amount of arsenic dust on this plate marked for the chief, the assassin is trying to complete the deed. Perhaps because

I've arrived and might figure out that you aren't succumbing to an illness." Grace pinched her lips, while all four males in the room stared at her. She needed a reason for a gathering. "It is February," she said, her words slow, and looked to Keir. "I think we shall have a St. Valentine's Day feast in the hall."

"To celebrate my near death?" Rab asked. His face turned red, and he coughed for several long moments into his fist.

"Dara has mentioned before that we don't celebrate holidays," Keir said. "Not since Bradana died—"

"Don't say her name," Rab said, his voice forceful even as he gasped, recovering from the coughing fit.

"If we have the gathering, the fiend is likely to try to poison you there," Grace said. "We will be watching, and you will make sure not to let anything pass your lips." She tipped her head, studying Rab as a plan solidified in her mind. "How well can you act?"

• • •

Keir stood in the decorated great hall. Over the last two days he'd seen Grace only in Lachlan's room. When the circles around her eyes darkened with exhaustion, he'd convinced her to sleep in his bed while he guarded his nephew. He'd asked Dara to instruct the cooks to make a small feast for St. Valentine's Day. She'd seemed surprised but pleased, rushing off to the kitchens. He'd asked his *seanmhair* to find a gown that Grace could alter for the celebration.

Meanwhile, the kitchen staff must think Grace was the clumsiest lass to walk the halls of Dunakin. She went by several times each day to replace the bowls and plates of food that she'd spilled in Lachlan's room.

Keir kept the tankard he'd been careful to wash himself. He filled it from a common butt of ale and sipped while watching two maids scurry about with linens, dressing the table that ran the length of the hall. In the corner, three musicians gathered with their instruments, discussing the folk songs they would perform. Keir ignored their cautious glances. When one passed the sign of the cross before his chest, Keir snorted softly. Aonghus Mackinnon would be pleased. He took a swig of the brew, realizing that every time he thought of the man who'd raised him, he craved a strong drink.

Dara entered the hall from the back corridor, wearing a dark red dress, the color like old blood. But what tainted the air more than the grim reminder of the lives he'd taken was the man leading her in. Normond MacInnes was not someone with whom his sister should tangle. If Keir had been chief, Normond MacInnes would be in Dunakin's dungeon right now instead of strutting across the room, a belligerent smirk on his face.

"No fighting, Keir," Dara said, her voice sharp.

"'Tis a day to commemorate the beheading of a saint," Keir said with a shrug. "Blood spilling seems appropriate."

"Ye best get used to me being here, Devil," MacInnes said and patted Dara's arm. "I will soon be part of the family."

Keir watched the man saunter off with Dara, parading as if he were waiting to swoop in and take over. Aye, Normond MacInnes dripped smug deceit.

Wooden plates were placed at each station, with a gold one set before Rab's chair in the center of the long table. Keir would sit to the right of Rab and Dara to the left. Grace announced that Lachlan was still too weak to be from bed.

Keir walked along the table, scanning for the fine dusting that Grace had found on the plates in the kitchen, but the napkins looked clean and had been taken from a common stack, and Rab's gold plate glinted with the candlelight. Grace's plan was rash and could make them look like fools, but if it worked, they would unmask the bastard tonight.

Keir turned toward the steps, as if a noise had called to

him over the sound of the musicians. When he turned, Grace stood at the bottom, staring his way. Had he felt her gaze?

She tipped her head to him, the delicate fall of pale blue silk of her hood sliding over her shoulder where it reached down her back, covering her hair, hair he knew to be soft with fragrant waves. She wore a blue bodice and skirt, to match the color of her eyes, a gown that his *seanmhair* said had belonged to his mother long ago. Just the sight of Grace sent strange sensations through his gut. He'd played a part his whole life, seeking confirmation of his success in the worried glances and pale faces of those he encountered. But Grace was the first person, since his mother, to see him for who he was, or who he hoped he still was. A man, not a devil. Perhaps… Was there a chance for a future with her? Hope cracked a small chink in the Devil's mantle.

Cream-colored flowers were embroidered along the blue silk of her gown, giving her the appearance of a walking garden as she neared. An underskirt skimmed the tops of her slippers, the cream-colored silk embroidered with blue thread into the pattern of dragonflies. Small puffs of fabric sat at her shoulders, the material hugging her slender arms down to her wrists. She looked every bit the proper English lady. Only the mischievous tilt of her lips, her gaze meeting his, changed the angel to a siren. With her natural grace, the gown flowed around her as she walked forward, and the rest of the hall seemed to fade away.

Grace's gaze traveled over his clean plaid. "You look good enough to eat," she said, stopping before him. Bloody hell, he wished to sweep her away that very moment, loving her all night. Her cheeks flushed beautifully. "It's an expression. I mean, you look quite handsome."

His lips curved into a smile, one he rarely showed anywhere near his family. "Ye look like an angel straight from King James's court." He leaned in to her ear, inhaling the floral scent of her skin. "And ye look delicious, too."

Her lips quivered on a little laugh. "I hardly believe there would be any angels at a royal court. I've heard from a friend, quite acquainted with the French court, that royal abodes are viper pits where slithering, gold-bedecked serpents breed and kill."

Keir wished he could listen to Grace speak the whole evening, but that wasn't the plan nor his duty. Letting his grin fade, he turned to take her elbow and glanced about the room. MacInnes stood with Dara, talking with the head of the archers, Edward Mackinnon, a distant cousin. Keir's *seanmhair* came in from the kitchens, speaking with the cook, Nora MacDonald. "I see Rab made it down," Keir said as his brother walked in from the bailey, his face still pale, though he looked better after two days of untainted food and ale. Brodie entered, talking with Will Mackinnon and Angus Macleod, two prominent men in the village who could possibly want Rab and his son out of the way.

"Yes, he looks better," Grace said, the smile in her voice also gone. "As does Lachlan, although Rab will say he looks worse if anyone asks."

Keir watched the village woodworker, Hamish Mackinnon, walk in, hat clutched in his hands. His wife stood beside him, both with wide eyes. They had to be wondering why they'd been invited up to the castle to dine. When questioned earlier in the week about the plates, Hamish said he hadn't made any specific plates for Rab and Lachlan. Either he lied and was terrified at being caught, or the true assassin had carried them to Dunakin.

Keir's gaze shifted to Normond MacInnes. The man had brought a trunk with him when he'd arrived last fall, and he'd made several trips off the isle since. Aye, he was the most likely traitor. But could Dara know about it?

The thought clenched inside his ribs. When his sister

had discovered the truth about their mother during one of Rab's drunken rantings, she'd questioned Rab's sanity more and more. It was true that their brother took after Aonghus Mackinnon in temperament: rash, brutal, and quick to judge. But until his wife, Bradana, had died two years ago, Rab had been a fair chief. Now though, Keir agreed that some of Rab's dictates were questionable, and he called on the Devil of Dunakin more and more.

"Let us sit," Rab called, bringing people toward the long table. He made an exaggerated gesture toward his stomach as if it pained him, carrying on the ruse. Grace had instructed them on their rolls in this performance, but Rab had little talent for acting.

The platemaker and his wife took seats at the end of the table, farthest away, as was their station. With a nod from Keir, Brodie sat down near the couple, his merry disposition sure to put them at ease. Unless, of course, they were guilty of a heinous crime that would see them executed.

Keir claimed Grace's arm, leading her with him toward the top of the table, which was reserved for family. The gentle pressure of her hand was like an anchor in the surging tensions and suspicions in the hall. Even the music seemed to be theatrically dark as Keir brought Grace to the chair next to his.

"*Seanmhair* should sit next to Keir," Dara said from the other side of Rab. She frowned at Grace. Had his sister picked up on her betrothed's interest in Grace, or was Dara still angry over their earlier interactions?

Keir ignored her and held the chair for Grace.

"Ye have your man, Dara. Let Keir choose his woman," Rab said and threw his weight down into his chair. The solid strength of oak kept the chair from buckling. Fiona moved down to sit on the other side of Grace, nodding to her as they both pulled up to the table.

Grace leaned around Keir to frown at Rab. "Are you feeling well? You look pale," she said without lowering her voice.

He dismissed her question with a wave of his hand, carrying off his performance with an authentic frown. Food was brought in, and Keir saw Grace run a finger over the surface of his wooden trencher, but she found nothing. He leaned toward her ear. "Rab's gold plate is clean as well, and I watched the napkins dispersed from a common stack."

Grace smiled as if he'd whispered something sweet. The lass could add acting to her list of talents, along with healing, cursing, and making his blood run hot. Her scent and the closeness of her soft skin were making it difficult to concentrate on their prearranged drama. Keir's body had a different plan for the night, and he reached under to adjust his rigid member. Bloody hell, but Grace turned him into an undisciplined lad. He grabbed his ale cup, but Grace's gentle touch on his wrist stayed his hand. They were not to eat or drink at this meal.

Nora, the cook, stood near the archway, watching the male attendants bring out the courses of roast venison and goose, dark and light rolls, cheese, and cooked vegetables. She looked anxious, and Keir studied her for several moments. Food was placed upon plates by the servers, starting with Rab as was custom. Everyone waited for his short blessing and watched for him to take the first bite.

Obviously irritated, Rab looked around the room. "We will share food tonight." He gestured toward Grace. Keir felt her arm go rigid against him. Rab hadn't recited anything that she'd told him to say.

In the stilted silence, Grace inhaled and slowly spoke, her lips set in a calm smile. "How gracious." She bowed her head toward Rab and looked at the confused diners. "I was telling your chief about a custom we adhered to in York, to celebrate the day of St. Valentine." She folded her small hands before her, resting them on the table. "My father, the Earl of Somerset, would pass around his own plate to those he favored. It was a cherished practice."

Rab nodded. "Aye, 'tis a noble gesture."

"'Tis an English gesture if an English earl practiced it," Angus MacLeod said, his frown fierce.

"Aye," said Will Mackinnon. "It sounds dangerous. Don't Englishmen poison those who are a nuisance?"

Rab coughed and cleared his throat. "But we are Scotsmen." He met Will's stare. "We lop off heads, not kill in the shadows with poison."

Keir kept his face neutral yet quickly scanned the guests. Dara looked down at the napkin lying in her lap. Coincidence, or did shame make her bow her head?

"In fact, I think ye, Will Mackinnon, will be the first to receive my reward," Rab said and gestured for the liveryman to take his gold plate down the table to the man.

Will chuckled. "I have no doubt that you'd dispatch your Devil to lop off my head, Rab, if ye wanted me dead." He stuck his eating dagger into a slice of venison and placed it in his mouth, chewing. The room seemed to wait, but Will smiled as he swallowed. "Quite flavorful."

Beside him, Keir heard Grace curse under her breath. Rab hadn't followed the plan. While he called upon Normond MacInnes to eat next, they knew the food wasn't tainted.

"I am honored," MacInnes said with a lopsided smile and shoved a large piece of venison between his lips. He chewed without worry, as if he knew for certain the meat was untainted.

Once Rab's plate was refilled, the others began to eat. MacInnes pushed back his chair and stood, helping Dara stand. The man cleared his throat. "Since this is a feast to celebrate St. Valentine's sacrifice in the name of mortal love,

Dara and I have an announcement."

There was a pause, and Keir watched concern flicker across Dara's smooth features. Gone in an instant, she smiled sweetly. "Normond and I are betrothed."

MacInnes laughed. "Go on, woman. Tell them the rest." She glanced at him with wide eyes, and he looked along the table. "We are already wed."

Chapter Twenty

Normond MacInnes stood tall, the gash across his face stark in the candlelight from the chandelier overhead.

Grace's stomach tightened at his words. Dara had no idea what type of monster she had pledged to be true to until death. And from the shock on her face, she wasn't expecting the revelation at tonight's feast.

Keir shifted, ready to stand, but Grace placed her hand on his arm. Amazingly, he stilled, waiting with all of them to see what happened next.

"We can still observe a church wedding," Dara said, her gaze shifting from Rab to Keir. "But we thought it best to take our vows now."

"Already consummated," Normond said with a flourish and a leering grin, which brought a rare blush to Dara's cheeks.

"We haven't finalized the bride price yet," Rab said, his voice low.

Keir perched his tight fists on the edge of the table but didn't stir. He reminded Grace of a horse, waiting with determined focus for the start of a joust.

Normond waved off Rab's concern. "A conversation for later tonight. First, my love and I bring ye a gift together."

Dara smiled and stepped away from her chair to pluck two cloth-wrapped items from behind a reed basket in the corner. She brought them forth, setting one before Rab and one before Keir. Dara bent near Keir's ear, and Grace barely heard her whisper. "I would not forget my true brother."

Rab was the first to open the cloth, revealing a polished pewter goblet. The candles before him, reflected flames in the mirrorlike side. Grace gave Keir a little nudge with her elbow, and he unwrapped an identical goblet. "It is a set," Dara said. "I have one, too." She raised a hand, and one of the liverymen brought a third goblet from the archway.

Normond placed a wooden cask on the table and untied the leather cord holding the wineskin on top. "I obtained this wine from a monk who felt it was holy in its deliciousness." He grinned. "I would share it with you all to lift in celebration over our union."

He handed the small wooden cask to the liveryman near him and indicated their cups. "See that it stretches to at least the family," he said. "And don't forget Dara and me."

The man poured the wine into Normond's cup, then Dara's, moving down the table to Rab. Before he reached Keir's cup, Grace picked it up, glancing inside. *Blast.* She couldn't see the bottom of the vessel in the low light. She set it down, frowning, and squeezed her nails into Keir's leg. He must assume there was arsenic in the bottom. Would he follow Grace's risky plan or not, for fear of looking foolish?

"I am not fond of wine," Rab said. "Whisky is a Scotsman's drink."

Normond brought his cup to his lips and took a long swallow, his tongue coming out to lick a red drop from his bottom lip. The gesture turned Grace's stomach. Her friend, Mairi, had fought against the man for months. What a horror.

"'Tis from a sweet vine," Normond said. "For your sister, Rab, raise a cup to her health."

Rab lifted his cup, and everyone around the table followed suit, including Keir. "*Slàinte mhath!*"

"*Slàinte mhath!*" followed from the people in the hall. Everyone raised their cups, and Grace held hers to her lips. Although she was certain her ordinary cup wasn't poisoned, she performed the act she'd told Keir and Rab to follow. She slipped a small bit of bread into her mouth as she raised the cup. Keeping her lips tightly closed, she tipped the wine against her lips, but stopped it from entering her mouth. Instead, she let her throat work to swallow the bread and lowered the cup, quickly wiping away the excess with the napkin. Rab used his sleeve to wipe his mouth. Keir stared at Normond, watching, the stain of wine on his lips.

Don't lick your lips, Grace screamed in her head.

Normond's smile grew as he watched them all. Was he actually waiting?

"Uhhh…" Rab groaned, his mouth falling open, and with a thump, he fell forward, his arm hitting the goblet to spill red wine across the bleached linen. The platemaker's wife screamed, and everyone jumped up, except for Keir.

He leaned back as if dizzy, his eyes shutting before falling off to the side of his chair to the floor. "Keir!" Grace yelled, dropping to paw at his lips with her napkin. When his eyes opened, meeting hers, she pulled in a breath to smother her panic. He shut his eyes again.

"No," she yelled. "Keir."

Chaos erupted around the table. "The sickness," the older man that Rab had given the first bite to yelled. "They both have it." He covered his mouth with his napkin, backing up. Keir's grandmother dove down to touch Keir's face. Would she give away the fact that he still lived?

Grace dropped to her ear. "We are catching a traitor. Keir

and Rab are dead."

Fiona's wide eyes snapped toward her. Despite her age, she was as sharp in wit and mind as a young warrior. She stood, tears gathering in her narrowed eyes. "He is dead. They are both dead. Stay back." She spread her arms wide.

Grace watched Dara's openmouthed stare. Her eyes welled with tears, and she blinked rapidly as if trying to retain them. "Nay," she said, hand to her breast. "Nay. They were well." Unless the woman was a practiced actress, Grace read real anguish and shock in her expression.

"The bodies will be burned," Normond said, grabbing Dara's arm to pull her away as if fearing a contagion. "And Dara Mackinnon, being the last of Aonghus Mackinnon's children, and I, will lead the clan until Lachlan returns to health."

Fiona stepped around the table, striding right up to Normond, her arm back. With power, she slapped him across his bristly cheek, mouth open, voice strong. "*Mortair!*"

Normond's face contorted in rage with the sting of the woman's slap. His fist came around and struck her, sending the old woman toppling backward even as Dara tried to catch her grandmother. "I will cut off your lying tongue, old woman," he yelled.

"Nay," Dara called back, but her word was overridden by the fierce battle cry from Keir as he rose behind Grace, pulling his sword.

"Traitor," Keir said, and Grace watched Normond's face turn from brutal conqueror to panicked prey. Without an ounce of dignity, the man turned to run, but Keir leaped up onto the table, his boots knocking off most of the dishes as he ran its length.

Grace dropped beside Fiona with Dara, her hand going to the line in the old woman's neck in search of a pulse. Dara said nothing, just looked to Grace. Grace swallowed and met her anxious eyes. "She lives."

Dara's eyes closed, and she murmured something that sounded like a prayer, her inhale shaking. She opened her eyes to stare at Grace. "There was no Spotting Sickness, was there?"

Grace shook her head, and Dara blinked back tears, her eyes growing cold. She inhaled through her nose, nostrils flaring, and she turned to stand. "Normond MacInnes," she yelled, but it was too late.

Grace turned in time to see Keir's sword swing down, clanging against Normond's blade, making it fly from his hands to skitter across the floor. "The Devil of Dunakin sends ye to Hell," Keir said. His claymore changed directions, the blade whistling through the air as if time itself couldn't keep up with it. The glinting edge met Normond MacInnes's neck. The blade was lethally sharp, and Keir's swing was so powerful that the head teetered upon his shoulders before finally falling as his body slumped to the floor.

The platemaker's wife, along with several maids in the hall, shrieked. Grace stared at Keir. He stood ready for another attack, the polished steel of his sword streaked red. He swung around, but the room was frozen in shock. Normond's blood seeped out to pool in the rushes, wetting the fragrant clumps of rosemary. Keir's face was filled with the promise of death, making Grace's head feel numb and stars blink around the edges of her sight. At that moment, Keir Mackinnon was the most frightening being she had ever seen, in life or in her nightmares.

Feeling the prickles of a swoon start, Grace forced her eyes down to Fiona, who seemed to be rousing. A bruise had begun to darken the left side of her face. A sharp *crack* behind Grace made her jump, her head snapping up. Rab sat in his seat, his large hands smacking together in a slow applause. The smile on his face was more frightening than the sight of

Normond's ragged, bleeding neck. "*Slainte*, MacInnes." He laughed. "Good health to ye." He looked to Keir. "Seems we've paid appropriate tribute to St. Valentine, since he too lost his head on this day for being a traitor to Rome as this man was a traitor to clan Mackinnon."

"Brother," Dara said, standing up to face Rab.

He held up a hand to stop her speech as his face slowly came around to her. Grace swallowed hard at the hatred she saw there. "Don't call me brother," he said low.

"I didn't know," she said and looked toward Keir. Brodie stood beside him as if ready to battle a horde, even though there were only half a dozen people in the hall, all of whom had abject fear etched into the lines of their faces.

Dara turned back to Rab as Grace helped Fiona off the floor, sitting her gently into a chair. The woman was dazed but seemed to be recovering. "Go to your room, Odara MacInnes," Rab said. "Remain there until I decide your fate."

Without a word, Dara squared her shoulders and marched toward the stairs leading above. Decide her fate? The words sent chill bumps along Grace's arms, because the madman, who watched his sister walk away, had only death in his gaze.

• • •

Keir stood outside his room. Grace was inside, and she would have questions.

He ran a hand over his forehead, digging his fingers into his scalp through his hair. Cold. For the first time since he'd seen his mother, bruised and bloody on the floor of her bedroom, he felt the cold of death. It was different from battle. Battle and war, protecting his clan, it heated his blood to create a focused rage. This was different, and he shivered there, alone in the darkness of the corridor.

He always knew he would die with a sword in his hand,

but he'd hoped that it would be his body's death before his soul's. He inhaled, pushing the chill down where his heart still beat, past the pain that had filled him inside Rab's bedroom as he ranted and made his proclamations. The same room where Aonghus Mackinnon had brought down judgment on his wife, Keir's mother. And once again, the Devil of Dunakin had been called into service, the service of slaughter.

He raised his knuckle and rapped on the door. "Grace?"

Without a word, the bar scraped along the inside, and she opened the door, standing in her smock. The light of the fire glowed behind her, and her hair was down, free to flow like water over tumbled rocks in the stream outside the castle. She moved aside, and he walked in, shutting the door behind him. If she didn't want him, he would leave, even though this was his bedroom. In truth, nothing at Dunakin was his. It all belonged to the Devil who served the clan.

She gazed up into his face. Was she frightened by what she'd seen him do to Normond MacInnes? Her hand lifted, and warm fingers touched his cheek. "You are cold," she said, concern tugging at her lovely arched brows. "You are never cold."

She brought both hands up, placing them on his forehead and cheeks. The feel of her touch, the sound of her concern, for him…it was as if he were a normal man, not the evil he was becoming. "Keir," she said. "What happened?"

"He's condemned Dara to death," he said, his words a whisper.

"But she's innocent," Grace said. "I feel it."

"Rab doesn't see it that way." Keir walked to the bed and sat on the edge. He stared down at his boots, unsure yet if he should take them off.

Grace slid up onto the bed. "We will sway him." Her hands flew up and down his arms, rubbing them, and she leaned in to hug him. The contact was almost his undoing. No one hugged him, not like Grace, giving him her warmth instead of trying to take something from him. He'd been raised to be the ultimate pillar of strength, a boulder to crush all those The Mackinnon found guilty as a threat to the clan. And yet now…Keir felt weak with regret for an atrocity he hadn't even committed. Yet.

Keir caught Grace's hand and met her worried gaze. "If…things turn badly, Brodie will get ye home to Aros or to Kisimul."

Her face pinched in stubborn denial. "We will sway him, Lachlan will heal, and you will escort me as you promised."

"Ye have a very simple way of looking at things," he said, his frown relaxing.

"Right and wrong are usually simple if one looks at the problem for what it is," she said. "It is the fallacy of human perception that makes everything complicated."

He touched the soft waves sitting along her shoulder. "Beautiful and filled with brilliant wit. Someone should put ye on a throne, Grace Ellington." He leaned forward and kissed her forehead, pulling back.

She leaned, following him, and her hands slid from his shoulders down his back. "You can't say something utterly wonderful and pull away," she whispered. "Not when I can warm you."

He shouldn't love her. Could a cursed devil even love? Yet the sincerity in her touch, in her smile, kept him still. Not with hope, because he had none, but with a desperate effort to grasp onto the last shreds of humanity he still possessed. He drew her in to him, and she naturally bent her face up to his. "What are ye saying, lass?"

Her worry thinned until a smile broke through. "I can say a lot," she said and hoisted herself up onto her knees to be level with his face. "Like what I want to do to you and then exactly what I want you to do to me."

The teasing lilt in her voice was like a balm to his brittle mind, his body responding to the promise in the stroke of her fingers down his chest. "What exactly do ye want to do to me?"

"Let me warm you, Keir," she whispered, and a wicked smile spread slowly along her lips. She pressed him back among the pillows on his large bed, stroking his legs until her hands slid under his kilt. "I seem to remember quite a few things the maid in the barn did with her mouth that drove the groom absolutely mad." Keir jerked in sweet agony as she wrapped around him, boldly gliding up and down.

"For such an angelic-looking lass, ye do have a deliciously wicked tongue," he said between his teeth as he fought to control his impulse to throw her over and drive into her.

Shrugging her shoulders, the smock fell off, sliding all the way down past her hips to the floor. He inhaled as his blood rushed through his body. "Let us forget about the human world tonight," she whispered as she straddled his legs, rubbing herself against him in a rhythm that drove him mad. "No angels. No devils. Just Grace and Keir."

"Aye," he said, unhooking the belt that held his kilt in place. "And nothing between us." *For one last night.*

Chapter Twenty-One

Grace rolled over in the bed and nuzzled into the warmth that still held Keir's scent. She sighed, a smile spreading over her lips. *Ravished lips*, she thought. She smoothed her hands down her naked body under the blankets. *Ravished everything*. Rolling onto her back, she glanced at the window where the sun was overpowering the dawn's gray pallet.

Their night was over, and they had to face Rab and his lethal judgment of Dara. Grace's sigh turned to a groan as she slipped her feet out of bed. The fire was kindled yet looked to have burned low again, indicating that Keir had left before dawn. Had he even slept?

Grace stepped out from behind the privacy screen and found her smock, throwing it over her head. Next came the day dress she'd borrowed. As she worked at pulling the cording closed, she stared at the portrait of the woman on the mantel. She had the same dark eyes as Keir and his siblings. This was surely his mother, Margaret Mackinnon. Picking it up, she met the woman's gaze. There was something sad about it, as if she pleaded from the thin canvas. "I won't leave him," she whispered, setting it down. "I promise." She pivoted, searching for her slippers, suddenly anxious to find Keir.

The corridor was quiet as if everyone had already dressed and departed, ready to get on with the day. Grace hurried down a level to Lachlan's door, knocking lightly.

"Aye," came a voice, and she pushed in to find the boy sitting up in bed, eating cooked eggs and pork.

The sight lifted a bit of dread she was carrying. "You look well this morning."

He nodded, swallowing. "Better each day." His smile faded. "When I'm not being poisoned by my aunt and her lover."

Good God. Grace sat down on the edge of the boy's bed. "I don't think your aunt had anything to do with it. Normond MacInnes is the villain, and he has paid for his sins."

Lachlan shook his head like a typical stubborn boy and tipped his chin higher. "My da said Aunt Dara carried the poison to me that the bastard MacInnes gave her."

Grace frowned. Rab had certainly made up his mind about Dara, and had held nothing of his judgment back from his young son. She patted Lachlan's arm. "You concern yourself with getting well and strong again while we adults worry about who is to blame."

He shrugged, but Grace picked up on the wetness in his downcast eyes. "Aunt Dara will follow MacInnes to Hell tonight."

"Tonight?" The word fell out of Grace's open mouth.

"Aye," he answered, meeting her gaze. "When the Devil of Dunakin lops off her head."

. . .

The great hall was empty as Grace flew into it from the stairs. Had Keir known last night? Been given the order to kill his own sister? Was that why he'd been physically chilled, the cold reflecting his pain?

Bloody hell, where are you? She jumped when Brodie seemed to appear from the dark entryway.

"Ballocks, Brodie, you scared the breath from me," she said. "Do you always lurk at the door?"

He smiled, but it didn't hide the tension in his eyes. "Only when I've been ordered to carry ye to safety."

His words shot through Grace, choking her. She coughed. "Safety? Meaning…"

"Aros or Kisimul, your choice." He moved closer, crossing his arms like a sentry.

Completely alert, she tucked her arms to imitate his stance. "And who would give you an order that would see you slain, or at least horribly maimed?" Of course, she knew the answer.

Brodie's smile broadened into near authenticity. "'Tis a good thing I am a brave warrior, or your threat would surely make me quake."

Grace stared directly into Brodie's eyes. "Where is he?"

His smile faded. "Either at the bloody execution circle or sharpening his claymore at the smithy."

Was he trying to frighten her? "So Keir is going to kill his own sister?"

"Nay," Brodie said, his jaw set. "The Devil of Dunakin will carry out the order of his chief."

"How could Rab order his own sister killed?" Grace asked, although her mind was already on to solving her immediate problem. She had absolutely no intention of going peacefully with Brodie away from Dunakin and Keir. After all, she'd just made a promise to his mother.

Brodie rubbed his jaw as if it ached. "She's only Rab's half sister."

Grace stared hard at him, wishing she could pluck from

his brain all the information that the man possessed. "Half?"

"Aye, Aonghus Mackinnon isn't her father," Brodie said, lowering his voice. He scanned the empty hall and shifted his feet like he regretted bringing up the topic.

Grace narrowed her eyes. "I think you are very bad at keeping secrets, Brodie. If Dara isn't the descendent of a bloodletting chief, I'm guessing neither is Keir. And yet, he was thrown into the job from the cradle."

Brodie pinched his lips tighter as if to say that she couldn't pry anything else from him. She waved her hand. "It doesn't matter anyway. Even if they were linked by blood to Aonghus Mackinnon, it doesn't mean they must become warlike tyrants, too. And being only a half sister doesn't make an innocent woman guilty."

"We should go," Brodie said.

"He doesn't want me to see him do the misdeed," she answered. When Brodie didn't say anything, she continued. "You do know this will kill him."

"The Devil of Dunakin—"

"I'm not bloody talking about…that thing in the mask who walks around in winter half naked," she broke in, her hands flying with her frustration. "I'm talking about Keir, your best friend. The man who protects baby wolves, and hungry men, and foolish lads."

Brodie's gaze shifted past Grace, so she stepped over, putting herself in his view again. "Killing an innocent woman, his sister, possibly his only kin left…" Grace blinked back the tears swelling in her eyes. "He remembers every person he's killed, etches them on his skin. If he slays Dara, it will kill his soul, Brodie. You know that as well as I do." She caught his gaze. "Don't you?"

His voice seemed clogged in his throat. "There…is no choice."

Grace's mouth dropped open for a long second. Throwing

her hands in the air, she stomped her feet, something she hadn't done since she was a child. "Of course there is a choice! What the bloody hell do you mean?" She deepened her voice and frowned, imitating Brodie's words. "There is no choice." Pivoting on the heel of her slipper she turned, paced, and turned again. "That's the most ridiculous thing I've ever heard. He can choose *not* to kill his sister. What will happen if he says no, sir idiot chief, I will not kill an innocent woman who is also my sister?" she asked, using a very poor Scottish accent.

Grace knew her face was red. It felt flushed with her fevered pulse and gesturing arms. She stopped, taking two large breaths, in and out, to gain control. Brodie stood there watching as if he wasn't sure what to do in the face of a shrieking female. She propped her hands on her hips, giving up all her formal upbringing.

"Listen to me, Brodie Mackinnon," she said, her words coming through clenched teeth. "I am not leaving here without talking to him, even if that means I must scratch your eyes out and kick your ballocks up into your throat." She watched his eyes open slightly. "Is he really where you said, or is he at the cabin on the border?"

Brodie's eyes opened even wider. "He took ye there? Inside?"

"Yes."

"That was his mother's cottage, where she would escape to be with Keir's father. He lets no one in there."

"Well, he let me in there," she said. Could Brodie tell from her flaming cheeks that Keir had done much more to her than merely giving her a tour of the interior?

Brodie's shoulders lowered with his exhale. He rubbed a hand at the back of his neck. "Keir ran off. He does that sometimes, likes to run. Says it helps him stay fit." He shook his head. "But if I were in his position, I might keep running."

He met her gaze. "Aye, he goes to the cabin to think. Ye talk to him, but as soon as anything looks dangerous, I'm hauling ye off Skye even if it means my ballocks."

Without a thank-you, Grace dodged around him and out the door into the clear winter air. With all the turmoil at Dunakin, she expected mist or storm clouds, but the sky was blue, the sun shining. She ran to the stables and spotted Little Warrior still in his stall. Grabbing his tack from the wall she walked over with a handful of oats. He nuzzled her palm, lipping up the treat. "You remember your way back to that cabin, don't you," she said, looking up into the black face of the warhorse.

Grace had been around horses since she was a young girl, but none this large. Steeling herself with a breath, she opened the stall and slid the bridle over Little Warrior's face. There wasn't time for a saddle. She threw on a saddle blanket and clicked her tongue, leading him to an overturned bucket to use as a step.

"There now," she whispered, fisting a bunch of his mane while hitching her skirts high. With a quick thrust she threw herself up, her leg swinging over the tall horse's back. Her muscles strained, but Little Warrior stood completely still while she righted herself.

She exhaled, her heart pumping wildly. Step one completed. Now, to find Keir.

· · ·

Keir stood inside his mother's cottage, his gaze on the bed where he'd shared the day with Grace. His gut was full of twisting eels, and his chest clenched. *Duty before everything.* The words of the man he'd always thought of as his brutal, warlike father slammed around in his head. Aonghus Mackinnon may not have sired Keir, but he'd raised him as his second son, to be the Devil of Dunakin. Until the day Keir had killed him.

The Mackinnon chief had molded Keir's heart into cold stone, approving of him only when he killed or defended. It was all Keir had ever known, until Grace.

He let his sword tip touch the wooden floorboards, his arm suddenly weak as he thought of the beautiful Englishwoman who had treated him like a man and not a devil. She named herself a coward, yet she was the bravest person he'd met in his nearly thirty years. He exhaled, feeling the crush of her loathing even before she condemned him, for she would certainly hate him for the task he must do.

He was an executioner. Grace argued that Dara was innocent, based on his sister's reactions that Keir hadn't seen and Grace's perceived feeling about Dara's goodness. But Rab was certain she'd colluded with Normond MacInnes, marrying him in secret so he could rule the clan with her upon their deaths. Keir had argued, but his brother would not be swayed.

Ye will do your duty, Devil of Dunakin. Dara is a traitor. His brother's words echoed in his ear, sending ice through his body, ice that only Grace's tender touch could melt. But if she witnessed this act, she'd never touch him again, and he couldn't blame her for condemning him.

Rab's haunting words faded as the thud of hoofbeats broke through. Keir opened the door, his sword raised, and his breath hitched. Grace. Couldn't Brodie follow a single bloody order?

He stood in silence as she nearly fell from Cogadh's tall back. *Magairlean!* She'd ridden his warhorse bareback.

Keir's frown nearly broke as she cursed her way across the yard to him, her fists swinging. "Leave? You want me to leave without even saying good-bye? After last night, all night, and this morning?" She punctuated her words with wild gestures.

Grace's cheeks were red, her bosom heaving. She was angry and glorious.

"Aye," he answered.

She waited, but he didn't say anything else. "Aye?" she yelled. "That's all I get?" Stepping forward she poked him in the chest with her finger. He wore black leather, the devil's suit, and barely felt her attack. "Dara is innocent," she yelled.

"Ye don't know that, and Rab has decided."

"Rab is mad, and you know it." She grabbed his leather vest in her fists. "You are not a killer, Keir. You don't have a legacy of murder like Aonghus Mackinnon. Break away from the Devil of Dunakin. In truth, this isn't even your clan."

Her words struck him hard. "Brodie told ye," he said low, but she ignored him.

"Even if he were your father, you don't need to follow his dictates. He's dead."

Keir inhaled through his nostrils, filling his lungs before they could freeze with his next words. "Aye, he's dead, and I became the Devil of Dunakin the day I killed Aonghus Mackinnon."

Grace stared up at him, her gaze shifting along his features. He could almost see the truth surfacing in her eyes. "He killed your mother, didn't he?" she said. "When he found out you and Dara weren't his children." Her eyes narrowed as if she were deciphering small script. "You were there, and you tried to stop him and killed him because of it."

Memories flashed to the surface like dead fish floating up from the depths, exposed by the sun. He'd never talked of that night ten years ago, not even to Brodie. Only Rab knew some of the truth. But something in Grace's strong face made his lips part.

"She was gentle and kind," he said. "And perfectly miserable married to a cruel man." He stepped to the cold hearth. "This was the only place she was happy, a sanctuary where she would escape Dunakin with my real father, Graham MacLeod. This cottage was his before Aonghus killed him."

Grace kept silent, and the words continued to tumble from his mouth. "Dara and I are bastards. When Aonghus found out, he sentenced our mother to death. I was ordered to execute her."

"Good God," she whispered.

"I could hear him yelling in their bedchamber at Dunakin, and when I went in, he ordered me to kill her right there." He forced the words out. "Finish her off."

Grace touched his arm, but he wouldn't look at her. "You didn't kill her," Grace said. "No matter what everyone thinks. You loved her. Still do."

He raked a hand through his hair. "Aonghus lunged for her when I wouldn't. His sword was drawn... I grabbed his thick neck and gutted him. He died cursing my name."

Several heartbeats passed before Grace's words broke the silence. "And your mother?"

Keir glanced up at the sky, which was a lighter shade than his mother's eyes. "Her wounds were great. I held her while she died."

"But you let everyone think you'd done your duty," Grace said. He listened for the condemnation that he felt, but he didn't hear it. No pity, no judgment. Just a statement.

"When I came out, covered in blood, Rab announced that I'd executed both for treasonous acts against Dunakin and that he was taking the chiefdom."

Grace's pretty cheeks rounded, and she let the air out in a puff. "Damnation," she whispered. "That's bloody awful."

Her words were like knives, but he pushed past the pain. "I am damned, and ye need to continue on your journey."

"What? No," she said, her brows gathering. "You need to tell Rab that you won't kill your sister, whether she's guilty or not. And she's not, by the way. I can tell, like I can tell that you are not damned and not a killer in your heart."

With two clicks of Keir's tongue, Cogadh trotted toward him. He looked one last time at the beautiful woman whom he realized he loved, loved too much to withstand the look in her eyes after he completed his duty to his clan and chief. "Ye do not know people like ye think, Grace Ellington. Go home." He swung up onto the saddle pad. He turned the horse toward Dunakin. "I will send Brodie to fetch ye here."

"And where will Dara's cross be etched on your skin, Keir?" she asked. "Not with the hundreds you've killed. You will etch her over your heart, because killing her will surely skewer it."

Without looking at her, he leaned forward. Cogadh leaped into a gallop, leaving Keir's heart standing before his mother's cottage, hating him as much as he hated himself.

Chapter Twenty-Two

Grace's heart sank into her stomach as she watched Keir gallop away. The vital organ felt as heavy as the boulders that rose from the Highland landscape like giants' knobby bones. She wobbled. Any second she would fall to the dirt in desolate defeat. Bracing her hands on her knees, she forced herself to breathe as tears gathered in her eyes. She watched them as they dropped out to dot the dirt beneath her, physical evidence of her pain.

She thought of the promise she'd made to the picture kept lovingly on Keir's mantel. The poor woman had lived in secret and fear her whole life, protecting her children as best she could and seeking out love here at this small cottage on the border.

Grace slowly walked her hands up her legs, pressing palms against her thighs for support until she stood straight. If she waited until Brodie came to drag her home, Margaret Mackinnon's three children would suffer. Dara would die, Rab would be responsible for ordering the death of his half sister, and Keir would never be able to wash Dara's blood from his hands. Grace couldn't let it happen.

"I need help," she whispered. Her mind flitted to the people she'd met at Dunakin, searching for someone strong, someone who might love Keir enough to help her save him. "Fiona," she said. She wasn't his grandmother by blood, since his father was a MacLeod, and she was Aonghus Mackinnon's mother, but she seemed to care for Dara. Would she help Grace save her and Keir?

Grace gathered her skirts and ran toward the path she'd ridden along to find the cottage. "Ballocks," she cursed as her ankle twisted slightly on the edge of a rock, but she kept going, holding her skirts high to see the ground. If she'd known she'd be running through the woods, she'd have worn boots instead of slippers. Pebbles and twigs poked through the thin soles, bruising her feet. She ran and ran, stopping periodically for breath and to search for landmarks. Over the rushing in her ears, she heard the thud of hooves ahead, and Grace dodged behind a thick oak in time to avoid Brodie's gaze. Her lips grazed the rough bark as she sucked in gulps of air and prayed for him not to turn around.

When the thuds faded, Grace pushed away from the tree. Hands out before her, to slap away the branches determined to rake her eyes, she charged down the hillside, breaking out at the edge of the forest. Just as she had when riding on Little Warrior, she gulped a last breath of untainted air and tipped her gaze to the ground. Concentrating on her footfalls along the uneven ground, she ran between the torches holding the rotting heads. There was no time for shock. She needed to reach Fiona.

Off to the left, she could see the wide river flowing beside the castle, on its journey to the ocean. A small island sat in the middle of the river, a circle with a narrow bridge on one side. "Oh God," she breathed at the crack of hammers hitting pegs. The execution platform.

With renewed determination, Grace raced into the village. "Fiona!" she yelled as she ran along the path between the thatched cottages. "Fiona Mackinnon!" A door opened, and a man peeked out. He pointed toward the cottage on the far end. "Thank you," Grace called, running to pound on the door.

It flew open, but Grace was too out of breath to say anything. Fiona stared, her eyes hard. She looked behind Grace and yanked her forward into her cottage, slamming the door. "Find your breath, lass," she said. "And tell me ye are here to save my granddaughter."

Grace plopped into a chair. "And Keir."

"Aye." She shook her head. "Rab is as insane as my son, Aonghus, I fear. The deaths of his wife and bairn have addled his head."

"What can I do?" Grace asked, still gasping for breath. "Brodie's hunting for me to carry me back to Aros. No one else will stand up to the bloody Devil of Dunakin."

Fiona took Grace's hands. Her fingers felt hot against Grace's frigid skin. "Ye can."

"I tried. Keir wouldn't listen to me." Grace felt panic press tears in her eyes until Fiona's image swam before her.

"Ye must stop the Devil of Dunakin, not Keir," Fiona said, bringing her a cup of light ale. For the first time ever, Grace wished it was whisky, strong whisky.

"How can I do that?"

"The Devil of Dunakin will be killed by an angel, ending the long line of Mackinnon devils," Fiona answered, nodding. "He calls you an angel. Ye must pierce his heart."

Grace pressed upward out of her seat. "I'm not killing him or anyone."

Fiona frowned at her as if she were being stubborn. "Not Keir," she snapped. "Ye will kill the Devil of Dunakin."

Fiona was as insane as her grandson. Grace stared after

her as the woman rushed to a wardrobe, throwing it open and rummaging in the bottom. "Ye will wear my warrior clothes."

"What?" Grace asked, her mouth hanging open.

Fiona turned around, a smile cracking her nearly permanent frown. She held up a suit made of bleached doeskin with a white linen shirt. Three straps with buckles encircled the waist, and the breeches tapered to the ankle. A broad collar rose up to lay flat against the breast up to the neck. "Put it on. I have white boots to go with it."

"What?" Grace said again, staring aghast at the costume.

"Is that all ye can say?" Fiona snapped, throwing the boots out from the wardrobe to clunk against the floorboards. "Put the damn things on."

Grace worked her fingers into her bodice laces, loosening them. She kicked off her muddied shoes. "I don't think they will fit." She'd never tried to stuff her legs and hips into such tight clothing.

Fiona gestured toward the costume. "Leather stretches. And ye look about the size I was when I wore it decades ago."

"In battle?" Grace asked, sitting on the bed to shimmy the trousers up her legs. Her heart beat fast, but she persisted, yanking the pliable leather.

"Aye." Fiona threw the linen shirt over Grace's head and tied the bodice into place.

"I am not brave enough for battle," Grace whispered.

Fiona's hands landed on Grace's shoulder. She stared directly into her eyes. "Ye need to learn the circle of *caim*."

"Wh—" Grace stopped herself from saying the word again. "I'm not familiar with 'cime.'"

"The word is said kie-em," Fiona said, stepping back to draw a circle around herself with one extended finger moving through the air. "*Caim*. 'Tis Gaelic for sanctuary, or an invisible circle of protection drawn about yourself to remind you that you are safe and loved, even in the darkest of moments. 'Tis what makes a warrior brave."

Grace exhaled and, with Fiona's encouraging nod, she drew a circle around herself. "*Caim*," she repeated, stressing the two syllables, for she needed all the bravery she could find.

• • •

Where will you etch your sister's cross? Grace's words flew at Keir like poison-tipped arrows, and he could do nothing to dodge them. Rab had judged her guilty, and she could be. Dara had certainly had ample opportunity. She'd handed out the cups at the table. After her initial plea of innocence, Dara had kept her lips clamped shut. Maybe her guilt wouldn't allow her to speak. Or her pride. Their mother had done the same thing when Aonghus had accused her of adultery, and she'd admitted to her crime. Keir would never have put his mother to death, so how could he put Dara to death?

"Damnation." He tugged his black leather mask into place, walking toward the river where the entire clan stood silently. Wearing the costume of the Dunakin Devil, he strode over the foot-wide bridge to the execution island. Blazing torches lit the scene where Dara stood on the platform next to…Brodie? *Bloody hell!* He should be miles away with Grace. Was she with the villagers now? Watching him stalk toward his sister, an unforgivable monster?

Brodie and Dara stood before a thick tree stump, set for her to place her neck. As he walked closer, she sneered. "Aonghus Mackinnon would be proud of ye, Devil."

Her words hit him like a blow, but he shoved the ache away, his gaze turning to Brodie. "Why the bloody hell are ye here?"

Brodie's mouth puckered with frustration. He shook his head. "I am always by the Devil of Dunakin."

"Your damned henchman can join ye in Hell," Dara said.

Rab stood from his seat next to Lachlan on the far side of the river. "For your crimes against me, my son, and the Devil of Dunakin, ye, Dara Macleod MacInnes, shall die for your sins." Stripping her of his father's name, Rab was letting everyone know she was a bastard.

The wind blew dead leaves about the bottom of the scaffold as if nature itself felt the icy hand of condemnation against Keir's nape. Bare to show the dark etchings on his skin, chill bumps rose. Keir's breath rushed in his ears, and he stepped to stand before Rab. *Reasonable judgment to accompany strength and strategic prowess...* Grace's words about leadership beat through the conditioning of many brutal years. There hadn't been a chance to weigh Dara's true guilt. Rab was not showing the reasonable judgment of a good leader, and Grace was right. Keir did have a choice.

"Commence the execution," Rab yelled, his lips pulled back in grim determination.

Keir stood before his chief and brother, his fist tight around his sword. "Rab Mackinnon, as your brother and chief advisor, I ask once more that you consider the lack of proof against Dara. Normond MacInnes may have acted completely on his own, and ye will be condemning an innocent woman. I ask ye to show your wisdom and sound judgment."

Rab's eyes narrowed, and he stepped to the edge of the river. The two brothers faced each other over the surging current. "Does the Devil dare to question my decision and rule before the clan?" Rab's words seethed from between clenched teeth. Wildness lurked in his gaze.

"Nay," Keir said, his battle stance tall and full of strength. Familiar heat surged through his body at the promise of war. "But I, Keir Macleod, do." Keir reached his arm over his head to grab the back of his mask.

"Stop!"

The familiar voice reached Keir's ears, shooting like

burning lightning through him. He dropped his hand, leaving his mask in place, and turned, his eyes falling on Grace, standing on the other side of the river beside the narrow bridge. But she wasn't dressed like Grace. Clothed in white, she stood like an Amazon warrior woman holding a short sword. Tight-fitting trousers of pale leather curved along her hips and thighs, tapering down her perfectly shaped legs, which Keir had feasted upon the night before. Buckles of brass cinched her trim waist, accenting her full breasts. Tall boots, made of the same doeskin, rose up her legs to an inch past her knees.

She wore a face shield similar to his own but out of white leather. It curved upward, leaving only her eyes open, and a drape of white material covered her hair. Like Joan of Arc leading an invisible army behind her, Grace stood, a cross between a warrior and…an angel in white.

• • •

Grace glanced below the edge of the dark, flowing river that surrounded the flame-lit island. Forcing an inhale, she looked across to Dara, who stood on a platform with Brodie. But her focus swept to the man hidden behind the black mask, standing across the river from Rab.

"Who the bloody hell are ye?" Rab yelled, where he stood at the water's edge.

"Grace Ellington," she called. Her heart pounded in her chest, making a tremor run through her limbs. She inhaled, filling her lungs. Slow breaths would help the tingling recede in her chin. She placed one boot on the thin plank that ran across the river. "I have come to stop the Devil of Dunakin from killing an innocent woman," she yelled. "And losing his soul."

"Good bloody hell," Dara said from her spot on the

platform. She didn't sound confident. Neither was Grace, but she wasn't turning back now. Not when the man she loved stood there, ready to forfeit his compassion and honor to follow the order of an insane tyrant. Love? Yes, this was certainly love. To risk humiliation before a crowd, drowning in a freezing river, and confronting the deadliest man of whom she'd ever heard… Love was the only explanation for this insanity.

Grace stared down at the rushing water. She could hear her sadistic brother's taunts, teasing her that he would hold her under the water again. She swallowed hard. God save her! If she swooned now, she'd surely drown. She could turn back, run, and hide somewhere, wait for Brodie to come find her and take her back to Aros to…cry in shame forever. The thought of retreat twisted her gut harder than the fear of the water.

Grace let the tip of her sword lower as she took even breaths. *Caim. Caim*, a circle of protection. She recited the word, summoning any power she could from the ancient belief that it could keep her safe.

With slow movements, Grace raised her empty gloved hand, drawing an invisible circle above her, encompassing her entire frame. She imagined it draping down as a column of protective light and stepped forward. *Caim. Caim. Caim. Love is stronger than fear.*

The rushing noise of the water receded, and her heartbeat slowed. She looked straight at the Devil of Dunakin, but she didn't see him there in the mask. She envisioned Keir's face, his strong jaw, full cheekbones, sloped nose, and his deep brown eyes.

Rab's voice rang out. "If she interferes with Mackinnon law, she is also a traitor. I command the Devil of Dunakin to execute the healer, too."

His words didn't penetrate Grace at all, sliding away as

she murmured the powerful Gaelic word. One more step, then another, and finally… Grace jumped down from the end of the plank, her boots thudding softly on the trampled winter grass.

"I am here to stop the Devil of Dunakin," she called through the leather, wondering if she should take it off so he could see the determination in her face.

"Kill her first," Rab demanded.

Lachlan left his seat to join his father at the river's edge. "Nay, she healed me."

With a backward swipe, Rab slammed his arm against his young son, sending him sprawling. Gasps rose behind Grace from the crowd on the bank.

"I will not back down, Keir," Grace said. "Surrender Dara."

"He isn't Keir!" Rab yelled. "He is the Devil of Dunakin, protector of the Mackinnon clan and the weapon of the chief. Do your duty, Devil."

Grace paused, staring at Keir, who stood like black, carved ice. She couldn't tell anything about his thoughts behind the damn mask. "I know you are Keir behind that mask," she whispered.

Keir held his sword tip to the night sky. Grace walked around him, and he turned with her. With a flick of his sword, he could disarm her, but what would he do then? Kill her? Knock her down, vault onto the platform, and behead his sister? Grace shook her head. "You have the choice not to do this, Keir," she said, her voice low, but he remained silent, watching her.

Grace brought the point of her sword to the pebbly ground. With a quick step, she dragged it in a circle around the two of them. "I summon *Caim*, sanctuary, around the two of us," she said with all the confidence she could muster.

Keeping her sword tip lowered, Grace grasped the edge

of her mask under her chin, yanking it from her face. The hood followed, releasing her long hair. She stepped closer to him and lifted her sword with both hands. Leaning forward she pressed the tip to his bare skin, right over his heart where the intricate crosses lay etched.

Her lips parted, pulling in air, and all else around them seemed to vanish. It was only Grace and Keir in the circle. She swallowed and inhaled. "Keir Mackinnon, *is tù gaol mo chridhe*."

Keir's sword lowered to the side. "Grace, do ye know what ye are saying?"

A smile flitted to her lips at the sound of his voice, the way he said her name. Her heart pounded with relief. There was no Devil here, only Keir. She wet her lips. "I walked all the way across that bloody board," she said. "Of course, I know what I'm saying. *Tha gaol agam ort*," she continued. "I love you, Keir."

Grace barely heard Rab yell from his spot. Her complete focus was on the man before her. Keir raised his hand to his mask and slowly pulled it off. Arms spread wide, he pressed forward, her blade tip piercing his skin. "*Is tù gaol mo chridhe*," he repeated as a drop of blood slid down his bare chest.

"What is happening?" Rab yelled, running over another bridge, spanning the river, to push through the crowd.

Grace could barely draw a breath as she stared into Keir's intense gaze. His lips parted, his words calling out on the night breeze. "An angel has pierced the Devil of Dunakin's heart." His biceps hardened as he threw his mighty claymore away from him. "The Devil is vanquished," he yelled, his voice resounding across the island.

Grace's vision swam with tears, and she blinked, throwing her own sword toward his in the grass. A small sound issued from her lips as she rushed forward. Keir grasped her face in his hands, staring down into her eyes. "I love ye, Grace." A small sob of joy came from her, and he lowered to kiss her.

"Keir!" Brodie yelled from the platform, making Keir whirl to tuck Grace behind him.

Rab had run over the narrow bridge to the island, kicking their swords away while holding his own pointed at Keir's chest. "Ye are a bastard and a traitor against the Mackinnons," he said.

Grace slid to the side where she could see Rab's contorted features. Pinched tight, lips pulled back to show gritted teeth, spittle wetting his mouth. Fury and bitterness had stolen his sense. Could Keir unarm his brother without a weapon? She wasn't taking a chance.

With subtle movements, Grace slid the *sgian dubh* from her boot, the same one she'd carried from Aros. Her throw was never perfect, but the thought of losing Keir squashed the embarrassment and fear of failure out of her mind.

"Ye've gone mad, Rabbie," Keir said, holding his arms outward calmly. "Losing Bradana—"

"Shut your bastard mouth!" Rab yelled, lifting his sword as if to swing.

Without the hindrance of skirts, Grace threw her weight into a forceful step like Gavin Maclean had taught her back at Aros. Arm and wrist snapping forward, she released the dagger into the air. End over end, it flew toward Rab.

Crack! The heavy, dull end of the handle hit Rab's nose. The blade snapped upward, its razor-sharp edge scoring Rab's forehead before falling to the ground.

"Shite," he yelled, blood gushing from his nose as his empty hand came up.

Seizing the opportunity, Keir leaped forward to knock the weapon from his brother's grasp. Grace watched, her palms pressing against her cheeks, as Keir's leg swung behind Rab. At the same time, Keir shoved him in the chest, sending Rab crashing to the ground. Keir stepped over him, pinning his brother with one solid boot in the middle of his chest.

"This is finished, Rab," Keir said. Rab turned his head to spit out blood as he held his nose. "From this moment on, the Devil of Dunakin is no more, and ye aren't the chief of the Mackinnons." Keir glanced to where Brodie stood, sword drawn, face grim. He turned his focus to the silent, wide-eyed villagers. "Until Lachlan has aged and earned the respect of his clan, Brodie Mackinnon will rule Dunakin as chief."

Brodie stepped up to him as Keir signaled several of his warriors to come across to take Rab. "Keir," Brodie said. "Ye should be—"

"I am leaving Dunakin," Keir said. Grace's breath caught with a twist of hope. "Ye should lead." He turned to meet Grace's gaze. "A sound leader is intelligent and thoughtful, using reasonable judgment, strength, and strategic prowess to earn the respect of his warriors. Not brutality and fear."

Grace felt the ache of tears as Keir used her own words. She gave a small nod to him, and he turned back to Brodie.

"Ye've earned the respect and trust of the clan, Brodie," Keir continued. "Ye will make a strong chief for the Mackinnons of Dunakin."

Stepping forward, Brodie extended his arm. Keir grasped it, linking it in solid approval as Brodie accepted. A shiver rose up Grace's back, as around the island a soft rumble grew among the villagers until the dark glade echoed with cheers of acceptance and something Dunakin had been lacking for many generations. Hope.

Keir turned to Grace, pulling her into his arms. He touched her cheek and looked down into her eyes. "I'm going to teach ye to throw a *sgian dubh*," he said, his perfect lips turning up at the corners.

She smiled back and gave him a quick shake of her head. "I hit him exactly how I'd planned."

He chuckled softly. "Ye are a wise woman, Grace

Ellington. And I love ye." He leaned in to kiss a tear that had escaped her eyes. Pulling her around to face the crowd, Grace saw Fiona. Rab's grandmother nodded to her. Grace held her hand to her heart and bowed her head to the woman who had helped her, even when it meant removing her grandson from power. Fiona let a sad smile touch her lips and followed behind Rab as he was forcefully led away by Keir's men.

Keir's voice rose. "Ye are all witnesses," he said and turned to stand before Grace. "I pledge my heart to ye, Grace Ellington. Forever."

A giddiness bubbled through Grace, a mix of joy, hope, and love. "I, too," she said, her voice clear in the once again silent, watching night, "pledge my heart to you, Keir Macleod Mackinnon. Forever."

Keir leaned in, one eyebrow raised. "Ye do know that ye just wed me?"

She tipped her chin higher to give him a mischievous look. "With the night I have planned with you, I certainly hope so." Keir's grin grew into a full smile, lighting his face with the same happiness that made Grace laugh. Keir pulled her to him, and Grace reached up on her toes to wrap her hands behind his neck, surrendering to his powerful, oath-sealing kiss.

Epilogue

Grace swayed in the seat of the white mare that Brodie had given her the morning she, Keir, and Dara had departed Dunakin. Ferried over to the mainland, they had ridden to Kilchoan. Grace had been ready to obtain passage to Barra Island to help Mairi, her original course. But once Thomas had regained his head after the fever broke, he'd sent to Aros for help. Macleans and MacDonalds had been searching the countryside around Kilchoan for more than a week.

Grace and Keir decided it best to return to Aros first, after sending a message to Mairi. Another ferry ride brought them and their horses to the Isle of Mull, and they rode across the familiar path toward Aros.

"You can live with us, Dara, in my cottage, until you decide if you'd like to stay at Aros," Grace said.

"Only if she wants to hear the creative things ye like to yell out at night," Keir said. Grace wrinkled her nose at him but couldn't help her grin.

"Ugh," Dara huffed, a frown souring her pretty face. "I'd rather sleep in a dungeon."

"I'm sure we can find you a *quiet* bed somewhere," Grace said. She tucked one of her loose locks of hair behind her ear and pointed toward the village. "Aros." Her heart squeezed at the sight of home. "And no heads on spikes surrounding it."

"It certainly smells better," Dara murmured.

Grace laughed and leaned into the saddle, the comfortable white leather trousers making it easy to keep her seat as they galloped across the moor, her hair flying out to match her horse's tail. She looked to the side to see Keir smiling at her from Little Warrior's back. They slowed as they rode through the winding path of the village and up to the open gate of Aros Castle.

"Halt! *Stad*!" came the voice of the gatekeeper.

"Hamish Maclean, it is Grace Ellington," she called.

"Bloody hell," Hamish said, quickly climbing down the ladder. "Where have ye been? And who are they?" Without waiting for a reply, he pointed at one of the stableboys. "Ye there. Go tell Lady Maclean her sister has returned."

"Grace?" Gavin Maclean ran over from the other side of the bailey. "Good God, ye're sound."

Hands encircled her waist before she could say a word, and Gavin lifted her down. *Oh hell.* Keir's large hand landed on Gavin's shoulder. "Take ye're hands off my wife." The intent sat in his tone, but he kept the death threat back.

"Who the hell…?" Gavin's words trailed off as he turned to see Keir looming over him. Gavin wasn't a small man, but next to Keir he looked like a scrawny lad.

Grace stepped around him and took Keir's arm. "I am well, Gavin, and this is Keir Macleod, my husband." She indicated Dara. "And his sister, Dara."

"Grace!" Ava waddled down the steps of the keep, still quite pregnant. Grace met her halfway, hugging her. Ava pulled back. "What are you wearing?"

Grace laughed. "Trousers are really much more

comfortable than skirts."

Tor came out behind his wife. "Grace Ellington?" He looked shocked. "Where have ye been?"

"The Isle of Skye," Grace said. "At Dunakin Castle."

Tor frowned. "'Tis dangerous there. Did ye run into the Devil of Dunakin?" His eyes shifted to Keir.

"Aye, she did," Keir said, taking her arm. Grace looked up at him as he spoke, her smile full.

"Goodness," Ava said, her eyes wide. "What happened?"

Keir's mouth relaxed into a grin. "She confronted him in battle and destroyed him."

"Grace Ellington killed the infamous Devil of Dunakin?" Tor asked, his jaw open in disbelief.

"I pierced his heart," Grace said.

Ava let out a little laugh. "I knew you were courageous, Grace, but I didn't know you were that courageous."

Keir pulled her in to his side. "My wife is the bravest person I know." He bent to kiss her gently. Even brief, the touch caused a warmth to flow into Grace's middle, anticipation for their first night alone after the journey.

Grace looked up into Keir's warm brown eyes. "Love grows courage out of fear."

"This sounds like a wonderful adventure," Ava said. "Come in and tell us."

Grace squeezed Keir's arm as they walked together toward Aros Castle, ready to begin their new life together.

Acknowledgments

Thank you to all my readers who asked me to write Grace's story. I must confess that when I started, I was concerned that she didn't have it in her to be the heroine. But her courage was always there, buried beneath her self-doubt. Love helped her dig her way out, putting everything on the line to save the man she'd grown to love. Grace's story has reminded me that everyone can be a heroine, we just need love and *caim*. (And a pair of white leather trousers can always help!)

• • •

As at the end of each of my books, I please ask that you, my awesome readers, remind yourselves of the whispered symptoms of ovarian cancer. I am now a six-year survivor, one of the lucky ones. Please don't rely on luck. If you experience any of these symptoms, consistently for three weeks or more, go see your GYN.

Bloating
Eating less and feeling full faster
Abdominal pain
Trouble with your bladder

Other symptoms may include: indigestion, back pain, pain with intercourse, constipation, fatigue, and menstrual irregularities.

About the Author

Heather McCollum is an award-winning historical romance writer. She is a member of Romance Writers of America and the Ruby Slippered Sisterhood of 2009 Golden Heart finalists.

The ancient magic and lush beauty of Great Britain entrances Ms. McCollum's heart and imagination every time she visits. The country's history and landscape have been a backdrop for her writing ever since her first journey across the pond.

When she is not creating vibrant characters and magical adventures on the page, she is roaring her own battle cry in the war against ovarian cancer. Ms. McCollum recently slayed the cancer beast and resides with her very own Highland hero, rescued golden retriever, and three kids in the wilds of suburbia on the mid-Atlantic coast. For more information about Ms. McCollum, please visit www.HeatherMcCollum.com.

URL and Social Media links:

Website: HeatherMcCollum.com
Facebook: facebook.com/HeatherMcCollumAuthor
Twitter: twitter.com/HMcCollumAuthor
Pinterest: pinterest.com/hmccollumauthor/
Instagram: instagram.com/heathermccollumauthor/

Discover the **Highland Isle** *series...*

THE BEAST OF AROS CASTLE

THE ROGUE OF ISLAY ISLE

THE WOLF OF KISIMUL CASTLE

Also by Heather McCollum

HIGHLAND HEART

CAPTURED HEART

TANGLED HEARTS

UNTAMED HEARTS

CRIMSON HEART

Get Scandalous with these historical reads…

DUCHESS BY DAY, MISTRESS BY NIGHT
a *Rebellious Desires* novel by Stacy Reid

Georgiana Rutherford, the Duchess of Hardcastle, seemingly has it all—wealth, pedigree, and the admiration of the *ton*, except her heart hungers for a passionate affair. She meets the enigmatic and ruthless Mr. Rhys Tremayne, a man known to low and high society as *the Broker*. The attraction between them is impossible to deny, but she cannot be feeling it for *this* man.

THE ROGUE'S CONQUEST
a *Townsends* novel by Lily Maxton

Former prizefighter James MacGregor wants to be a gentleman, like the men he trains in his boxing saloon. A chance encounter with Eleanor Townsend gives him the leverage he needs. She'll gain him entry to high society and help him with his atrocious manners, and in return, he won't reveal her secret. It's the perfect arrangement. At least until the sparks between them become more than just their personalities clashing.

How to Bewilder a Lord
a *How To* novel by Ally Broadfield

Gavin Corey, the Earl of Thornbrook, has shed his rakish ways in the hope of winning Lady Louisa Adair's heart, but neither she nor her parents consider him a suitable match. He convinces her to join forces with him to locate a missing family treasure by proposing a wager: if he finds the jewels, Lady Louisa must allow him to court her, but if she prevails, he must reveal the secret he's keeping from her.

The Highlander's Choice
a *Marriage Mart Mayhem* novel by Callie Hutton

Lady Sybil Lacey is properly horrified to attend her best friend's wedding in the Scottish Highlands. For Sybil is quite certain that Scots are little more than brutish, whiskey-swilling lechers. Yet she's secretly attracted to Liam MacBride—the tall and devastatingly handsome Scottish laird of Bedlay Castle, who believes English ladies are silly sassenachs. All they can do is quarrel, until loathing turns into sweet, undeniable lust…but a tempestuous, fiery romance between an English lady and Scottish laird cannot end well.

Printed in Great Britain
by Amazon